Trail of Storms

Book 5: The Owen Family Saga

Also by Marsha Ward

That Tender Light
Gone for a Soldier
The Man from Shenandoah
Spinster's Folly
Ride to Raton
Trail of Storms

Mended by Moonlight

The Zion Trail

Trail of Storms

Book 5: The Owen Family Saga

Marsha Ward

WestWard Books

Payson, Arizona

WestWard Books
P O Box 53
Payson, Arizona 85547
www.westwardbooks.com

Publisher's Note: This is a work of fiction. Names, characters, places, and incidents are a product of the author's imagination. Locales and public names are sometimes used for atmospheric purposes. Any resemblance to actual people, living or dead, or to businesses, companies, events, institutions, or locales is completely coincidental.

Cover Design: SelfPubBookCovers.com/FrozenStar
Book Layout © 2017 BookDesignTemplates.com

Originally published in trade paperback by iUniverse, Inc. This second edition contains bonus material not found in the original, and features new cover art and interior layout, as well as revised placement in the Owen Family Saga book order.

Trail of Storms / Marsha Ward -- 2nd ed.
ISBN 978-1-947306-07-3

Dedication
To my children, Audra, Jeremy, Gregory, Karen, and Kevin,
whose examples amidst trials and troubles have led me to know
that I must go forward in faith, believing that a better day
is just beyond the horizon.
Thank you for your encouragement and support.

Notes and Acknowledgements

Several years ago, I was solicited to donate something of value for an auction to benefit the local Scout troop. I offered to name a character after the winning bidder. My friend Jeff Julander bid high, and threw in five dollars more if I would name a goat after his friend. Thanks Jeff! A pivotal character bears the name of Jeff Julander, and the Julander family's goat is named Mike. I rounded out the fictional family by using some actual family names, as well as some fakes ones. Be it known to all, however, that beyond names and general physical descriptions, my Julander characters are not the same as the actual people whose names they bear. The characters are purely a product of my imagination.

Albuquerque, New Mexico Territory, is mentioned frequently in this work. At the time in which our characters lived, it was called "Alburquerque," with an extra "r." In 1706, Don Francisco Cuervo y Valdés, the provincial Governor of New Mexico, named the settlement in honor of the Viceroy of New Spain, Don Francisco Fernández de la Cueva, Duke of Alburquerque. It is generally believed that sometime after the coming of the railroad in the 1880s, an Anglo station master dropped the first "r" because he couldn't correctly pronounce the Spanish name of the town. "Albuquerque" became the common spelling thereafter.

Despite the historical time frame, I have used the modern spelling as a convenience to my readers (and also to prevent Microsoft Word from going crazy with spelling error underlines as I typed).

One of my characters speaks Spanish only a little, and that badly. The word *henti* is his approximation of the correct word *gente*, meaning "people."

My grateful thanks goes out to the ever-gracious Connie

Wolfe and Kerry Blair for their invaluable brainstorming and characterization suggestions; to the dozens of readers from American Night Writers Association who gave initial critiques; to C.K. Crigger for title suggestions; to Betty Wilson for her encouragement; to Josi S. Kilpack for the liberal use of her red pen; to Elizabeth Petty Bentley for her advice on edits; to Dan Olsen for checking the testosterone content; to Shirley Bahlmann, Robert J. Randisi, and Pat Decker Nipper for their endorsements; and to the many generous readers who contributed praise for my work.

Contents

Chapter 1

"You girls stick tight together. Those blasted Yankee riders are still botherin' folks."

Jessica Bingham paused outside the bakery's front door, letting Ma's words roll off her shoulders as she rearranged the loaves of freshly baked bread in her basket. She looked down the quiet street. The rising sun's pink and gold rays chased night's shadows from the cracks and crannies of Mount Jackson's storefronts. She inhaled the fresh scents of the morning to clear the heavy odor of yeast from her nose. Spring was here. "Hmmm," she sighed, and felt a smile of satisfaction lift her mouth. Ma was wrong to worry. This perfect day could hold no danger to her or her sisters.

And yet . . . the previous week, two young married ladies had been knocked to the ground by a band of cavalrymen of the occupation force. One merely had the wind knocked out of her, but the other had lost her unborn babe. Her husband had protested. He'd been badly beaten. A feeling of unease crept over Jessica. Perhaps there were no perfect days in Virginia anymore?

Her older, recently married sister, Hannah, pushed past, saying, "Jessie, get yourself out of my way. This bread won't deliver itself."

Jessie stepped aside and let Hannah pass, since she always seemed to be in a hurry. She had to take the lead in every endeavor, and couldn't abide being late. Maybe that's why she was born first of the twins.

The other twin, Hepzibah, came out of the door and stopped at Jessie's side. She nudged Jessie and said, rolling her eyes,

"Hannah's just so rude. Don't give in to her. Ever since she got married, she thinks she's the queen of the world."

Jessie shrugged and stepped out into the street, Hepzibah following after. "Maybe she is, in Robert Fletcher's eyes. He treats her like a fine lady."

Hepzibah made a small, anguished sound. Jessie looked around at her sister, whose expression had changed to chagrin.

Jessie said in a rush, "Oh Heppie, don't mind my prattle. I reckon George loves you just as much as Robert does Hannah. He's bound to say so real soon."

This time, Heppie's sound was definitely a sigh, and her eyes began to redden.

Jessie, trying to divert Heppie from having a crying spell in the middle of the street, called out to Hannah, who strode along five yards ahead of them. "Wait for us. Ma will have a conniption if we don't stay together." She looked around the deserted street, her nerves beginning to twang. "Do you see any riders down the road?"

"No," Hannah replied. "It's too early for those lazy bums to be out. Besides, I ain't seen 'em for days. Ma's just got a bug in her ear." Hannah carried her basket of baked goods on her hip. She stopped walking and gave it a little hitch to make it ride higher.

"Do you reckon they've left town?" Heppie asked Jessie as they followed Hannah.

Jessie shrugged. "I don't know. Maybe a customer told Ma they're still here." She turned her head to look behind her. "I don't see them."

"That don't mean they're not around the corner," Heppie said, sniffing, then wiping her nose with a tiny scrap of a handkerchief. "Look sharp."

Jessie shivered. Her stomach began to ache, and she felt vulnerable and unsafe. The Yankees had already won the war, ravaging the country in the process. It was terribly hard to make ends meet these days. She'd heard Ma crying at night on that score. Why didn't the Yankees go home and leave the people of Mount Jackson alone?

She thought of Hannah, who lived with Robert in a house on the other side of town. During the time he worked at the bank, Hannah was all alone. *She may lord it over Heppie and me for not being married, but maybe she's afraid too. She does spend an awful lot of each day at our house.*

Jessie stepped over a stick in her path. *I reckon I don't blame her*, she thought. She hesitated a moment, sniffing the air. Was that dust she smelled? *Don't panic. Likely a wagon passed on the Valley Pike.* At that moment, the sound of hoof beats coming up behind them raised chills along her spine. She whirled and faced four mounted Yankees, who had seemed to rise out of the very ground.

The men caught up and circled the three women before they could take another step. Two of them spat tobacco juice near the girls' shoes. One failed to launch his mouthful properly, dribbling juice down the front of his shirt.

"Cal, you can't hit a tin can with a turnip," said one man whose dirty red hair poked out in points where it escaped his cap. His laughter rang through the empty street.

Jessie grabbed hold of Hannah's arm with her free hand. She felt Heppie clutching at her skirt band. Jessie looked around, frantic. Where were the Miller brothers? They were always up early, coming down the street as the girls left the bakery.

"Sez you, Red," the Yankee named Cal said, spitting a fresh stream that landed on Heppie's shoulder.

Heppie screamed, dropped her basket, and tried to wipe the juice off.

Cal chewed on his wad of tobacco, turned, and shot a spurt of juice in Hannah's direction. She shrieked as it hit her cheek.

Red laughed again, and waved his cap in the air.

"Hannah!" Jessie shouted, and pulled her sister closer to her. The stink of the tobacco filled her nose as she dashed it away from Hannah's eye with her hand.

The third man, whose black moustache contained bits of food, said to Heppie, "Here, let me wipe that for you." He leaned down and grabbed a lock of Heppie's blonde hair. She cried out as he yanked on it, pulling her closer to his horse.

"You need a knife, Bull?" asked the fourth Yankee, reaching into his pocket.

Bull swore. "I can get my own trophies, Foster. Put away your knife."

"Get away from her!" Jessie shouted. Her heart thrummed in her chest. She tried to think of what to do even as she shoved at the man's arm, getting the juice from her hand on his uniform sleeve. He let go of Heppie's hair and turned on Jessie, trying to swat at her hand, but she evaded his reach. Hannah was cowering away from Foster, who called her unpleasant names. The other men rode in circles around the three young women, laughing, whistling, and making rude talk.

"Go back to the store," Jessie urged her sisters. She stripped the white towel from her basket and flapped it in the face of the nearest horse. It reared, dumping Red, and galloped off down the road. The girls pushed their way through the interrupted circle and ran for the front door of the bakery. Behind them, Jessie heard the laughter and catcalls the other men showered on the unseated rider, who swore at them, his horse, and Jessie herself.

Heppie made it to the door first, wrenching it open. Hannah followed hard on her heels, and Jessie brought up the rear.

"Lock it, Jessie," shrieked Heppie. Her big blue eyes seemed ready to leap out of her face.

Jessie twisted the lock, wondering if it would keep the men

out if they wanted to enter. "Ma," she cried out as her mother rushed into the shop from the kitchen. "Those Yankees! They spit tobacco juice at us. Just look at Heppie's dress!"

"They're so crude," Heppie moaned, swiping at her shoulder. "I'll never get this stain off me!"

"There, there, girls." Ma gathered the young women into her arms. "Did they hurt you?" Jessie felt her mother's body shaking.

Hannah loosed herself from Ma's grasp and dabbed at her cheek with a handkerchief. "I hate tobacco!"

Ma let go of the girls. "Jessie? You ain't been harmed?"

"No, Ma." Jessie started to hug herself to control her quaking, but remembered in time that her hand was still smeared with slime. She walked behind the bakery display case, found a cloth, and wiped her hand with it. The day had just begun, and already it was a disaster.

Ma went to the window and looked out. "Are the Yankees still out there?" She craned her neck to the right. "Looks like they're goin' off down the street," she said. "One of 'em is chasin' a horse. What happened?"

"Jessie spooked his mount and got us out of there," Hannah said. Her voice sounded calmer. "Heppie, let's go clean ourselves up." She took Heppie's arm, and the twins went into the kitchen.

"Ma." Jessie joined her mother at the window. "Do we have to go out there again?"

Ma took a deep, shuddering breath, then let it out slowly. It seemed to steady her. "Folks'll be lookin' for their bread and pastries. If you leave by the back door, it's most likely the Yankees won't even spot you." She gave Jessie a pat on the shoulder. "I know those Yankee louts are mighty rude to folks, but I don't think you'll come to real harm if you stay together. When Hannah and Heppie have cleaned up, you three scoot."

Jessie sighed. *Ma's right. Folks need their baked goods, and heaven knows we need the money.* She shivered. They would have to go back out. Without a protector. Her brother Luke was too young to do much good. Her heart pounded in her chest. *Oh Pa! Why did you have to die and leave us so helpless?*

Jessie looked over her shoulder at Hannah and Heppie, who walked away from her toward the street corner, leaving Jessie to collect payment for a pie. Mrs. Wiggins, however, seemed inclined to chat.

Please just pay me, Jessie thought, looking the other way down the street. *I don't want us running into those Yankees again.* She turned back to Mrs. Wiggins, anxious about the distance between her and her sisters. She didn't want to be alone, even for the few seconds it would take her to catch up.

Mrs. Wiggins looked at Jessie expectantly. She must have asked a question.

Shrugging her shoulders to shake off her reverie, Jessie said, "I'm so sorry, ma'am, I fear I was woolgathering. What's that you said?"

The stout little woman sighed. "Jessie dear, I was askin' if your ma could bake me a loaf of sourdough bread for tomorrow morning."

"I'll need payment for the pie first, ma'am," Jessie said, hoping it didn't sound too rude.

"Can't y'all wait to the end of the week?" Mrs. Wiggins looked flustered.

"Times are hard, ma'am. Ma needs to buy supplies." Jessie glanced over her shoulder again. Hannah and Heppie were a half block away. A cold chill ran through her.

"That's right, Jessie dear. Times are hard indeed, but Mr. Wiggins wanted an apple pie for his birthday." Mrs. Wiggins sighed. "I'll get your money." She turned her back, left the door open, and took the pie into the house.

Jessie tapped her toe as she waited, watching her sisters grow smaller and smaller. Her stomach tightened on her breakfast and made her queasy. *Hurry up!* she thought, and mentally berated the twins for leaving her here. She was the "little sister." More often than not, they stuck together and left her to do the more distasteful things like collect money from customers.

After what seemed like forever, Mrs. Wiggins returned with a few coins and counted out the price of the pie.

"Thank you, ma'am. I'll tell Ma about your bread," Jessie said as she put the money into her pocket.

Mrs. Wiggins closed the door forcefully, as if to protest Jessie's insistence on being paid.

Jessie snorted. *Silly old bat! Of course she has to pay Ma now. How does she expect—* Jessie left the thought alone and went on to her more immediate worry. With one hand she scooped up the basket she'd put on the porch while she waited, and with the other she grabbed her skirt, racing off after her sisters. "Hannah," she called out. "Heppie! Wait for me."

Jessie had covered half the distance that separated her from the twins when she tripped on a root and fell, landing on the hard dirt with her forearms straddling the basket.

Pain lanced through her arms but was instantly supplanted by the smart of her embarrassment. *Oh, what mortification! You'd think I was twelve years old instead of eighteen, trippin' over a danged root.*

Heppie had looked back in time to see the fall. "Jessie," she cried out, and started toward her, motioning for her to get up—as if Jessie were perfectly content to lie sprawled across the path as she was. Hannah continued on to the corner, then turned and waited while Jessie scrambled to her feet and Heppie helped her brush off her skirts.

"Jessie! Are you hurt?"

She rubbed her sore arms, getting the dirt off. "I reckon I'll be—"

Jessie saw the man at that moment, the rider the Yankees called Red. In what seemed only a few seconds, he jumped off his horse, grabbed Hannah around the waist, and was back in his saddle, having thrown Hannah over the front of his horse like a sack of grain. Her basket tumbled through the air, spewing loaves of bread onto the ground. Jessie cried out and pointed, unable to form words to describe what she was seeing. Heppie turned and began to scream. Jessie lifted her skirts and ran toward the corner as fast as she could. *He can't be takin' her*, she thought, her heart pounding in her ears.

Jessie shoved open the door of the bank with such force that it banged against the wall. Several customers turned to gaze at her in surprise. The clerks and tellers looked up from their work.

Jessie located Hannah's husband, Robert Fletcher, in the teller's cage at the end of the row. She ran across the tile floor and pushed aside the woman standing opposite him.

"You must come, now!" Jessie said to the man, gasping as she struggled to draw air into her burning lungs.

"Miss Jessica—" He turned to his customer. "I'm sorry, Miz Addison. I'm sure she didn't mean—" He broke off and faced Jessie again, frown lines deeply creasing his face and sweat breaking out on his forehead. "What happened to you? You're quite . . . untidy." Robert took out a handkerchief and dabbed at the brow on both sides of his pronounced widow's peak.

"Mr. Fletcher—Robert—Hannah's been taken!" Jessie put out a shaking hand and grasped the counter to support herself. "We've got to get help."

Robert took in a sharp breath. He stuffed the handkerchief in his pocket as he turned and leaped over the gate separating the teller's cages from the customer area.

Before Jessie could blink, he grasped her by the elbow and shook her arm. "What do you mean, 'Hannah's been taken'?"

Jessie's trembling almost overcame her. She forced herself to find her voice, still breathing with difficulty as Robert's grip tightened. "You know those Yankee riders? One of them grabbed her and took her off. Oh, Mr. Fletcher, Heppie's in such a state I had—"

An oath escaped Robert Fletcher's lips as he dropped her arm. "Take me there," he grunted, barging through the door to the street. She caught up to him and led off at a run, lifting her skirts out of the way of her feet.

They cut across the street, darting between vehicles and horses, bumping without apology into passersby, their silent haste fed by adrenaline and fear.

When they arrived at the street where Hannah had been abducted, Heppie bolted out of Mrs. Wiggins's door, crying into her handkerchief. "Oh, Mr. Fletcher, I'm so glad to see you."

Robert nodded briefly to Heppie, then turned and asked Jessie, "Which way did he go?"

Jessie pointed south on the Valley Pike. "It's the redheaded one."

Robert thrust Jessie into Heppie's arms, saying, "Go to your ma's. I'll bring her there," and ran down the street.

"Jessie, did you see his face?" Heppie wailed.

Jessie shook in her sister's embrace as new fear enveloped her. "Yes. I'm afraid he'll kill that Yankee."

Chapter 2

Hannah screamed as the Yankee carried her away from her sisters. She took a breath to scream again. The odor of tobacco and sweaty clothes worn too long without washing almost gagged her.

"Don't bother yelling. Nobody's going to help you," said the man in a rasping voice. He jammed his free arm underneath her stomach and yanked her roughly against him. "None of your yellow-bellied rebel men have the guts."

Hannah twisted and turned in the man's grasp. She tried to get her fingers to his face to gouge his eyes, but he swatted her arm down with his rein hand and pinned it to her side.

"No more of that, missy," he growled, and prodded his horse to a faster pace with a few kicks.

"My husband will come. He'll find you, and he'll kill you," Hannah gasped, struggling anew to find a way to hurt the man.

"You won't be worth the bother when I'm done with you."

The Yankee's words ripped through Hannah's mind. *Oh dear God, no! Help me! Don't let him do this.* "Robert!" she shrieked between sobs that seemed to tear all the flesh from her throat.

"Your Bobbie-boy can't help you, missy," the man growled, and punched Hannah on the side of her head. "Behave now. We've got a ways to go."

Pain sent Hannah slumping forward against the horse's neck as she tried not to lose consciousness. Her ears rang. Her nose filled with dust thrown from the horse's hooves. She closed her eyes and coughed. *I won't let him kill me, she thought. I'll be strong. No matter what he does, I'll be strong until Robert comes.*

After a long time, the horseman pulled up and pushed Hannah to the ground. She rolled to her knees. Three startled chickens ran into the brush at the edge of a stable yard. Before she could arise and follow them, the man was beside her, grasping her around the waist. He dragged her to her feet and into the stable, tugging on a rein to make sure his horse followed. He kicked the door, but not hard enough to close it, and it stood open a ways, letting in a stream of sunlight.

Hannah screamed, lashing out at the man, pulling his hair with both hands. *I'll mark him*, she thought. *If he's gone when Robert comes, I'll tell him what to look for.*

The Yankee hit Hannah across the mouth, and she lost her grip on his hair with one hand. She tasted salt against her tongue and knew she was bleeding, but she tugged on the man's rusty-colored hair with her other fist. They whirled around, struggling back and forth in the alleyway of the stable. Hair came loose in her hand. She spit her blood on his shirt. He hit her again and she spun and went down onto the straw-covered floor of a stall.

Hannah choked and coughed at the dust her fall had raised. She heard the man coming toward her and tried to curl into a ball, but he knelt on top of her, ripping her blouse until her flesh was exposed and pulling at her skirt. She smelled his rank breath as he tried to kiss her. "No!" she screamed. He slapped her, but she only cried out again. "Help me!"

The man swore at her, calling her vile names as he unbuckled his belt and slid down his trousers. Hannah thrashed back and forth, clawing him with her nails and calling for help as he tore at her skirt, ripping it open nearly to her waist. She screamed again when he shredded her underclothes, then wrestled with her until he restrained her hands above her head.

The pain of his assault wrenched through her body, tore at the sanctity of her womanhood, and bludgeoned her soul until

she believed that neither her body nor her spirit would survive.
She clenched her eyes shut, as if that could hide what was
happening, and felt tears leaking from the corners of her eyes.
He is a fiend of hell, her thoughts shrieked as he slumped on top
of her.

Hannah shivered under him, too spent to cry out any longer.
She could not avoid inhaling the stench of his hair lying on her
face. It seemed that hours passed while his loathsome body
pinned hers into the straw. At last he raised himself above her.
She kept her eyes closed, but couldn't hold back the sob that
rose in her throat.

"What's the matter? You don't like my looks?" he growled.
"That's too bad, missy. You've got to bear them until I'm
finished with you." He reached down and touched her breast,
laughing at her. "I told you no one was coming for you. I've got
as long as I want."

Robert ran down the Pike, his heart thudding in his chest.
Where would the man take Hannah? If he was intent on doing
her harm, he'd want a private place, like a barn or a grove of
trees, even though the occupation soldiers and cavalry were
doing pretty much as they liked these days. He'd have to ask if
Hannah and the rider had been seen passing by. That might be
useless—folks were staying out of each other's business. His
breath rattled in his throat. His side burned with pain. His legs
seemed made of lead. *No matter*, he thought, and continued his
headlong dash. *Hannah needs me.*

When he stumbled and fell, Robert lay with his face in the
dust for a moment, then raised his head and eyed the road. The
marks of horses' hooves mocked him. *I don't know how to
track. I don't know what's fresh and what might be five days
old.* He scrambled to his knees, got to his feet, and looked

around. He was outside of town and had passed two farms already. *Have I gone too far?* He took a steadying breath. No. Those farms had been burned out by the Yankees. Their barns hadn't been rebuilt yet and the woodlots were gone. No privacy there. Robert began to run again. George Heizer's dairy farm was next. He had a barn.

Robert approached the Heizer place. From the lane he could see two men standing by a wagon in the barnyard, talking. They seemed calm, not looking over their shoulders or fidgeting. *No Yankee's been there*, he decided, and continued down the pike. *I'll try at McNeely's.*

Robert ran another two hundred yards, turned into McNeely's farmyard, skidded to a stop at the door of the house and rapped. His windpipe wheezed and his lungs burned as he sucked breath into them. After a moment, Mistress Maude moved the curtain to one side and peered out. She opened the door a crack, her white face telling of her fear.

Before he could say a word, the woman began.

"Mr. Fletcher! Oh, please, can you look? My Patrick won't be home until after dark."

"Look where, Mrs. McNeely?"

"Oh my! Out in the stable. There's been the most horrid sounds coming from out there for such a long time. Screams, very terrible sounds, they were."

He ground his teeth. "Do you have a gun?"

"A gun? Oh, no, Mr. Fletcher. We had to give it up."

"A knife, then. Lend me your butcher knife."

Her gasp told Robert how she felt about that idea as she closed the door in his face. He heard the lock snapping into place.

He found a stout stick of firewood he could wrap his fingers around, not thinking what he would do with it, but somehow needing to feel the wood's heft, needing to have a weapon. He strode toward the stable.

The door stood open enough to let him through, and he stopped a moment to let his eyes adjust to the semidarkness. The Yankee's horse munched straw to one side, still saddled, reins hanging loose. A rack of farm implements hung on the wall, next to a couple of saddle blankets arranged over a rail. The burly redheaded Yankee knelt over Hannah in a stall, pants at his ankles.

Hannah! What has he done? I'm too late to spare you that—

Robert swallowed hard, his thoughts a torment. The sight of Hannah's bare knees being forced apart for the brute's pleasure enraged him, pushing him past reason, past honor, and he ran toward the man, raising his bludgeon to strike him from behind.

Hannah opened her eyes. With his last vestige of wits, Robert saw hope spring into them, then she turned her head away, but not before he recognized the look of shame on her face.

Robert swung his club down toward the Yankee's head, but Hannah shrieked at his attack. The sound startled him, causing him to miss his target. The blow glanced off the side of the man's skull, and he fell on top of Hannah. Robert threw away his club, grasped the back of the man's jacket, and hauled him to his feet.

Robert turned the Yankee around. Hannah had done damage with her nails. One of the man's cheeks was striped with raw lesions.

The Yankee groaned, wagged his head, and then spat in Robert's face. "I'll kill you, rebel scum," the man rasped through his patchy beard. He threw a punch at Robert, striking him on the chin and knocking him backward. Robert crumpled to the floor. The Yankee loomed over him, and gave a gargling laugh as he pulled up and buttoned his trousers. "She wasn't even that good," he said, and stomped on Robert's cheek. "I've had better times with a whore."

A red blur swam before Robert's eyes. *My sweet Hannah, compared to a whore?* He cried out, "She was good at defending herself." Rage flashed through his body, giving him strength he didn't know he possessed. He leaped up and connected with a blow that sent the man staggering into the aisle of the stable. Robert followed, punching him time and again until his knuckles bled. He jabbed the man's ribbon-slashed cheek with a thumb. The man yowled.

Robert's fingers closed around the man's throat. "I'm here to finish the job."

The Yankee clawed at Robert's fingers, finally breaking their hold. Then he retreated, stumbling backward until he found a pitchfork and jabbed it toward Robert, murderous intent glittering in his bloodshot eyes. "You'll finish nothing, you slimy reb. I ain't through with you, nor with her."

Robert lunged back in time to avoid the lethal tines. *If he kills me, he'll continue with Hannah until she's dead. I can't let that happen.*

The man came at him again, and Robert's hand closed over the handle of an ax that he swung blindly at the oncoming fork. The clash of metal on metal split the air. The pitchfork flew from the man's hands and landed against a partition near where Hannah crouched with her hands covering her ears, shrieking.

Robert swung the ax once more to keep the Yankee at a distance, but underestimated his strength and turned himself half around.

The man rushed Robert, grabbing him by an arm and a leg, then spun and threw him against a wall. Momentum carried the man in another circle, until he screamed in agony and fell silent.

Robert lay in a heap, wondering at the cessation of the man's cry. He pushed himself to his knees, his own panting sounding loud in his ears, louder than Hannah's hysterical sobs. The Yankee hadn't returned to the fray. Robert staggered to his feet, wary, looking for his enemy.

The man stood close to a partition, bent over a bit, his face a mask of astonishment. His mouth gaped open, and his arms hung at his sides, but he didn't move.

Robert could hear Hannah, weeping uncontrollably, but he couldn't see her anywhere. *I've got to deal with him first*, he told himself, struggling with his instinct to find her, to gather her into his arms and console her.

Robert searched for a weapon, located and picked up the ax from where it had fallen, and approached the man, on guard. "You ain't through with me, you say?" he challenged. Hannah's cries filled his ears, louder than ever, but the Yankee made no reply. A fly buzzed down from the ceiling and settled on the man's eye. He didn't blink.

Robert did blink, finally seeing the streams of blood trailing down the front of the Yankee's chest from where small black iron points emerged from his shirt. Hannah squatted behind him against the partition, the handle of the pitchfork clutched in her hands.

Almost stuttering between crying and speech, Hannah gasped out, "Is . . . he . . . dead?"

Robert nodded. He dropped the ax, reached behind the man and forcibly uncurled Hannah's fingers from the pitchfork so he could push the Yankee aside. He pulled her to her feet, dragging her away from the sight. As they reached the other side of the stable, he snatched up a saddle blanket, and drew her into his arms.

"Hannah," he crooned in her ear. "Hannah love." He pulled her blouse closed and covered her with the blanket.

His wife shook in his embrace, sobbing out, "I wanted him to stop hurting you."

He stroked her hair. "I . . . Hannah, he can't hurt anybody anymore."

"I killed him." Hannah's cry came out strangled.

Robert swallowed, wishing he could take her burden upon himself. He glanced over at the dead Yankee, face down in the straw. Bile rose in his throat, and he wanted to vomit. Instead, he steeled himself and said, "We have to leave."

He stood up and helped Hannah to her feet. She stopped crying, but swayed against him, at the point of collapse. He picked her up, but his own strength was spent and he staggered, almost dropping her. How would he get her home?

The Yankee's horse.

Robert set Hannah down and went to the wild-eyed animal. "Hey, boy, quiet now. Come here." He mounted with some effort, then kneed the animal forward to where his wife stood. "Put your arms up, love," he murmured, and as she did, he reached down and, grunting, pulled her onto the horse.

As Hannah settled against him, he stiffened involuntarily. Hannah whimpered, "You're hurt, ain't you?"

Robert bit his lip against the pain throbbing through his head and body. "Some little bit," he agreed. "But I reckon we can make it as far as the Heizer place."

Chapter 3

George Heizer leaned his head against the warm flank of the cow, his fingers squeezing in the age-old rhythm of milking. When the knock came on the barn door, he paused, not sure he'd heard it. When it came again, he stood up and grabbed his pitchfork. Who knocked on the door of a barn?

Before he had sorted out in his mind whether the visitor could be a customer or someone bent on doing harm, the knock came again. He waited a moment, but no one spoke to offer him a greeting.

George crept out of the stall, stepping as quietly as he could. "Who's there?" he called.

"Robert Fletcher. George, I need your help."

Robert Fletcher was his good friend. They'd seen action in the same company during the war. Robert had come home unwounded, but George's right ear was half gone from a close shave with a Yankee bullet. Robert had tied his own handkerchief around the bleeding ear. Later, in the same battle, he had saved George's bacon when he was wounded in the leg.

George went to the small door and wrenched it open. A horse stood in the shade before the opening, two people hunched over its withers. One slid to the ground, fell to one knee, and struggled to get to his feet. It was indeed Robert, his brown hair darkened by sweat, and— was that blood?

Robert held out his hands to the other figure, still sitting on the horse. That person half fell into his arms, and the two of them went to the ground.

The horse moved aside. Again, Robert climbed to his feet, stooped, and tried to raise the other person. At length he stood, his arms around what was clearly a woman in a high state of disarray. Robert had married not long ago, and George finally recognized the second person as Robert's wife, Hannah.

George cried out in dismay. Robert had taken a beating, and Hannah had obviously suffered a great deal of misuse. Her pale yellow hair was matted to her head. Her face was bloodied. Her clothing was torn. Although she tried to clasp the pieces about her, she was having difficulty remaining covered. George stared at her, knowing he should look away, but unable to do so.

He finally shook himself free of the fascination and asked, "What happened to you? Yankees?" The mere thought of the occupation forces made him shudder and look down the lane. "Come inside," he said, backing through the door.

Robert bent to retrieve a saddle blanket on the ground. When he straightened up and draped it around Hannah, he grimaced in pain. "Yes. I had a set-to with one of those riders." He shepherded Hannah through the door, paused and coughed, then examined a spot on his head with careful fingers.

George slammed the door shut. "I hope you killed him."

"He's dead," Robert said, and spat out a gob of blood. "Can you help us get to Mrs. Bingham's bakery?" He paused, wiped the blood from his lips, and blurted out, "I hate getting you involved in this, George, but I don't know where else to go." After a moment, Robert continued, "Unless you can't see your way clear."

George swore to himself. Yes, helping Robert was risky. The Yankees would find their crony dead. If they discovered Robert had killed him, then learned that George helped Robert, who knew what they would do in reprisal.

Hannah moaned in Robert's arms.

Robert had pulled George off the battlefield when he'd been shot in the leg and lay bleeding and stunned by the force of the blow and the pain. No matter what happened, he owed Robert a debt.

"I'll hitch the team to the milk wagon. It's covered, so no one will see you."

"Thank you," Robert said.

George said nothing, but shook his head as he hurried to get the harness.

A hard knock on the back door made Jessie jump. She looked through the curtain of the back window. "Oh, thank God," she said, unlocking the door and throwing it wide. "Hurry in," she whispered, unable to take her eyes off her bedraggled sister, who sagged between Robert Fletcher and George Heizer. "Hannah?" she asked as she locked the door behind them. But she couldn't continue. She didn't know what words to use in asking what had happened.

Jessie followed the group into the kitchen. Her younger brother Luke sat at the table, fiddling with a half-eaten plate of food. George said to him, "Give Hannah your chair," and Luke hopped up as Heppie screamed. George and Robert get Hannah into the seat, then George stepped away and went to Heppie. "Shh," he said, putting his hand on her shoulder.

Jessie heard her mother gasp repeatedly behind her. *Ma isn't dealing well*, she thought. *George is distracting Heppie. Who's going to tend to Hannah?* She threw back her shoulders. *Me*, she told herself, and went to her sister's side. Hannah's head hung low, but her hand flew up and gripped Jessie's forearm.

"Steady," Jessie said. "You're home safe."

"There's nowhere safe," Hannah got out through lips crusted with blood. "Nowhere in Virginia."

"Oh, my dear daughter," Ma said, breathing in great rasping breaths. She elbowed Jessie to one side, and hugged Hannah around her head.

Jessie peeled Hannah's fingers from her arm and went to

find a cloth to wet. She heard her mother's wild questions to Robert, and his soft answers.

"She was in McNeely's barn. I pulled the Yankee off her, and he's still there."

"Still there?" Luke asked. "Didn't you fight him?"

Jessie came back with the wet cloth and caught Robert nodding in answer to Luke's question. *Luke's stupid question*, she thought. *Anyone with eyes can see Robert's been in a fight!* She said a quiet word to her mother and got her to release Hannah. She started cleaning the blood from her sister's face. Her eyes smarted as she struggled to hold back tears. What kind of monster had done this? Her stomach lurched as she cleaned a clot of blood off Hannah's ear. She'd always had an aversion to blood. *This isn't so bad*, she told herself, trying to contain her tendency to gag. *It's dried, not flowing.*

"How come he's still there? Isn't he looking for you?" Ma's voice soared, and Jessie wanted to hush her as she would a wailing child.

"He's dead."

"Thank the Lord. Thank the Lord." Ma stood by the stove, rocking back and forth, her voice uplifted in prayer.

"Ma, softly now," Jessie said. She glanced at Heppie. "Can you get some water for Mr. Fletcher to clean up?" What an impossible event, having to prompt her older sister into action. The whole world was coming apart.

Ma finally stopped praying, came back to Jessie, and took the cloth from her. Jessie began to pace, rubbing her arm where Hannah had clasped it so hard, wondering what would happen to them, how they would go on.

"Now everything will be fine," Ma said.

Robert shook his head as he took a basin of water that Heppie gave him. "I have to leave, Mrs. Bingham. As soon as someone finds that dead Yankee, the commander will investigate. Mrs. McNeely knew I was there, and with so many Yankees still around—"

"No. We'll be safe now that the Yankee is dead." Ma said. "You did the right thing, Mr. Fletcher, exactly the right thing." Her voice broke, and she blinked back tears, wiping Hannah's face vigorously.

"That hurts, Ma." Hannah's voice was feeble.

"Ma'am, folks will remember Mrs. Fletcher was kidnapped. When Miss Jessie fetched me, the bank was full of people. They all saw us leave in a hurry." Robert put one of his hands into the water to soak and with the other scrubbed his face with a cloth. "Folks are frightened. Someone's going to say something."

"But what of Hannah?" Mrs. Bingham asked.

Robert looked up, his face hard with offense. "I'll not leave her behind!"

As the buzz of the discussion continued behind her, Jessie paced between the stove and the back door, trying to wrap her mind around how different her world was from what it had been when she woke up this morning. Hannah had been carried off in broad daylight. From the looks of her, she had been terribly abused by the Yankee. Could Heppie, could Jessie herself expect any better treatment in the months to come? Jessie kneaded her hands together. What could they do to keep safe? Nothing. Hannah was right. There was no safety for women in Virginia. They were all subject to Yankee whims and carpetbagger tricks. If the Yankees didn't leave Mount Jackson, why couldn't the whole family leave instead? She stopped pacing and stood still. She held her breath. What if they left with Mr. Fletcher and Hannah? Yes. Yes! That was the answer.

"Ma!" she interrupted. "Do you have that letter Max sent you?"

Mrs. Bingham turned her head sharply. "What?"

"The letter. Didn't Max ask us to join him in"—Jessie made

circles beside her head, frustrated with the mental fog the day had brought to her mind—"that town with the strange name?"

"Oh Jessie, you don't mean—"

"Ma, let's all go. George, I mean Mr. Heizer too, if he wants— if he must."

"Albuquerque is far away, Jessie," her mother argued. "It's almost to California."

"Isn't that a good thing? We'll get lost to these troublesome, hateful—" She couldn't think of a word bad enough to describe their tormentors. Her eyes settled on Hannah, her broken countenance. "Conquerors!" she spat.

"Miss Jessie," George began. He stopped and pursed his lips for a moment. "I'd like that better than anything, but I can't leave. I've had a letter from my brother Ned. He was in the hospital for a long time, but they finally released him. He's not very strong, but he's on his way home." He glanced over at Heppie with a somber expression on his face.

Jessie looked from George to Robert, who was bent over Hannah, patting her on the arm and murmuring soothing words to her. He straightened up when George finished speaking. One of his eyes was swollen and blackened. His lips were cracked.

"As many of you as wants to go with us can do so, but if you're coming, you need to pack up right away. We're leaving tonight. Miss Jessie's right. After all—" He looked at Hannah again, and Jessie thought she might have seen tears in his eyes before he regained control. "After all that's happened, leaving this place, leaving all of this behind is the only way to go on."

Heppie gave a little shrug. "I'm goin' with you. Hannah needs nursing, and I can do that."

"Heppie," George said, disappointment strong in his voice.

She looked at Hannah, then back to George. "Hannah needs me more," she said, her voice cracking.

Jessie knew that was not an easy thing for her sister to say.

Heppie whispered to her each night before they fell asleep about her growing affection for George Heizer. Leaving him behind was no trifling act on Heppie's part. But what else could they do?

"Ma," Jessie said. "I'm goin' too. There's been nothing here for me since . . ." She stopped herself, unwilling to say it out loud. The wound of James Owen's leaving her to go west with his family was still raw, even if it had been almost a year ago. "What about you and Luke?"

Ma clasped her hands together. Jessie saw her knuckles turn white with the pressure. Her shoulders hunched together. At last she sighed and let them relax. "Lucas, cut your pa's picture from the frame. We're going to New Mexico."

Heppie sat with George on the floor of the darkened bakery, her knees drawn up to her chin. The others were still packing, but he had insisted they take a little break and talk one more time.

George lifted her hand and stroked it. "Stay here with me, Heppie," he whispered. "We'll get married and you can help me run the farm. I'll keep you safe from the Yankees."

Tears ran down Heppie's cheeks as she blinked her eyes. What should she do? Hannah needed her so desperately. Besides, she was Hannah's twin. Hannah's marriage had caused the greatest parting they'd ever experienced, but they still managed to see each other almost every day. George was complicating her life with his plea. If she married him and stayed here, she'd never see Hannah or her family again.

"My family needs me. I want to be with them. They love me." She swiped at the tears.

"I love you, Heppie. I've loved you for years."

She shook her head and took her hand away from George's

fingers. "You never said that before. You talked of us marrying but never declared yourself to love me. Maybe that's why I didn't give you an answer." Her words trailed off into the void between them.

George hung his head. "That was wrong of me. I meant not to pressure you." He looked up at her, his blue eyes pleading. "Heppie, don't go off and leave me alone."

"You won't be alone for long. You said your brother's comin' home. You said that's why you can't leave." Her voice sounded flat, expressionless, devoid of hope.

"Heppie, please. He's still not recovered. How can I up and take off when he expects me to welcome him home? And the cows. I wouldn't do them a service to leave 'em without someone to take care of them."

Heppie waited for a long time before she spoke in a terse voice. "I need to be with my family. You need to take care of your brother and your cows. I reckon that puts us on different paths, Mr. Heizer."

"Heppie, don't say that."

She struggled to her feet, and he also arose. "Good-bye, George," she managed to say, and walked back into the kitchen.

Chapter 4

George headed back to the farm in the milk wagon. He'd had a busy morning making deliveries, just barely busy enough to keep him from thinking too much about Heppie. She and her family had been gone for several days, and every single one of those days had been an agony of despair to him. He should have told her a long time ago that he loved her. He should have insisted that he needed her more than her sister did. He should have, he should have, he should have.

Hoof beats drummed on the road behind him. His baleful thoughts faded into the protective recesses of his mind as he wondered who was coming down the Valley Pike in such a hurry. Whoever they were, they were riding hard and quick, not sparing their horses. He craned his neck to see around the box of the milk wagon, and spotted three men, lashing their mounts unmercifully.

I'd best get out of their way, he thought, and guided the team to the side of the road and halted them. He waited for the riders to pass by, but instead, he heard rough voices yelling as they drew near.

"It's him," one said. "Catch up that team."

A man rode up and grabbed hold of the harness. Another, whose dirty blond hair flew around his face, circled his mount in front of the team, blocking their way. The third, wearing a full black beard that covered the collar front of his Union uniform blouse, reined to a stop beside the seat and hit George in the face with his fist. "Where are they, rebel scum?"

George recoiled from the blow, almost toppling off the other side of the seat. "Who?" he grunted, trying to catch his breath.

The black-bearded man swore. "You know who. That bastard banker, that's who, and his whore of a wife." The man struck George again, then hauled him off the seat and dropped him in the road. He dismounted and kicked George, who curled into a ball to absorb the blow.

By this time, all three men were off their horses. The one with the blond hair unhooked the team from the wagon, and gave the horses a swat on their rumps so they ran off, dragging the lines behind them.

"Don't kill him, Bull," said the man who had grabbed the team. "He knows where they are."

"Where did they go, you miserable rebel dog? Tell me now." Bull kicked George again, reached down, and pulled him to his feet.

"Where's that bakery lady at?" asked the man with the blond hair. "Did they all go off together?" He punched George over the kidney, and he reeled across the roadbed, moaning with the pain that radiated throughout his body.

"Cal, let me beat him some," whined the third man to the blond.

"No, you grab him and hold him, Foster," said Bull. Foster shrugged, then caught George by the arms. He wrestled him back to Bull, who hit George in the jaw, muttering "Where is Fletcher? We know he killed Red." His black beard twitched as he clouted George again.

"I don't know what you're talkin' about," George mumbled through the pain, just before Cal hit him in the eye.

"We know different," said Bull. "People saw you making a late delivery to the bakery. We figure it wasn't milk."

"Bull's right, Heizer," said Foster, twisting George's arms. "You helped him get away."

"We want to know where they went," Cal said, and followed his words with a punch to George's belly.

George yelled, "I don't know where they are," and tried to keep himself upright, tried to raise a foot to kick one of his tormenters. He failed, as another fist plowed into his face. The blows came without much talk from the riders. His mind focused on trying to blank out the pain. At last it overwhelmed him, and he wished for death before he betrayed his friend . . . and Heppie. These men would treat her as their crony had treated Robert's wife.

Bull planted another blow on George's other kidney, and he sagged in Foster's grip. "Where did they go?" the lout asked again.

"I don't know," he shouted with the last of his strength. "I don't know." He heard sobs and, after a few more punches landed, realized they were his own. His lips were swollen from the blows that had split them. He could barely breathe, but he sucked in air and forced out a word. "Richmond."

"Ha," Cal said, with another jab. "If you're lying, we'll come kill you." He turned away, then back again, "We're done, Foster. Let him loose."

Foster released his grasp, and George staggered forward and collapsed in the dust. He dimly heard the creak of leather when the men climbed into their saddles. The sound of hoofbeats on the hard pike receded as they rode back the way they'd come.

He didn't know how long he lay there before he mastered the pain enough to get to his hands and knees. His face throbbed. His ribs ached where he'd been kicked. His kidneys burned. A question flitted through his mind. Would he pee blood? Anger roiled into his body, and it gave him the strength to get one foot flat on the road. He couldn't get the other under him, and he fell back onto his knees, feeble from the pain.

At least I bought Heppie a few more days, he thought. *They'll look in the wrong direction.*

He crawled to the side of the road, wondering if he had the

strength to get home. Probably not, but he'd be damned if he didn't try. The cows would need milking by the time he could get there. The infernal cows he'd chosen over Heppie. No, it wasn't only the cows. Ned was coming home. Ned, who would need tending to finish healing up. Ned, who had gone North at the beginning of the war. Ned, the Yankee officer.

"Hannah love, you have to eat," Robert said, holding a spoonful of gruel to his wife's lips.

Hannah moaned, closed her eyes, then opened them. "I'll just lose it again," she whispered.

"Heppie tells me you haven't eaten much of anything for three days." Robert found Hannah's mouth by the light of the campfire and tried to put the spoon inside her lips.

She shook her head. "Don't make me."

"You're so weak, darlin'. You won't mend if you don't eat something."

Hannah gave a tiny negative shake of her head. "Who cares if I mend? I don't. God don't. If He cared I wouldn't have . . . That man . . . I killed him, Robert."

Robert swallowed down the bitter gall that rose in his throat as his mind flashed over that horrible day. He put down the bowl and started to cup his hands around Hannah's face, but she turned away. He looked at his scabbed-over knuckles and dropped them to his sides. When he tried to speak, his voice seemed to choke on a lump in his throat, but he pushed the words through, noting how hoarse they sounded in his ears. "He deserved to die," he said. "If God was there, He had you pick up the fork. You were defending me."

"I should be sorry I killed him." Hannah was sobbing, gulping for breath. "I'm not. It's all mixed up. He hurt me so much!"

Robert reached out to gather Hannah into his arms, but she froze with her arms crossed over her chest. Again, he dropped his hands, wondering how long she would lock him out, rejecting his consolation. She didn't want his comfort.

No, she doesn't want your touch, he thought. *You're a man. Her mind was hurt as badly as her body, and a man did that to her.* His stomach churned. *How long will it take for Hannah's mind to heal?* He took a deep breath, remembering his wedding vows. *In sickness or in health.* He let out a long, shuddering sigh. *However long it is, however long it takes, I've got to stand alongside her, ready to help her fight the trouble in her mind.*

Hannah choked back her sobs as Robert walked away, banging one fist into the other. She longed with all her heart to feel his arms around her, but she couldn't bear that. Not now. The violation of her body had damaged her spirit and her mind, as well. Perhaps that was the worst part. She couldn't abide the comfort that she needed the most.

She flinched, gagging, and turned on her side to locate the basin Heppie had placed there. Hannah brought it to her mouth, but her heaving stomach was empty. She had nothing to throw up, not even bile.

Finished, Hannah dropped the basin. Retching had left her too weak to hold it. *Am I dying? Has that wicked man mortally wounded me?* Her eyes leaked tears that she had no strength to wipe away. *I don't want to leave Robert alone. What will he do without me? Who will take care of him? No one can cherish him as I do.*

As she lay there, exhausted and feeble, a seed of determination grew in her heart. *I won't let that evil Yankee kill me,* she thought. *I must hold on for Robert's sake.* With a jolt, she realized she had made similar oaths on the day she had been attacked. *I had the strength at that time. I'll find it again.*

She rolled onto her back and slid her hand toward the bowl with the gruel Robert had tried to feed her. She knew if she tried to raise it, she would spill the contents, so she located the spoon, filled it, and lifted it toward her mouth. The nearer the spoon came, the more she feared she would drop it, but when she did, most of the gruel ended up in her open mouth.

She closed it, holding the cold, mushy liquid on her tongue until she dared to swallow. Her hand fell to her side as her body shook from the effort she had made. The spoon slid down her cheek to her bosom. She ignored it and the gobs of gruel on her face and in her hair. They didn't matter. Someone would come back soon, and they would clean her up. All that mattered was that she had eaten a bite of food. She was not going to die.

George made it to the narrow road leading to the farmhouse after dark had fallen. He'd rolled into the ditch beside the Pike every time someone came along. Crawling up the lane on bleeding hands and elbows, and knees that poked through his trousers, he saw lamplight streaming through a crack in the shutters covering the kitchen window.

He stopped. *What on earth?* He blinked, not trusting the sight of his injured eyes. Yes, that was light, not an illusion. Someone was in the house. *Who is it? The Yankees didn't come back down here by the pike.*

There was no ditch to roll into for protection. Only trees lined the path. He hunkered down to the ground, not knowing what else to do to. He waited for an eternity.

At length, a hunched figure carrying a lantern stepped out the side door and limped toward the barn. He stopped once, turned toward the lane, and held the light high. Then he continued on his original path, whistling a few bars of a tune.

Ned!

If the fleeting look at the man's face hadn't been enough for George, the tune was confirmation. His brother had made up that melody years ago when they were boys playing games in the dusk. *Ned is home.*

George pursed his swollen lips, but couldn't manage a whistle. He tried again, but it was useless. He'd have to cry out, if he had enough strength. He tried breathing deeply, and pain penalized his efforts. *Busted ribs.*

"Ned," he exhaled, and thought he saw his brother pause. "Ned," he tried again, with a little more force.

This time Ned turned around and held up the light again. "Who's there?" he asked, his other arm sliding down to a holstered weapon.

"George. Come get me," he whispered, rising to his hands and knees.

"Who's out there?" Ned asked again, setting down the lantern and drawing his pistol. George heard the click of the hammer being pulled back.

Weakness overwhelmed George, and a sob came out of his throat. "Help . . . me," he tried again. Unable to look up, he heard Ned's hesitant footfalls as he approached. They stopped a fair distance away.

"Friend or foe?" Ned challenged.

"Friend," he moaned, trying to raise his face out of the dust.

Footsteps. Ned had gained courage. George sensed, rather than saw, a circle of light through his closed eyelids. Ned must be carrying the lantern. Something settled into the dust nearby. Maybe the lantern. A hand turned him over. He heard the creak of the lantern's handle and the light rose above him.

"George!" Ned exclaimed, and swore. "What happened?" George heard him ease down the hammer on his pistol and holster it.

"Riders," he said, trying to open his eyes. "The occupiers." He coughed, and his ribs flamed with pain.

"Why?"

George shook his head a fraction. This was his brother, but the war might have changed him into someone he couldn't trust. "Can you . . . get me . . . to the house?" he gasped.

"I can try." Ned blew out the lantern and set it down. "No point in borrowing trouble," he said, and knelt on one knee, grunting as he got his hands under George's shoulders. "Hold on, brother. This is going to hurt."

"Me, or you?" George could see the shape above him dimly outlined against the dark.

"Ha!" Ned barked a laugh. "Both of us, I reckon." He began to haul George slowly toward the house, stopping every few paces to catch his breath.

When he reached the stoop at the house, Ned stopped and stood up. He swiveled his neck and shook his arms, then opened the door and bent to help George to his feet. "Come on up. Lean on me."

George shook his head and said, "I'll have to crawl. I don't reckon I can stay on my feet, even with help. Go fetch the lantern, but hold off lightin' it until you're inside."

Ned went back down the lane to get the lamp, and George got into the house and was working at getting onto a chair in the kitchen when his brother returned. Ned put the lantern on the table, tugged George onto the chair, and lit the lamp. He said, "You weren't around when I got here and I was some worried. Then the team came trottin' into the yard by itself, and I worried a lot more." He positioned the lantern on a hook hanging from the ceiling of the kitchen and began to examine George's wounds. "I put up the horses, but was tryin' to decide which way I should go to look for you when the cows started making a fuss to be milked."

George sighed. "You chose right." He gasped in pain as Ned's fingers probed his side.

"These ribs is busted, brother."

"Tell me something I don't know," George said, his breath rasping.

Ned frowned. "Here's the news from town. I reported to the commander of the occupiers, as you call them, before I came here. There's a big fuss about a cavalryman who got killed a few days back. Looked like he was in a fight. He died quick from a pitchfork in his back." He eyed George. "They're searching for his murderer."

George said nothing. He fingered his swollen eye.

"I reckon the war is past business. I'm home now. You're my brother. Those are the two things that matter to me." He found a rag and water, and began to clean George's face. "Why'd they beat you up?"

George swallowed and breathed through his mouth while Ned worked on his nose. Could he trust Ned? Tell him why he'd been beaten? No. It was too early to settle on where his loyalties lay. He had to let Heppie and the Bingham family get clear out of the South.

"They must have had a reason."

George groaned as Ned found a tender spot—split skin over his cheekbone. "Do they need one?"

Ned grimaced. "It's a wonder you're alive. Whatever their reckoning, they didn't care if they killed you or not."

"No. I don't guess they did."

Ned suddenly sat down.

George squinted at him. Ned's face had gone gray. "Where does it hurt you?" he asked.

"Mostly my legs. I lost a lot of muscle when the shell exploded." He shook himself.

"Where else?"

"I get kinks in my back. Spasms."

"Anything I can do to help?"

Ned laughed, a bitter sound. "Not in your shape, brother. Let me take a minute to rest, then I'll get back to nursin' you."

"I had it all worked out that I was going to nurse you," George said. "I let Heppie leave here—" Aghast at his slip, George shut his mouth and let his head hang down to hide his face.

After a moment, Ned asked, "Who's Heppie?" When George didn't answer, he paused for a long moment, and finally said, "Hepzibah Bingham? Are you sweet on her?"

George said nothing, his heart sick. If his brother put the pieces together and reported them to the occupation commander, his own stupid big mouth might mean a prison sentence for the girl he loved. She didn't do anything wrong, either. *No, please*, he thought, and realized that he was shaking, but not from the pain of his injuries.

Ned was speaking again, wringing out the bloody cloth over a bowl of water. "When I came through town, I didn't get a brass band and a 'welcome home' speech." His voice sounded strained. "Folks didn't seem happy to see me. Old Man Calkins spit on me before I made it out of town." He paused for a moment and began again, his intonation carrying a note of despair. "I stopped at the Bingham's bakery to see how Miss Jessie would receive me, but it was locked up, so I didn't get to see her."

George looked up. "James Owen edged you out of the running with Miss Jessie last year," he said. "I heard tell they were fixin' to marry. Ended up he went west with his folks."

Ned's face twisted in anxiety. "James Owen? Jessie's gone with him?"

George shook his head. "No. He left her here."

Ned called James a few choice names even as he heaved a

sigh of relief. He straightened up in his chair, his face furrowed. "Where is she? Nobody was at the bakery. It looked"—he compressed his lips for a moment, then blurted out—"abandoned."

George shook his head again. "I don't know where she is."

Ned swore. "George, you're hiding something. You'd know where she was if she was anywhere nearby. That means she's gone. What happened?"

George licked his split lips. "I can't say."

"Does it have anything to do with those riders beatin' you near to death?" Ned was hovering over George, looking intently into his eyes. "Don't tell me you don't trust me."

George put his hands over his face. "War changes folks," he muttered, ashamed of his misgivings. "I don't know where you stand." He heard Ned's sharp exhalation and the creak of the chair as he sat once more. After a while, George dropped his hands into his lap and looked at his brother. To his surprise, tears trickled down Ned's cheeks.

Ned swiped at his cheeks before he opened his mouth and said, "I fought for the Union because I believe in it. That didn't make me love my family less than I did before I left. George, you're all the family I got now, and I don't want to be at odds with you." Ned swallowed, his Adam's apple moving up his throat, then down again. "I won't press you more than to ask this favor. If you know Jessie's in trouble, and you know where she is, you've got to tell me."

Chapter 5

During the next few days, Hannah fought her fears and strengthened her resolve to live. She ate everything Heppie gave her, and soon she became strong enough to walk for short periods.

The morning was bright and sunny when Hannah decided she wanted to get off the wagon seat and see how long she could keep pace with the others.

"Luke," she said to her brother, who was driving. "Can you pull up for a minute? I'd like to walk."

"Are you sure, Sis?"

"I reckon so."

He halted the team and helped her down. "Holler when you're tired out," he said. He slapped the lines on the rumps of the horses and yelled, "Hi-yup! Get up there!"

Hannah took a deep breath of spring-scented air as the wagon lumbered into motion. Soon, however, she coughed, as the dust left in the wagon's wake filled her lungs. She moved to the side of the road, coughing and gagging, and clutched a sapling for support.

The air cleared as the wagon and its brown cloud moved on down the pike. Hannah stood straight, breathing in the newly freshened air. Suddenly she bent double and threw up her breakfast.

No! she thought, as her head and stomach roiled in a crazy dance. *Not again. I can't be ill again.* But the nasty sickness came down on her, forcing her to gag and heave until she had no strength to stand. With her last bit of energy, she wrenched herself away from the foul results of her ailment and fell to her knees, forehead against a tree.

She took shallow breaths, trying to avoid vomiting again. After a while, her stomach calmed, but she couldn't get to her feet. She let go of the tree and fell sideways, then rolled a bit away from the pool of vomit.

As Hannah lay by the side of the pike, she began to worry that the wagon and her family were getting farther away each moment. *Will they miss me? Luke will daydream. He won't take notice that I'm gone for hours.* Her anxiety increased until she had to wrap her arms around her stomach to keep herself from vomiting again. Then she thought, *Robert will come for me.* She sighed, relief sweeping through her body.

Why do I feel ill? she asked herself. *I'm not feverish. Not even a little bit. These spells come out of nowhere.*

Half-hidden thoughts ran like skittering mice through the hallways of her mind. She swallowed, dipping her head and making a grand effort to force saliva through her dry throat. Half-recalled whispers, timidly giggled from the mouth of a girlfriend into her conspiratorial ear wafted by her consciousness. One thought took root, and she shuddered violently. *No!* She rolled into a ball. *This is impossible!*

She lay curled on the earth and leaves, unable to believe the caprice of her brain. "No!" she cried out, feeling like her body would explode. The awful truth bombarded her realization, but she thrust it from her, out of her thoughts, out of her actuality. Her fists flew to guard her ears, as though someone were speaking to her in gross, disgusting words. "No!" she shrieked. "No, I won't let it be so. You can't make me. God, you can't make me bear a child from that loathsome, hairy monster! It's not true! It's not true! It's not true."

She began to sob wildly. What would Robert think of her, bearing a bastard child? The child of a bastard Yankee? *He'll never love me again!*

Chapter 6

Several days after he'd met the Yankee riders on the turnpike, George hauled himself into the milk wagon, wincing at the pain in his ribs. Although Ned had wrapped them well with strips of soft cotton material, any movement of his torso gave him sharp reminders of the beating he'd taken. Just as George gathered the lines, Ned came into the barnyard and stood in front of the horses, glowering as though he'd drunk sour milk.

"Where do you reckon you're off to?" He took hold of the headstall of the nearest horse.

George took a shallow breath. "I'm sick of you pouring most of the milk down the garden rows 'cause I can't deliver it."

Ned shook his head. "Come down off that seat. You're not healed up enough to drive into town. I'm sorry I don't know the customers, but that can't be helped."

"I'm goin', Ned. If you want to come spell me on the driving, climb up. If not, step out of the way."

"Do you deliver to the Yankee camp?"

"Ha," George barked, a single laugh at Ned's reference. His brother, the Yankee. "Yes, I do. They pay on time, too."

Ned moved aside, hesitated a moment, then got up onto the wagon seat. "I'll go along. I have business there."

George got the horses underway before he handed the lines to Ned. "Do you reckon you remember how to drive?"

"Does the sun come up in the east?" Ned countered, his face serious.

George arranged himself more comfortably on the seat, and after Ned had turned the team onto the Pike, he asked, "What's your business at the camp?"

Ned's face was blank and he didn't answer.

"Are you fixin' to tattle on those riders?"

This time, Ned grimaced. After a bit, he nodded. "You're the only brother I got, George. Those louts ain't my brothers-in-arms. I got no loyalty to them." He paused to guide the horses around a pothole in the road. "If my service as a Union officer counts for anything with the commander, I'll use it."

"You reckon he'll shake his finger at Bull and them and give 'em what for?"

"I'm hopin' for more like a court martial."

"A court martial? For beating a Johnny Reb?" George laughed. "You been cooped up in that hospital for too long, Ned. Mount Jackson, hell, the whole Shenandoah Valley is occupied territory." He touched his swollen, yellowing cheek. "They'll probably get medals."

Ned growled, "The war's over. The troops are supposed to treat the population with respect."

"You're askin' too much." George sat back on the seat. "Those riders are rough men. I know they don't care about giving respect. Not after what I seen."

Ned looked sideways at George. "Are you ready to tell me what you seen?"

"I'm thinkin' about it."

"It was pretty bad?"

George's face twisted at his memories. "My friend's wife was raped!" He looked over at Ned. "You can't say that to the commander. I'll let you tell him I was beaten, but that's as far as it goes."

"Tell me their names."

"Bull, Cal, Foster. I don't have first and last names for you. That's all I heard."

"I reckon that will do." Ned shook the lines over the backs of the horses and lapsed into silence for the rest of the trip to town.

Their first stop was at the Union camp. Gritting his teeth against the pain in his ribs, George hauled down the milk cans and delivered them while Ned talked to the commander.

George returned to the wagon and waited on the seat, his hands tightly gripped together. What was Ned telling the commander? Would he mention Mrs. Fletcher's violation? Ned was no dummy. George figured his brother had made out most of the story from the bits of information George had let slip. How much would he reveal to the Union commander?

When Ned finally limped toward the milk wagon, his set face didn't give away much of what was in his mind. He climbed aboard, and George slapped the horses' backs with the lines, urging them to get started into town.

After a period of silence that stretched into forever, George asked, "Well?"

Ned leaned over and rested his elbows on his knees. "He listened. He's likely going to drum them out of the army. There's been reports about their cruel deeds before, and I reckon this was the final straw." He picked at a thread of weed clinging to his boot. "I still should have taken you in with me to show what they did."

"What does it matter if you convinced him they're treating folks poorly?"

Ned threw the weed onto the passing roadway. "No matter, I reckon. You'd have made an almighty good witness, though, just to look at you." He grinned at last. "I might not have had to jaw at him so long."

George clucked to the team, and they went about their deliveries. They were finished by midafternoon, and headed back to the farm.

Ned saw the smoke first, black and billowing, far down the Valley Pike.

"No!" he exclaimed, and swore.

George shouted at the team, but the horses were weary and couldn't keep up more than a shambling trot. Ned threw himself out of the wagon seat and ran along the pike. Soon, the injuries to his legs proved too much, and he pulled up at the side of the road, bent over and panting.

When George reached him, Ned climbed aboard and gasped out, "I reckon it's our place."

George bellowed "Damn Yankees!" and then looked at his brother's white face. "No offence," he muttered.

"They're louts," Ned replied, shaking his head.

George turned into the lane, and pulled up the horses when they were halfway down, aghast at the devastation. The barn had burned to the ground, the wellhead had been tipped over, and the house had been set afire. Being made of stone, it had not burned entirely. Smoke drifted on a breeze. George sat in stunned silence for two minutes. At last he got out of the wagon to follow Ned, who was attempting to enter the barn.

"It's still too hot to get inside," Ned said, wiping sweat from his forehead. He kicked a timber that had fallen into the barnyard with the collapse of the roof and swore bitterly. "How many cows did you have?" he asked.

"Six. They should be in the pasture."

"I don't see any out there."

"Where are they?" George stumbled toward the pasture fence.

By then Ned was inside the barn, moving debris out of his way. He stopped working and let loose a string of impassioned swear words, beckoning to George. "You have to see this."

George followed Ned, his stomach roiling at the stench. His six cows lay on their sides, throats cut, the hair on their hides burned. George emptied his lunch onto the embers of what had been a stall.

Once he could stand upright, he wiped his mouth with the

back of his hand and looked at his brother. The bleak, yet outraged expression on Ned's face helped him make up his mind. He cleared his throat and said, "I reckon I can tell you where Miss Jessie went. The Fletchers and all the Binghams are on their way to St. Louis. They're heading out for New Mexico Territory."

Ned let out a whoosh of air. He looked around and spread his hands. "There's nothing of value to keep us here, George. Let's follow them at first light."

As the glow of coming dawn lightened the eastern sky, George and Ned left the burned-out farm and walked their horses toward the Valley Pike. George rode the better of the two wagon horses, and used the other as a pack animal. Ned was astride the Union mount that had brought him home. They carried a bare minimum of supplies: a change of clothes, water, whatever food they could find in the ashes of the kitchen. George dug a hole in the garden to retrieve a buried rifle and ammunition he'd managed to bring home, and Ned had his weapons.

When they reached the end of the lane, George turned south and Ned turned north.

Wheeling his mount, Ned whistled a note to halt George, who waited for him to catch up.

"Where you goin'?" Ned asked.

"To Staunton."

"Wouldn't Fletcher take the Northwestern Pike out of Winchester? It would get them into West Virginia quicker."

"I reckon they took the Staunton and Parkersburg Pike." George slid his thumb along one of his reins.

"What makes you think that?"

"Miss Heppie sometimes talked about her cousin in

Monterey. They used to visit every couple of years before the war. Mrs. Bingham knows that road."

Ned rubbed the back of his neck. "The Northwestern is better traveling."

"Don't matter," George said. "I followed them a mite, and they turned south out of town."

Ned exhaled. "Let's get movin'."

They gigged their horses to a trot and followed the pike south, and soon approached the McNeely farm. Mrs. McNeely stood in the yard, throwing feed to her three scrawny hens. She stared after the brothers as they passed.

"That's a bad piece of fortune," George muttered.

"Old Miz McNeely?" Ned shook his head. "She's harmless."

"No, she'll make mention of our leaving. The dead rider was found in her barn, and I expect the other Yankees scared her pretty fair. I reckon she's afraid not to tell them anything they might be curious about."

Ned looked back over his shoulder. "She's just standin' there, watching us."

"We'd best be watchful, ourselves."

Neither brother said much the rest of the day. They reserved their strength for the journey, pressing forward as hard and as fast as George's ribs could bear.

On the third day, they passed through Staunton and turned northwest toward Monterey. Late in the day, they forded a stream that hadn't been re-bridged since the war ended, and found a camping place back in the forest away from the road. They kept their campfire low, just hot enough to warm the beans they'd cooked the night before. After they ate, they doused the fire and made ready for bed, aided by the light of a quarter moon.

George stood up from rolling out his bedroll. "Ned, my ribs ache something fierce. I'm going to scout around a bit before I turn in. Maybe I can work some kinks out with a walk."

Ned gave a nod and said, "I'd join you if I wasn't so tuckered out. Mind you, don't make a lot of noise and wake me up when you come back."

George chuckled. "You wouldn't hear a bear stumbling into camp over your snoring. Rest well, brother."

He left the camp and walked a short distance through the woods. Silver moonlight streaming through the trees dappled the ground before him. He wondered how Heppie would look with the light of the moon falling on her hair, over her shoulders, on the soft white skin of her throat. He swallowed hard. Heppie was somewhere on this road ahead of him. He would find her, maybe inside of a week. How would she receive him after the dim-witted things he'd said? Would she turn her back? Refuse to look at him? Meet him with harsh words?

How could a woman with such a fair face say anything unkind? Yet she had left him behind, coldly turning his loyalty to his brother and the dumb creatures in his care into ashes with a few stark sentences.

George leaned against a tree. He could see Heppie's face in his mind's eye as clearly as though she stood before him. Pale yellow hair rippling beside her cheek, nose turned up a tad bit on the tip, lips pink and soft— He backed away from that thought. She had chosen Hannah over him. They were like two halves of a split apple, those twins. Ever since he'd known them, he'd puzzled to figure out a way to distinguish which sister was who. Finally he had discovered the small pink spot on the side of Heppie's neck; a spot that pulsed with the beating of her heart.

He imagined he could hear her heart beating, throbbing, drumming like horses' hooves on a road. Her voice seemed raised in a strident complaint, then it lowered, then came forth again with a different timbre. He closed his eyes. Was this an omen of what lay before him?

He shook his head to clear away the unwelcome discordant noises and stood upright as he realized that he actually heard a party of riders coming along the road. He could hear them not only because of the usual sounds of horses traveling, but because the men were arguing as they rode along.

"All right!" one voice yelled, frustration evident in the shrillness of his voice. "We'll stop."

The road was not far from where George stood, and the riders turned off on his side of the track. He stepped behind the tree he leaned against, wishing he'd brought his rifle.

The quarrel continued as the men dismounted and prepared to camp.

"They're still at least a week ahead," one man grumbled, and George recognized the voice as that of the frustrated man who'd called the halt in spite of wanting to continue on.

"Nah, we've made up time," another said.

"If you'd let us sleep once in a while, my stomach would be in better shape." This objection came from a different voice, so there were at least three men in the party.

"If you'd stop nipping at your flask, your stomach would have no complaints," the first man bellowed.

"If you'd brought proper rations, my stomach wouldn't have a quarrel with you."

"Shut your trap, Foster. Bull's right. We can't make good time if you're too drunk to sit your horse."

George froze as the men continued wrangling over their differences. These men were the Yankee riders. How had they known— Of course. Mrs. McNeely had reported seeing Ned and him passing by. His mind whirled, sorting out what he heard the men say. He and Ned hadn't been on the road for a week. Somehow, they'd tracked down Robert and his wife . . . and Heppie. Cold chills ran between his shoulder blades. The men were close by. Would they hear him as he moved away toward his own camp?

". . . Heizer!" one man said, and spat. "It's all his doing."

George inhaled sharply and held his breath. They were after him, too.

"Thinks he's so high and mighty. Captain bloody rebel-born Heizer! When I get my hands on him, I'll snap his scrawny neck!"

"Not if I get to him first, you won't. That damned turncoat cost me my back pay."

George let out his breath slowly and crept away. He and Ned had to ride out immediately. They had to escape the wrath of these ruffians. They had to warn Robert and the Binghams.

George knelt beside Ned's bedroll, gently shook his shoulder with one hand, and rested his fingers on his brother's mouth with the other.

Ned came awake with wide eyes.

"Shh," George warned. "Them riders caught up with us."

"Riders?" Ned blinked. "Those occupiers?"

George nodded. "They know Robert and the family are on this road." He paused, then continued in a lower tone. "They're after you, too. And me, I reckon."

Ned was on his knees, rolling his bedding. He threw a whisper over his shoulder. "Well, we'd best not let them catch us or the girls. I'll saddle the horses while you break camp."

After leading their animals along the pike for a mile, George and Ned rode the rest of the night, the turnpike ever climbing into the foothills. As dawn broke they entered the outskirts of Monterey. George pulled his horse to a stop and looked to the west. Pink light coming from the east flooded the hills as far as his eyes could see. *What a fetchin' sight*, he thought. *A pity I won't be back to see it again.*

"Do you know the cousin's name?" Ned asked as he dismounted. He lifted one of his horse's hooves and took a look at it. He pried a stone loose with his thumb. "That should feel better," he said to the horse, then lowered its leg.

George had finished consulting his memory. "Emmy Lou. Emmy Lou Pitkin. This town ain't so large that we can't find her."

"Where do we start?"

George looked around. It was too early for the stores to be open, but a farm woman might be a good source of information. "How about over there?" he asked, pointing to a nearby house where light came through a window.

Ned mounted, and they rode to the dwelling. George knocked on the door, found a cautious reception, but got the information he sought. When he joined Ned, he said, "The lady told me the Pitkins live on a farm the other side of town. She gave me good directions. We don't need to bother anyone else in finding 'em." He yawned. "After we learn if they have news of the Binghams, I want about two hours sleep."

"Dang it, don't yawn, or I'll start in doin' it," Ned protested.

George grinned, but sobered as he climbed into his saddle. "Let's get goin'."

They found the Pitkin farm, as directed, and came upon several members of the family finishing morning chores before breakfast.

"How do," George called out, as he and Ned halted their horses in the yard. "Is this the Pitkin place?"

"Howdy, strangers," said an older man, looking the brothers over. "I'm Pitkin. You look like travelers." He gestured for George and Ned to alight from their horses, and they did so. Three teenage boys gathered nearby.

George offered his hand. Mr. Pitkin squeezed it in a farmer's grip.

"We are travelin', sir," George said, "hopin' to catch up with the Bingham family. How long ago did they come through here?"

"Well now," said the farmer, eyeing George's face. "That cut there on your cheek looks recent." He paused, took a pipe out of his pocket, and stuck it in his mouth. "What puts you in mind that the Binghams passed by?"

"I was at their home when they left Mount Jackson. I'm Miss Heppie's beau, sir."

"Well now," Mr. Pitkin repeated. "If you're Miss Heppie's beau, why aren't you at her side in her adversity?"

George felt himself flush. He took as deep a breath as he could manage and said, "I would have gone with the family, sir, except they left so sudden. I had obligations to take care of."

"Obligations." The man chewed on the word, squinted at the sky, took the unlit pipe from his mouth, and put it in his pocket again. "Did you get shed of your obligations?"

George nodded.

"Someone chasing you?"

"Yes sir. Three cashiered Yankee riders. They're also after the Binghams." George paused, and then added, "Robert Fletcher, mostly."

"Miss Hannah's man." It was a statement rather than a question.

George nodded again.

"By the age of his scars, you didn't beat on each other."

"No sir."

Mr. Pitkin nodded in his turn, appeared to be satisfied, and said, "My sister and her kin came in six days ago. Spent a night and left. I gave them my extra pistol and a shotgun. I figured they had more need of them than I do." He abruptly turned on his heel, then stopped and threw over his shoulder, "Want breakfast?"

"Thank you kindly, sir," said Ned. "If it's no trouble to the missus, we'd be pleased to join you for a bite."

They left before noon, fortified by a solid country breakfast and a couple of hours of sleep.

About a week into their travels, the brothers arrived at a small stream just before the sun went down. Exhausted, they made camp, keeping a good distance from a fire that told of other people nearby.

"Do you reckon they're friendly?" George asked.

Ned snorted. "I don't propose to find out. Mind you, give them plenty of space to move around."

"A man can't be too careful about his neighbors," George agreed. He arose from where he'd been scraping a bare spot for a fire. "I'll bring in some wood." Before Ned could offer a caution, he added, "Yes, I'll be wary."

George ranged about in the half light until he located a dry limb as thick as his arm. He put his foot in the center and lifted one end. It broke into two lengths with a snap. Somewhere behind him, a voice drew in a sharp breath, followed by, "Luke, is that you?" The voice was young, and female.

He whirled around. A bush screened most of a female's figure from his sight, but he could see a part of her skirt spread against the ground. "Sorry, ma'am, no, I'm not Luke. I'll be going on now." He turned away, his face burning at interrupting the girl at her private task.

The skirt rustled, then the voice came again, clearly Southern, not frightened, not embarrassed. A little amused. "You sound like someone my sister would like to see. Hmm, maybe not. She's riled that you prefer your cows over her."

George couldn't move. His arms had gone stiff as stone. His legs refused to shift to let him face the girl. He tried his jaw. It moved. "Miss Jessie?" he guessed. In case he was wrong, he tried again. "Miz Fletcher? Did we find you?"

"I'm Jessie. What took you so long, Mr. Heizer?"

Chapter 7

Heppie could scarcely believe the news Jessie brought her. George had come. Heppie smiled. He had followed her after all. He did love her! She'd started off to greet him, but Ma interrupted, fussing about getting the evening meal together in a hurry.

Heppie's fingers seemed to belong to someone else as she tried to do her part in carving venison steaks from the deer her brother had come across and shot just as they made camp. What would she say to George? Should she maintain her grievance against him, or should she welcome him with all her heart? Following several mishaps, and after she'd fumbled a chunk of the meat off the cutting board and into the grass, her mother thrust her to one side and gave her a different task: to clean up the wooden mixing bowl.

"You can't possibly hurt that, Heppie," Mrs. Bingham had said, irritation sharpening her voice. "Jessie, put this meat in the frying pan. No, you'll have to wash it a mite first. At least brush the dirt and grass off."

"Ma, I didn't mean to—" Heppie began, but her mother cut her off.

"Luke brought down that deer by the grace of Providence, and we need every last shred of the meat. Especially now that the Heizer boys have joined us."

Heppie sighed. Ma was going to talk all night about her clumsiness. As if that wouldn't make her all the more bungle fingered. All she could hope for was that George would pay Ma no mind. If Heppie forgave him, surely he would cast his thoughts on the future, and not on Ma's speech. Heppie smiled and played with a curl of hair that hung down her cheek. George was going to want to get married now that he had caught up with her.

She took a deep breath. Married! She thought of his broad shoulders and long arms. He would put those arms around her, cuddle her to his chest, maybe kiss her. She exhaled, her lips burning at the thought of kissing George. What else did married folks do? She knew very little of their amorous ways. Surely they didn't behave like mating animals! She shrugged. Hannah hadn't shared that part of her life. Heppie only knew about the occasions back in Mount Jackson when she'd caught her sister glowing with happiness after spending time alone with Robert. Being married must be . . . pleasurable.

Heppie dropped the bowl, startling herself back to reality. George might have come after her . . . no, them . . . well, maybe her, but he took his sweet time, and that proved she was second on his list of importance. No, make that third, she thought as she stooped to pick the bowl out of the weeds. *First the cows, next, his brother. I come third!*

Determined to punish George for his disloyalty, Heppie scowled all during supper, not once looking at him. She gave him the cold shoulder whenever he tried to make conversation with her. She frowned as she washed dishes. She wondered how on earth she was going to avoid him after cleanup was finished. Maybe she shouldn't avoid him. Maybe she should give him a piece of her mind, straight out. She attacked a pot with her brush, glaring into the dishpan.

"Heppie?"

Heppie jumped and dropped the brush. She knew that voice behind her, deep and resonant. She hunched her shoulders for a moment, then relaxed them, took her hands out of the water, wiped them on her apron, and faced George.

"George Heizer," she began, "you are a scoundrel!" She called him several other names.

He seemed concerned, but not repentant.

"That's not all. I don't know why you have the nerve to come after me when it's obvious to a pumpkin that you don't give me any thought." She half turned away, then faced him again. He stared back at her, almost somber, but strangely steadfast. He wasn't hanging his head under her onslaught of bitter words, scuffing the dirt, or fingering the poor little remnant of his ear. He should look more beaten down.

The resin in a log at the campfire flared up. Bright light played on George's face for a moment. He *did* look beaten down, physically. He had a cut on his cheek and discoloration around one eye, and his lips seemed to be misshapen. Heppie took in a quick breath and almost reached out to him before her anger overcame her again.

"How dare you come all this way to bother me with your protestations of love!" She resisted stomping her foot, feeling guilty that he hadn't, in fact, had a chance to make any such protestations since arriving. "And you brought your brother! I'd have thought you would leave him behind to tend your cows."

"You're throwing it in my face that I chose my brother over you." George's voice was so soft that Heppie strained to hear it. "Ain't it a fact you chose Hannah over me?" George bent his head and looked at the toes of his boots. He raised his eyes to look at Heppie again. "It appears we've both made mistakes."

Heppie sucked in her breath as her thoughts whirled. What was George saying? Her legs went mushy and she needed to sit down, but she steeled herself and stayed on her feet, although she swayed a bit.

"So I'm a pot calling the kettle black?" Heppie's hand went to her mouth. She'd said that too forcefully, too much like a challenge, when she'd meant it as a confession. She bit her lip, wanting to call the words back. A deep sense of sorrow engulfed her, making her shiver.

George stepped forward. He looked haggard, drawn down to a fine strand. He took her by the upper arms and held her still.

"That's enough! The cows are dead, the barn got burned, and the house is a shell. Those Yankee riders got thrown out of the army for"—he made a deprecating movement of his head—"beatin' me some, and they're comin' after Robert and y'all." He took a breath, and Heppie thought he grew taller. "Maybe I did wrong to stay behind, to put my brother and my animals over you. I've regretted that choice every day since you left. Every moment was misery, knowin' I'd lost you. That hurt more than the broken ribs." He let his hands fall from Heppie's arms and turned away as though he'd said too much.

Heppie touched his sleeve, and he turned back, his eyes burning with reflected firelight.

George stared at her, long moments passing before he spoke in a low tone. "I'm here now, come to save your life if I can. And marry you at the next town, if you'll have me."

Joy thrummed through her like a plucked fiddle string. She moved toward him, and his arms encircled her, those long, strong arms she'd been thinking about. *He loves me*, she thought. *As much as a practical man can. I reckon that's enough love for now.*

He held her still, not moving, and she realized he waited for her reply.

"Yes, George," she said, and wondered that her voice trembled. "If you can abide my mistakes and forgive me for them, I'll gladly have you."

Once they knew they were being followed, the Bingham party traveled on as quickly as they could. Hannah had recovered her strength enough to walk behind the wagon. The day after George and Ned found them, Robert strode along beside her, carrying a rifle. From time to time she glanced over at her husband's grave face.

"Do you reckon they'll catch up to us soon?" she asked.

Robert looked at Hannah, then directed his gaze forward again.

"It's likely. George said he and his brother were just a bit ahead of them." He turned to look back at the road they'd already traveled. "That's why they're riding behind us. They're what you call a rear guard."

Hannah tried to swallow the tightness in her throat. "What will they do to me for killing that . . . man?" Nausea built in her as she remembered the shock to her arms, to her whole body as her attacker's body hit the tines of the pitchfork. She wanted to clutch Robert or fling herself into his embrace for safety, and wondered if she would be able to stand having his arms around her. She fought with her fear and revulsion and kept walking.

"Hannah," Robert said. His voice was so tender that Hannah's breath caught in her throat. Robert paused for a long time before speaking again. "First of all, they're not going to do anything to you. We have four armed men, counting Luke. There are only three of them."

Hannah looked sideways at Robert. *He must be clenching his teeth,* she thought. *His jaw muscles are bunched up like grapes.*

"But you're worried?" she asked. The rhythm of her breathing increased with her anxiety, until Robert laid his hand on her hair.

"Concerned," he admitted. A shadow of a smile flitted over his mouth. "A man would be crazy not to have some reservations about a coming fight." His fingers dropped to Hannah's cheek and stroked it. "They don't know anything about your part. They think I killed that monster."

Hannah shivered, both at the venom in Robert's quiet voice and at his touch. He hated that man called Red. He surely must hate what had happened to her. Did he still love her? She stared at the tailgate of the wagon as Robert removed his hand. His actions said he did, but his voice was so . . . bitter, and he hadn't tried to share any physical intimacies since—

She shivered again. *How will Robert feel when he finds out that vicious cur planted his seed in me? He won't be able to love me when he learns of it. How can I keep this horrible baby a secret?*

A noise from behind brought Hannah out of her thoughts. She looked back, but it was only Ned Heizer on the road. The riotous curls of his yellow hair made a halo around his somber face. Her spine prickled with dread of the battle that would engulf them. The Yankees were coming.

The first hint that the riders had caught up to them came in the afternoon with the sound of rifle fire from back down the turnpike. Robert and Luke got the wagon stopped and pulled off into a screening stand of trees and brush. Luke unhooked the team from the wagon tongue, swatted the near horse on the rump, and the animals ran off.

The firing moved closer, but came sporadically. Robert got the shotgun from the rear of the wagon and handed it to Mrs. Bingham with a few words of instruction. He swept his arm toward the forest. "Ladies, get into the woods. Keep out of sight. George and Ned are bringing the fight to us."

"Robert—" Hannah started to say something, but he cut her off.

"Run, Hannah!"

Robert and Luke hunkered down behind what little shelter the wagon box gave them. "Don't fire until George and Ned are clear," Robert said. "If you can't get a good bead on a man, shoot his horse and bring it down. A moving man is a hard target."

Luke's voice shook when he answered, "I ain't shot a man before."

Robert felt as though his words would strangle him. "These are monsters. When you aim, think on what their buddy did to your sister."

Luke swallowed hard and nodded. He whispered, "Is she going to be all right?"

Robert didn't answer for a minute. Outwardly, Hannah looked the same. She had begun to eat better. Her bruises were healing. However, the light hadn't come back into her eyes. Instead, she looked haunted by bad memories. *It's going to take time*, he thought. He cleared his throat and said, "I don't know yet. Keep a good watch down that pike."

Hooves pounded. A bullet whizzed through the air. George came down the road, whipping the reins against his horse's flank. Ned was close behind, but turned and fired his sidearm before he approached Robert and Luke's position.

George pulled up his horse and vaulted to the ground where the wagon had turned off. He shoved his animal in the direction of the trees, then flopped to the ground behind a bush. "There's still three of them," he shouted to Robert. "I winged one, but he didn't fall."

Robert nodded. Luke screamed beside him, "Look out! Look out!" Ned wheeled his horse toward the forest. Luke's rifle boomed as three horsemen came into view.

One of the three horses faltered and bucked sideways, trying to unseat its rider. The man fell, but one foot didn't clear the stirrup, and the horse dragged him by, screaming.

"He's your lookout, Luke," Robert said. The boy turned and stood, bringing his rifle to his shoulder. The weapon spoke again. Luke raised his voice in an imitation of the rebel yell, then shouted, "I got him!"

The other two riders turned their horses in the road and sought shelter. Robert fired, but the bullet didn't find the target. He berated himself for wasting his shot, then ducked at evidence that one of the riders had taken up a position and thought well of shooting him. A yelp behind him made him turn. Luke lay sprawled on the side of the road. His hand flew up to clasp his left arm above the elbow. Blood seeped between his fingers.

George ran to the boy and dragged him into the brush. "I'll tend him," he called to Robert. "Ned, where are you?"

"Shh," came a soft response.

Robert squinted into the dust raised by the horses. Where had the two remaining men gone? He thought he saw movement in the woods to the left of where the men had turned off the road. Was that one of the men, or both? His stomach cramped with tension as time passed and the lull in the shooting grew longer. Where were the Yankees? Were they hunkered down as he was, or had they chosen to creep closer under cover of the trees? His back was exposed if the men passed his position. Did it matter where he was? Should he move? No, he wouldn't be able to spot movement down the turnpike if he abandoned his post. But who would choose to charge down the middle of the road into the rifle fire of your enemy? He wouldn't, and the men had already gone into the protection of the forest. Maybe it would be best to retrench back in the trees.

Robert lowered his weapon, and was in the act of shifting his feet to move when the shot came from across the road and down a piece, cutting a splinter of wood loose from the tailboard of the wagon.

He jerked his rifle to his shoulder and shot in the direction of the muzzle blast. One of the men in his party—Ned, maybe?—shot back as well.

An enraged cry came from a Yankee. Was he hit? He didn't fire again, and Robert took that moment to remove himself from the side of the wagon and back into the woods.

He came upon George, crouched beside Luke. The boy's arm

bore a crude bandage and splints made from segments of tree branches.

"How is he?" Robert asked.

"His arm's broke, but he'll live."

Robert nodded and looked around for Ned. Soon he spotted him to his right. Ned raised his hand and motioned toward the Yankee across the road. Taking the movement as a question, Robert shook his head and shrugged his shoulders. There was no telling if the Yankee was injured or not.

Jessie knelt in a circle of oak trees, her eyes darting from the direction of the road to her mother and sisters. Ma stood upright, her back to a tree, holding the shotgun so tightly in front of her face that her knuckles were white. Hannah and Heppie huddled together, their arms around each other. *The men will protect us*, Jessie thought. *There are four of them now.*

An errant thought flashed into her mind. *I'm glad I'm wearing this light-colored dress. It doesn't stick out like Ma's widow's weeds.* She looked down at her skirt, sprigs of flowers aligned in rows on a tan background. She shook her head slightly. *What on earth does it matter what I'm wearing?* she chided herself. *Three hell-raising Yankees are after us and I'm thinking about my clothing?* She looked at Ma again. The black clothes would be visible for a long distance.

A crashing noise in the woods behind them brought Jessie to her feet. She turned around to face the sound, aware that one of her sisters had caught her by the ankle.

"Leave go!" she said, shaking her foot at the same time as she tried to stay upright on her other.

"What is it, Jessie?" Hannah said in a wailing voice.

"Let me go so I can give attention to finding out," she said, hopping to keep her balance. As soon as her sister turned her loose, she said, "Ma, give me the shotgun and sit down!"

Her face white, her mother obediently handed her the weapon and sank into a heap.

Jessie lifted the shotgun until the barrels faced in the direction of the noise. Someone was walking toward them through the trees, and whoever it was didn't care how much racket he made. In a few moments, she would be able to see who it was.

She felt the strain in her arms and her back of keeping the weapon in position. Sweat dripped off the tip of her nose. Out of the corner of her eye she sensed movement within the circle of the oak trees, but didn't dare glance down to see what her sisters were doing. Someone was coming, and he probably wasn't one of their traveling party.

What if it's someone who lives around here? She thought. *Maybe he heard the shooting and is coming to investigate.* Dread of shooting a stranger filled her chest, squeezing her windpipe nearly closed.

A large man stepped out of the cover of the nearest copse of trees. His black-bearded face was familiar, seared into her memory by the tobacco-spitting incident in the street. "Bull!" slipped from between her lips like a swear word. She bit her lower lip to prevent saying more. This man wasn't a stranger come to see what was happening on his lands. This man had spit on Southern women, beaten Heppie's George, and now he was surely coming to hurt as many of them as he could.

In the next instant, a malevolent grin splitting the man's scruffy beard told Jessie he had seen her and the other women.

"Yep," he said, almost chortling in his glee, "we found you, all right. This is going to be fun." His voice became more threatening as he lifted his rifle in his hands. "Sort of a memorial for my brother, Red. I hope he got his licks in before that banker killed him." His voice turned into a snarl as he took notice of the shotgun in Jessie's hands. "Put down that scattergun, little lady. It won't stop me."

Jessie tightened her grip. Mr. Fletcher had told Ma to aim low and squeeze the triggers. She could do that.

The man advanced toward the circle of oaks, speaking in a wheedling tone of voice. "Give me the gun, sweetheart. It'll break your shoulder. You don't want a broken shoulder, now, do you?"

Better a broken shoulder than the horror your kin dealt to my sister, she thought.

The man put out his left hand, reaching for the shotgun, saying, "Give me the gun, sugar! I got a better plan for you."

Jessie's eyes locked on the man's leering face. He wanted to impose the same indignities on her as his brother had on Hannah. She squeezed both triggers and felt herself being thrown backward as the man disappeared from her view. The metallic smell of blood filled her nostrils, and she knew for certain the man named Bull was not a threat to her or her sisters any longer.

Ned heard the blast of the shotgun and looked over his shoulder in the direction of the noise. He half rose to his feet and looked back at Robert. "You get that one across the road," he shouted, then spun around and sprinted into the trees.

"Jessie," he cried out, wondering at the vehemence in his voice. He dodged a hanging tree branch and leaped over a downed log. A woman's high-pitched shriek came from ahead, and he adjusted his course, weaving between the trees as he ran. Someone ran behind him, but he figured it had to be George or maybe Robert, and he didn't look around. At last he could see the women, sheltered by oak trees. None were standing, and he increased his speed, drawn by the sharp wails made by one of them.

"Jessie, Miss Jessie," he called. In five more steps he skidded to a halt. Jessie lay on her back, blood spotting her dress. She clutched the shotgun with one hand and rubbed her shoulder with the other, while her sisters and mother crowded together, arms about each other. One of the twins continued to wail.

At that moment, Ned saw the mangled remains of a body on the opposite side of the tree circle. He shuddered at the nearness of the carnage and turned to stare at Jessie.

"He came so close," he said, the tightness of his throat almost strangling him. Jessie was trying to sit upright, and Ned took her hand to help her. Once she got situated, Ned reached for the shotgun. Jessie let it go without a word.

"That blood?" he asked, motioning to her dress. "Is any of it yours?"

Jessie shook her head. She didn't seem able to talk yet.

George came through the trees and went immediately to Heppie, quieting her outcry. Mrs. Bingham turned her loose, gathering Hannah to her bosom.

"Stay low," Ned said. "There's still one other man alive out there, but Mr. Fletcher's seeing to him."

"Luke?" Jessie whispered. She rubbed her neck.

George answered. "He took a slug through the arm. It's broken because he fell wrong when he went down, but he'll mend."

Ned removed Jessie's hand from her neck. "Do you mind if I test out your shoulder for injury?" he asked.

Jessie turned wide eyes to look at him. "He said"—she took a gulp of air—"he said it would break my shoulder. Maybe he was right. It hurts pretty fair."

"Let me check," Ned said. At Jessie's nod, he felt along the bones of her arm and shoulder with gentle fingers. Finally he smiled and patted her arm with great care. "No broken bones.

You'll bruise up and probably hurt like you do now for several days, but there are no broken bones."

Jessie must have been holding her breath, for she let out a long, shaky sigh. "Thank you, Mr. Heizer."

"You called me Ned back in school days."

Jessie slid a glance toward Mrs. Bingham and then looked back at Ned. "That was when we were children. Ma would take a switch to me if I did that now."

Ned chuckled. "Don't let her hear you." The smile she gave him warmed his soul.

Robert looked at Ned running toward the sound of the shotgun blast. *He's got the situation in hand,* he thought. *I've got someone to worry about across the road.*

He squinted through the brush but could detect no movement. He crouched and sidestepped to his left until he reached Luke's position.

"How are you doing?" he whispered to the young man.

Luke looked up, his face white. "It hurts a mite, but Mr. Heizer says I'll live."

"Good lad." Robert motioned down the road. "How far is your man?"

"About two hundred feet. The horse quit dragging him when it fell over dead."

"I'm going there to check."

"The Yankee's dead."

"Good. Making sure will give me a chance to get on the other side of the road."

"Oh." Luke nodded.

As Robert left Luke with a pat he heard, "Be careful."

Both man and horse were indeed dead. Robert crossed the road and started toward the spot from which the last Yankee had fired. He heard thrashing sounds. Huffing. Snorts. Not the man. He slowed his pace, peering into the underbrush before he changed position.

After a time, he came upon the horse, down on its side, barely moving. He gave it a pat and looked around warily. A breeze came through the trees, blowing against his face, bringing with it an acrid odor.

The man must be down. He's fouled himself. He continued in the direction of the smell, using the trees and bushes for cover. A few steps farther along, he spotted the Yankee propped against a tree trunk. He held his belly with blood-stained hands. The ground beside him was discolored with red pools.

Robert stayed where he was until he located the man's rifle. It lay out of reach in a blackberry bush, so he approached the man, watching for sudden movement toward a hidden weapon.

"What's your name?" Robert asked, standing over the mortally wounded Yankee.

"Jace Foster." He squinted at Robert. "What's yours?"

"Robert Fletcher." He looked around for the man's canteen. Instead, he found a flask half full of liquor. He squatted and held it to the man's lips.

Foster slowly took a sip, then spoke in a whisper. "You're the damned murderer we came after?" His drawn-out words spoke of coming death.

Robert shook his head. "He died in a fair fight. If it soothes your sensibilities any, I would have killed him for what he did to my wife."

"You killed me." Foster's voice faltered.

Robert considered for a long time. "Maybe I did." He shrugged one shoulder. "Maybe it was Heizer's bullet."

"Which brother?"

"The Yankee."

Foster choked, and blood spilled from the corners of his mouth. When he could speak again, he asked, "Where are my buddies?"

"You're the only one left."

"Finish me off!"

"No."

"I'll bleed to death."

Robert swirled the flask. "You'd better drink this down. It'll take the edge off the pain."

"Slit my throat. You'd do it for a dog."

"No. But when you're gone, I'll do it for your horse."

With a burst of energy, Foster reached for the liquor. He tipped the flask, rinsed his mouth, and spat. Then he drank, his Adam's apple bobbing in a steady rhythm. When he had drained the container, he threw it away and slumped forward.

Robert watched for a long time, but when Foster didn't right himself, he touched the man's neck. Then he walked away, drawing his knife.

When the riders were buried, Robert called the group together around Luke, who sat propped against a tree trunk.

"I don't want us to camp here for the night. My question to you is which way do we go, now that those . . . men are dead?"

Hannah asked, "What do you mean, 'which way'?"

"Do we go back to Virginia, or continue west?" He motioned with his head toward the common grave they'd dug back in the woods and filled with the remains of the Yankees. "They're not a threat to us now. We could go back." Robert looked at the somber faces around him. "Each of you has a vote. It's 'Virginia' if you want to go back, and 'west' if you want to go on." He stopped speaking for a moment, then gestured down the road. "Let me say it's a long journey to New Mexico Territory, and right now we're ill prepared for such an undertaking."

No one said anything, so Robert continued. "We'll start with Mrs. Bingham. What's your vote, ma'am?"

Mrs. Bingham looked down at her hands, clasping the edges of her apron. "West," she whispered. "Let's join Max."

"Mrs. Fletcher?"

"West!"

"Miss Hepzibah?"

Heppie looked at George, then down at her toes. Finally, she said, "West."

"Miss Jessica?"

"I want to go west."

"Master Lucas?"

The boy shifted his broken arm with his other hand. "I reckon Ma needs me. West."

"I vote to go west," Robert said, and turned to the Heizer brothers. "Mr. Ned?"

Ned glanced at Jessie, and said "West," with an emphatic nod of his head.

"Mr. George?"

George reached for Heppie's hand and drew her toward him. "I've asked Miss Heppie to marry me, and she has agreed. I'll go west with her."

"It's decided. Let's hitch up the team."

Chapter 8

Ned offered to drive the wagon in Luke's stead. "The youngster can't handle the lines with that busted wing," he reminded Mrs. Bingham. "If he's careful, he can ride my horse. If he'd rather, he can sit in the wagon." He looked around for Jessie. "Miss Jessie should ride until her shoulder stops hurting so much."

"Thank you kindly, Mr. Heizer," said Mrs. Bingham. "Luke, a few days in the wagon bed should speed your healing. See if you can crawl up there."

"Let me help," Ned said, and got Luke positioned to his liking in a few moments. Ned jumped out of the back of the wagon box and walked to the front. "Now Miss Jessie, let's get you up on the seat."

Jessie cradled her right arm with her left and shook her head. "I reckon I'd rather walk."

"But Miss Jessie—"

"I'm fine as can be, Mr. Heizer. Really I am. I'll tie something around my arm to keep it still, and I'll be fit as a fiddle. Besides, I don't want to displace Ma."

"I think Mr. Heizer is right, Jessie," Mrs. Bingham said. "Just you rest that shoulder. A few days of walking won't put me out none."

"Ma," Jessie protested, but Ned had his way, and soon Jessie was ensconced on the seat with Ned settled down beside her.

"Hi! Get up there!" Ned called to the horses. Once they were on the road, he turned to Jessie. "Your ma's walkin' back there with Robert and Miz Hannah. You can call me Ned now." He watched a pink glow light her cheeks.

"I haven't seen you for so long," Jessie said, ducking her head to one side.

"Yup." Ned moved his foot onto the brake lever. "I'm sorry I let some years get between us."

Jessie didn't reply.

"Do you remember that time I brought you a peck of mulberries, and we climbed the tree behind Miller's barn and ate the whole thing?"

Jessie smiled but said nothing.

"Our hands got all purple, and my belly ached something fierce, but the company was fine."

Jessie laughed. "As I recall, you threw up all over my skirt, and I had to hide it from Ma and wash it myself."

Ned grinned. "I don't remember that."

"It happened."

"Nah, it couldn't have. I was always a model citizen around you."

"It did."

"It didn't!"

"Did too!"

"Did not!"

Jessie gave Ned's arm a gentle shove as her laughter filled the road. "The purple stain never did come all the way out of my skirt. I had to cover it with an apron until I outgrew it."

"It does my heart good to hear you laugh, Jessie. I don't reckon you've had much to laugh about the last few years."

She shook her head. "Ma always tells us life ain't meant to be fair."

"But a fine-lookin' girl like you should have little things that give you pleasure, like fancy trinkets and good memories." He looked over at Jessie. She was blushing again. "Memories are precious gifts. I have a store of them I could share."

Jessie said nothing. After a while, Ned began to whistle a tune, and she turned to him, her face a picture of delight.

"That's the firefly song. You made it up."

"I made it up for you." Ned avoided looking at Jessie. He hadn't told her that, before now, and couldn't predict how she would react.

"You did?" A low chuckle escaped Jessie's throat. "I never knew." She tried out the tune, then laid her hand on his arm. "You never told me. What other secrets are you keeping from me?"

"Oh, lots and lots." Ned grinned, relieved. "Like the time I shut the Owen boys in the Bates's cellar for teasing you. Remember, I took you and Ellen Bates and Marie Owen into town on the buckboard to get candy at the store? That's so you wouldn't hear them rascals fussin' to be let out."

Jessie snatched her hand from Ned's arm. He looked at her. She had turned her face away again.

"Did I say something wrong?"

"N-no," she said, stumbling on the word.

"Are you in pain?" he asked. "This road ain't too smooth."

"Um, I'm a little tired," she said.

"I don't wonder," he said. "That shotgun sent you flyin'. Fear is mighty fatiguin', as well."

Jessie said nothing in return, and Ned lapsed into silence.

Jessie hadn't thought about James Owen for more than a week, but Ned's remembrance of secrets he'd kept had reopened the wound that never quite seemed to heal. *Precious mercy! Will I never stop thinking about him!* A cold chill ran through her body, and she shivered, fighting tears that she wouldn't be able to explain away.

Ned Heizer. Big-brother substitute Ned. Protector and friend while her own big brother, Max, played beau to the girls. Ned was acting like he wanted to court her.

That can't be. Ned is my friend. How can he possibly want more than that?

Trying to get her mind to think about a different sort of relationship with Ned, Jessie compared him to her vanished James. He and Ned were about the same height, but while Ned's hair was light colored and prone to corkscrew curls, James Owen had dark, crisp hair that curled around his ears only if it grew too long. How she'd loved to run her fingers through that ink-colored hair! James was handsome in a thoroughly different way from Ned, who limped when he walked. She'd heard Ned had received serious injuries to his legs. James had two perfectly good legs, although he had received a bayonet wound in one shoulder. His impairment had not kept him abed for long. Within two weeks of his return home, he had come courting, smiling and joking and singing songs of love that won her heart.

She sighed, remembering the nausea that had swept through her when James told her he was being forced to go west with his family and he could not take her with him. They clung together, hidden behind a clump of lilacs, tempted to fulfill their love, but when James's kisses grew hot and insistent, she pushed him away, weeping.

"I can't, James. You know why. You could leave me with a child. That'd be a dreadful situation for me." Tears ran down her cheeks, and she allowed him to kiss them away, but kept her body from touching his.

"Ah Jessie, Jessie." James's groan seemed to come from his toes. "How can I leave you?"

"It's your pa's doin'. I'll never forgive him." Jessie inhaled sharply as James kissed her neck. "Don't, oh, don't!" She struggled to think clearly. "The Bible says you've got to obey him, even if you don't like it. Go and take care of your ma," she whispered, and gave James a soft kiss and a shove. "Go away, James. Don't come again. Just go." She fled for the house.

James was gone, lost to her. She'd never see him again, and a sob rose in her throat, choking her. Even knowing Ned sat beside her, puzzled at her strong emotion, couldn't keep her from letting it free, for just a moment.

Ned watched Jessie that night. She surely had acted strange earlier, falling silent when he brought up memories they shared, then starting to cry. Oh, she tried to keep it secret, but he knew she was upset about something he said. He simply didn't know what had set her off.

She sat on the ground beside Luke, feeding him soup, a spoonful at a time. Her face, lit by the firelight, danced with animation, first smiling, and then frowning when Luke refused the remnants of the soup. She set aside the bowl and pulled up his blanket, patting it into place around his chin. She smiled again, and started to hum.

Ned recognized the tune. It was a lullaby, an old one his mother used to sing.

Jessie finished one hummed verse, then began to sing in a low voice. "Golden slumbers kiss your eyes, smiles awake you when you rise . . ."

He grinned in the dark. How was Luke taking this, a lullaby from his sister? He looked at the boy. His eyes were closed, his face slack. *No shame there*, Ned thought. *He's already asleep.*

Chapter 9

Several days later, Heppie stood at the altar in a strange church and gave a nervous giggle. *At last!* Her face felt warm, and she wondered if she was blushing. She took a deep breath to suppress another giggle. George stood, ramrod straight, clothes brushed free of dust, sandy hair combed carefully into place over his half ear, looking like he'd keel over if he didn't wiggle something soon. Heppie looked at the minister, who was thumbing through his prayer book. She couldn't read his expression and wondered if he objected to marrying two strangers. *Two shabby strangers.*

She wore the same dress as every day. It was all she had to wear. Ma had brushed at it with her hand, trying to get the worst of the dust off, before they stepped through the church door. Heppie wished she'd been able to wash her dress or at least take a bath, but time had run out when the bustling little minister arrived, shepherded by Robert Fletcher. Several curious townsfolk came in their wake—drawn by gossip that a traveling couple had asked the minister to marry them—and accompanied the wedding party into the church.

Fortunately my hair looks nice. Hannah had brushed it, braided it, and coiled it intricately at the back of Heppie's head. *I'll make a good appearance from the back.*

The minister looked from his prayer book to them and opened his mouth to begin the wedding ceremony. At first Heppie didn't hear a word he said. She knew he was talking, because his mouth moved, and she could hear a droning sound like a thousand bees circling her head, but nothing made sense because George was looking down at her, and she was drowning in the depths of his blue eyes.

When George finally broke eye contact to look at the minister, Heppie got her ears working again. George stuttered, "I . . . ah . . . do," and the minister looked at Heppie.

"Do you, Hepzibah Bingham, take George Heizer for your husband, to love, obey, and cherish him so long as life lasts?"

Heppie stared at the little man in the frock coat. Did she want to marry George? She swallowed, panicked. *Will I love him until I die? Do I have to obey everything he says?* She looked at George, her eyes drawn to his right ear. *Can I cherish that little half-shot-off ear as long as I live?* George squeezed Heppie's hand and smiled down at her. His touch steadied her, and she knew he loved her. *Settle down, Heppie*, she thought. *You can do this. Just be quick about it before you change your mind again!*

She turned to the minister and said in a rush, "Yes, I do. What's next?" As soon as the question left her lips, she gasped and clapped her hand over her mouth, mortified at her audacity.

The minister looked surprised and slapped his prayer book closed with his hand still inside. After a moment, he opened it again, moved his finger down the page, and found his place.

"By the power given to me by God Almighty, this county, and the state of West Virginia, I proclaim you husband and wife, duly and legally married according to the rite of the church. Two dollars, please."

As Robert took up a collection for the money, George wrapped his arms around Heppie. "The preacher forgot to mention this," he whispered, and lightly kissed her on the lips. "I'll never put cows ahead of you again," he vowed, then kissed Heppie with a thoroughness that dizzied her brain.

She clung to him, warmth spreading from her lips to the core of her being, a tingling wave that awakened an overwhelming need to somehow knit her body together with his. Frightened by the intensity of her feelings, Heppie broke away, her breathing short and quick. George winked at her, and she looked at her hands, still gripping his shirt. She dropped them to her sides, wondering, *Did Hannah feel like this on her wedding day?*

After the ceremony, the townsfolk gave the newlyweds energetic congratulations and several bits of advice. Heppie smiled, nodded, and wished they were on the road again, away from well-meaning strangers. She wanted to wash, to get at least her hands and face clean before nighttime came and George— What *was* George going to do? After they'd set up camp, Ma had taken Heppie aside for a moment and said that after the wedding Heppie would give herself to her husband. Tales she'd heard and things she'd seen crowded into her mind, but surely that wasn't what people did?

They finally arrived at their camping place with the other members of their party. George patted her hand and said, "I'm going to wash up a bit, but I'll be back soon." Heppie smiled in relief and took herself into the woods with a pan of water to do the same.

Later, the last supper dish had been dried and put away and everyone had gone off into the darkness, leaving the newlyweds alone at the campfire. Heppie sat beside the fire, stirring it back to life whenever the flames weakened.

After a time, she got up and leaned over the fire with her stick, and George asked, "Heppie, what are you doing?"

She jumped backward, righted herself, and looked at her husband. "Keeping the fire going."

"Why, my girl?"

"I like the light." She sat back down, fidgeting with the stick and wishing Hannah or Jessie would step into the firelight.

"Let it go out. It's time for bed."

"Allow me a few more minutes."

George got to his feet, moved behind her, and squatted down. He put his lips to her ear. "I'd rather you came to bed, my love," he whispered.

"It's dark away from the fire," she whispered back.

"That's fine with me. The darker the better." He slipped his arms around her waist.

"George!" she whispered. "What a thing to say!"

"Come on, honey. We have to get up early."

"I don't like the dark." She thought of animals in the darkness of the forest beyond their camp. Animals that lumbered through the trees, making noise.

"You'll be safe with me." He nuzzled her neck. "So safe and warm." He drew out the words, tantalizingly slow.

"Will I?" she asked, moving her neck slightly. "I'm fearful."

"Of me?"

She remembered seeing a tom cat mount a female at a friend's farm. The tom had been rough. "No, of things I don't know much about."

George kissed her throat. She thought her skin would melt.

Heppie swallowed hard. "The things I feel."

"Don't be afraid. I'll take care of you."

"Will you?"

"Yes." His drawl made the single syllable go on forever. His breath stirred the hairs below the coils of her tresses.

Heppie closed her eyes and took a deep breath. Yes, her skin was melting, and if he kept kissing her, she would want to flee into the darkness with him. *I'll be safe from these feelings beside the fire.*

George stood up and stepped to one side. Heppie also stood, bending toward the embers to stir them again. *I'm a married lady. I can have these feelings.* She put down her stick. She paused, thinking, *What if this is lust? Lust is sinful!* She picked up the stick again and stirred the fire. Sparks flew up, and she stepped back to avoid them. George moved in, took the stick from her hand, and led her away from the fire.

Those cats made a fearful racket. Heppie felt a bit of panic rise in her stomach. *Do married folk make noise? Will all the camp hear us?*

George drew her closer into the circle of his arm as they walked toward the bed she knew he had prepared for them. *He is strong,* she thought. *He is brave and warm and safe. I love him. I want to be with him.* An idea dawned on her. *This is what Ma meant.* Her panic diminished.

He chuckled. "You're so deep in thought, my dear. Where are you wandering?"

"Hold me close," she begged, suddenly clutching him around the neck.

"That's what I had in mind," he said, enclosing her in his embrace.

"No. Hold me for a minute or two right now." She let out a gust of air as he complied.

He bent his head and kissed her under the ear. "There's nothing to fear."

"Wolves?"

He shook his head against her.

"Bears?"

Again she felt the negative movement.

"Making noise?"

He was still for a moment, then whispered, "I can't guarantee that."

"George!"

"I *can* guarantee I'll take good care of you." His hug tightened.

The last of the panic left Heppie, and she let him lead her through the darkness toward their marriage bed.

Chapter 10

Several weeks of travel brought the Bingham party within sight of the Mississippi River. When they reached St. Louis, they rented quarters in a rooming house. Everyone got jobs to improve their condition. Robert hired on at a bank, while Ned took a job as a guard at a warehouse, and George joined the police force. Luke ran errands for a grocery, Mrs. Bingham sold dry goods, and Jessie worked in a millinery shop. Hannah took in mending and sewed men's shirts.

One day, Hannah sat in a chair, her still hands lying on trousers that needed mending, when Jessie returned early from work.

"Hello, Hannah," Jessie said, taking off her bonnet and hanging it on a hook by the door. "Miss Huckaby gave me a few hours off, as we've caught up on the latest piece work." She walked over to Hannah and looked down at her. "You look so pale. Why don't you take a stroll around the park, if you're finished there? The fresh air will do you good."

"No." Hannah glanced at Jessie, and then down to her lap. "I haven't finished the mending." One of her hands twitched, and she clasped both together. "Nothing will do me good, Jessie. Not a walk in the park, not a journey across the country, not anything!"

Hannah's voice had risen, and her sister stared. "What do you mean?" Jessie asked.

"I mean I'm not all right. I'll never be all right again." She turned her head away from Jessie. "You can't know what I endured that awful, horrible day. Why did you and Heppie leave me on that corner alone?"

"Hannah, I'm sorry. You can't know how bad I feel that you were . . . taken. And hurt so." Jessie knelt by the side of Hannah's chair and tried to grasp her hand.

Hannah pushed herself sideways in the chair, her back to Jessie. "You'll never feel as bad as I do. Never!" She bit off her words.

"I know that," Jessie said, getting to her feet. "It's been weeks since that happened to you, Hannah. Past time for you to get over your troubles." She squared her shoulders. "I'm going out. You may not want to walk around the park, but I do. Tell Ma I'll be home before dark." She rushed to the door, grabbed her bonnet, and left the room, slamming the door behind her.

Hannah stood up. The trousers and her mending supplies tumbled onto the floor as she ran into the bedchamber, snatched the pitcher out of the washbasin, and threw up.

After spewing her luncheon into the white ceramic bowl, she slowly raised her head, picked up the towel, and wiped her mouth. *That's twice today*, she thought, wringing the cloth in fisted hands. *It's getting so hard to keep this a secret.* She blew out slow breaths through pursed lips, hating the smell of the vomited material. She wrinkled her nose, but picked up the basin, went to the open window, closed her eyes, and threw out the waste. Someone below yelped in protest, and Hannah felt shame that she hadn't looked before she tossed out the vomit, but she moved out of sight and put the basin on the stand.

The odor remained in the room, filling it like the noxious fumes from a pile of manure. Taking small, slow actions so as not to alarm her stomach, Hannah poured a little water from the pitcher into the bowl, rinsed it with a slow swirling motion, looked out the window to be sure no one was below, and emptied the foul brew into the street. She lit a candle, blew it out, and moved it slowly through the air to kill the odor.

When she put the candle on the washstand, she sighed in

relief. The air seemed to be cleaner. Now no one would know she had thrown up.

Hannah backed to the bed, and slowly lay across it. *I'll just rest for a minute. Mrs. Coley won't be here for the mending until five o'clock.*

She woke to footsteps in the sitting room. The pall of sleep still rested heavy on her body and her mind, but she pushed herself to her feet and staggered from the room to see her mother taking off her bonnet.

"Ma! Why are you home?"

"It's time for me to be here, daughter. I imagine it's almost five."

"Oh no!" Hannah stumbled across the room to her chair and bent to retrieve the mending and her sewing materials from the floor. "This batch is due to be finished by five. How on earth did I nod off?"

Mrs. Bingham took the trousers from Hannah. "What is needed besides mending this hole?"

"That's all. I've finished everything else, but I went into the bedroom to—" Her eyes went wide, and she stood still.

"I'll complete this work, my dear," her mother said, sitting down. "You seem somehow frazzled. You say you were sleeping?"

"Yes. I just lay down for a moment, and I don't know what happened to me."

"You have suffered quite a deal of tumult, my dear. If you wish to finish your nap, I don't mind whipping a few stitches into these britches." She smiled, evidently pleased with her joke, and sat herself in the chair Hannah had occupied an hour previously.

"Thank you, Ma." Hannah stepped backward, turned, hurried into the bedroom, and approached the washstand.

"Oh," she gasped. Her stomach clenched, but there was

nothing within it to come forth, so she heaved helplessly as the convulsive waves racked her body. A small part of her mind wished she had closed the door behind her. *What if Ma hears?* she thought. *I can't bear it if she comes in and sees me.*

At last the nausea passed. Hannah went and shut the door, and sat on the bed. *If this baby were gone, I wouldn't throw up.*

The thought buzzed in her head, twisting and turning, mixed with denial that her mind had conjured such an idea. "That's a sin," she said, clapping her hands over her mouth, afraid her mother had heard. Afraid that if she came in, she would read the wicked thought hanging in the air.

If the baby were gone, I'd be rid of the shame.

Oh God, oh God, she prayed. *Take this evil thought out of my mind. I'll give the baby away. Some barren woman won't mind having the child of a monster. I won't tell her that's what it is.*

But if I carry the baby, Robert will hate me. He'll hate the child. He'll be so disgusted. Maybe he'll leave me. I can't bear that.

Hannah covered her eyes and sobbed, beaten down by her ghastly situation. *I can't tell Robert!* she thought, and mourned the loss of her close relationship with her husband.

At the table in the family's combination cooking-eating-sitting room one Sunday afternoon, Robert paused from doing sums with a stubby pencil and scrap paper and watched George count coins into stacks. Mrs. Bingham wrote a letter; Luke whittled softwood by the front door; and the young women on the sofa took turns modeling an unfinished shop hat Jessie had brought home. Meanwhile, Ned dozed in a window chair, and his soft snores punctuated the others' conversation.

"Do we have enough?" George asked.

Robert took up his pencil and finished the calculations. After a minute, he stood up and stretched. His shoulders ached, and the motion felt good. He twisted his head from side to side, and his neck cracked. "Ahhh," he said, letting his shoulders fall into place. Then he sat down.

"You're doin' that to keep me in suspense," George said, grinning. "Do we have enough?" His words were deliberate.

"Nearly so." Robert gave a short, barking laugh. "In all honesty, I want to purchase that prairie schooner from Mr. Grant." He moved a coin back and forth on the tabletop with his fingertip. He looked at the figures on the paper. Then he nodded at the pot of bean soup that stood on the stove. "I reckon if we work another week and continue to eat plain food, we can make our deals for wagons and supplies, and depart within a fortnight."

George smiled hugely. "That is good news, Robert. Thanks for doing the sums." He clapped Robert on the shoulder. "I can figure how much seed is needed to sow a field, but real money figures are beyond my understanding."

George rose from the table and looked at the women. "I'm going for a walk. Will you come with me, Mrs. Heizer?"

Heppie looked up, a smile quirking her mouth. "Yes," she said. "I think it's a lovely day." She got off the sofa and removed the apron she still wore from preparing dinner. "Will any of you come with us?"

Amid a widespread shaking of heads, George and Heppie prepared to depart for their stroll.

"Wait just one moment." Mrs. Bingham stopped them. "Can you post this letter for me? I've written at last to let Maxwell know we're on our way."

Heppie took the letter, and she and George left.

Robert scooped the cash and coins into a canvas bag, drew the cords shut, and knotted them together. He hid the bag behind a cracker tin on a shelf, and turned to survey the room.

Hannah and Jessie still sat on the sofa, measuring a feather affixed to the side of the hat.

"Is it just a mite too long?" Jessie asked. "Shall I snip it down?"

"I suppose it's fine," Hannah said, shrugging. "It's not to my taste. I've never liked feathers on a hat."

"You've never *had* feathers on a hat," Jessie joked, wiggling the plume against Hannah's upper lip.

"Don't do that!" Hannah shouted, and bounced to her feet. "You know I can't abide tickling."

Robert crossed the room and took Hannah by the hands. "I also need a walk, my dear. Come with me so I won't be alone."

"I don't want to—" she tried to protest, but Robert shushed her with a wave of his hand.

"I think you need the air," he said, gently tugging her toward the door. "You're looking a bit pale."

As Robert wouldn't listen to her protests, Hannah gave in.

Once outside, Robert bent his head to speak to Hannah in a low tone. "No feathers? No tickling? No taking the air? Where is the agreeable wife of my heart?"

She gave a huff and lifted her chin. Robert stopped. She looked away, avoiding his gaze.

"Hannah, have you lost flesh? Aren't you eating enough? You don't need to leave off eating to make our savings grow." He touched her hand, lifted it, and inspected her fingers. "You're too thin. Look how your wedding ring spins around. Hannah, you must eat. You would not want to lose that off your finger."

"Most days I have no appetite," she said, pulling her hand free. "If we must walk, let's get to it. I still have a bit of mending to accomplish."

"Not today," he said. "The customer can wait for a weekday."

"It's your mending," she murmured. "How did you manage to tear your sleeve so badly?"

"It was merely a slit a month ago. I don't know how it grew."

"Was it neglect? Wearing it each day? Not showing it to your wife in good time?" She seemed to make an effort to put on a jovial countenance.

"There's my smile," he said, coaxing the bud into full blossom with his fingertip. "You have such beautiful lips, my dear. Curving them into a smile makes them even more lovely."

"Robert, someone will see you. And you mustn't say such things. They'll hear you."

"Who?"

She looked around, but the street was nearly empty. She shrugged.

"Let's go to the park," Robert said. "There are several benches we can sit on if we grow tired. In fact, I know of a bench that's hidden in a grove of trees. I can say anything to you there." He grinned at her, and she ducked her head away from him. "Maybe I can get you to say something indiscreet back to me." He winked.

She shrugged again but let him lead her to the park.

Chapter 11

Ned awoke a few minutes later. He scrubbed at his face with one hand, feeling the stubble prickling his fingers, and looked over at Jessie, who sat on the sofa showing her mother a hat. *She sparkles like the evening star at twilight*, he thought. *She always has.* He dropped his hand on his thigh. *She's takin' a lot of joy in that hat. I wish I could buy it for her.* His pockets were empty, all his wages tossed in the common pot to purchase supplies for the journey ahead. He looked around the room. Only the two women and young Luke were there with him.

"Where is everybody?" he asked, getting to his feet.

"Mr. Heizer," Mrs. Bingham said, smiling up at him. "Did you enjoy your nap?"

Ned fidgeted with his thumbnail, embarrassed that he hadn't gone into the next room to sleep. "Ah, yes, ma'am," he said. "I hope I didn't disturb y'all."

"Certainly not. A little snore now and then can be curiously comforting."

He smiled and gritted his teeth. *I was snoring? Just the impression I want to leave on Jessie.* "What's my brother up to?"

"He went for a stroll with Heppie," Jessie answered. "It's a lovely day." She looked down at the hat in her lap, put it on her pale yellow hair, and fiddled with the feather.

Ned's heart turned over, and he caught himself breathing hard and fast. "Whew," he said in a whisper, then added aloud, "Would you enjoy a walk in the park, Miss Jessie?"

Jessie looked up, a slow smile spreading across her face. "I would, Mr. Heizer. Are you asking me to accompany you?" She took off the hat and gave it to her mother.

Ned gulped. "I am. That is, if your mother is willin'." He turned to Mrs. Bingham. "Is that agreeable with you, ma'am?"

Mrs. Bingham pushed herself to her feet and nodded. "I think Luke would enjoy stretching his legs. Wouldn't you, Luke." Her tone made her last words a statement.

Jessie rose to her feet. "It appears we will have company, Mr. Heizer." She turned to Mrs. Bingham. "Are you coming, Ma?"

"No, dear." Mrs. Bingham smiled as she shook her head. "Luke will be companion enough to make things proper. You young people have a good time."

With Jessie beside him and Luke following after, Ned limped down the stairs leading to the street. Once they were walking toward the park, Ned turned to look at Luke. He glanced at Jessie and waggled his eyebrows. Jessie grinned back at him, then looked over her shoulder at Luke.

"Lukie, I believe I left my little purse behind. Will you go fetch it? Please?"

"Ah sis, you're kidding me. You don't need a purse for a walk in the park."

"Yes I do."

"Do not!"

"Do too!"

"Do not."

Jessie stopped, turned around, and pointed her finger toward the rooming house. "Yes I do. Go get it for me, and I'll do one of your chores tomorrow."

"Take out the rubbish?"

"Well . . ."

Luke pulled his knife from his pocket and picked at the whittling stick he still held in his hand. "You don't need your purse. You're trying to get rid of me. I'll get rid of myself if you'll take out the rubbish tomorrow."

Jessie laughed. "I'll do it. Maybe Mr. Heizer will help me."

Ned nodded, and Luke grinned. "You promise?"

"I promise, Lukie." Jessie put out her hand and shook Luke's. "Good-bye."

Luke turned around and left. Ned took Jessie's hand and pulled it through the crook of his arm. "Ready for our walk?"

Jessie smiled. "It will be delightful, now that our chaperon is gone."

Ned grinned. "You got rid of him right handily, missie." He inhaled deeply as they entered the park, breathing in the heady scent of the lilacs lining the path.

"I've had lots of practice," Jessie said, almost skipping a little as she tried to keep up with Ned's longer stride. "Whenever Ma sent him out with us girls, we would take turns inventing errands to send him on." Her smile grew wistful. "It was more fun before he figured out we didn't want his company."

Ned threw back his head and laughed. When his mirth was spent and he had wiped tears from his eyes, he said, "Jessie Bingham, you're a caution. Poor Luke. It must be hard living with a bunch of girls. I'm glad I grew up havin' George."

Jessie looked thoughtful. "I reckon you're right. Max was so much older. By the time Luke wanted someone to play games with, Max was interested in girls, being a hero, and such. He didn't pay Luke any mind." She looked at Ned. "Do you suppose I'm being cruel to Lukie?"

Ned looked at Jessie and wanted to touch her on the nose, but he resisted, instead saying, "Maybe."

"Oh, do you think so?" She frowned. "I don't want to be mean. We've had good times together. We're the two youngest, you know."

"I know." They arrived at a bench situated in an intimate circle of trees beside the winding path, and Ned stopped and turned to face Jessie. "Shall we sit a spell?"

Jessie plopped on the bench and smoothed her skirt.

Ned watched her face as her emotions played over it. *She's got a tender heart*, he thought. "Luke will be all right," he said, sitting beside her. *Will she let me take her hand?* He decided to wait. "What do you think of St. Louis?'

"It's so much bigger than Mount Jackson," she said, crinkling her nose. "The river smells. If I lived here, I'd have to be away from the river."

Ned laughed. "I thought you were going to New Mexico Territory with your ma."

"I am," she said tilting her head to one side. "I wonder if Max found a wife out there. When he left, his head was filled with notions of making his fortune. I hope he did so."

"From what I remember of Max, I'm sure he's doin' fine." *Makin' a big impression with the ladies, no doubt*, he thought. *Max always liked the girls.*

"He wrote to Pa, inviting us to join him, so I reckon he's set up in some kind of business." Jessie looked down at her feet. "He didn't know Pa had died."

Ned looked at Jessie's somber face. He reached over and took her hand, sliding his fingers between hers. "What happy memory can I bring to your mind? You're thinking too hard on your pa."

"Not just Pa. All that's happened to us. That . . . man I killed back there. Is God angry with me?"

Ned gave Jessie's hand a little squeeze. "You been stewing about that since it happened?"

"It comes and goes. Some days I think I did the right thing. Some days . . . I don't know."

"Like today?"

"Yes."

Ned wondered if he could put his arm over Jessie's shoulder. It might comfort her. Then again, it might well offend her. He decided to wait. He was, after all, holding her hand without any protest from her.

"Here's what I think," he finally said, when Jessie had turned anxious eyes to him. "God ain't in favor of tyrants. He don't like bullies. I don't reckon he looks on rapists and such with high regard. From what you said at the time, he was threatening you and your sisters—maybe even your ma—with vile acts. Am I right?"

Ned felt Jessie's shiver through her hand. He squeezed it again and said, "I'm right. I reckon God knows your heart, that you were defendin' yourself and your kin. You did purely the right thing, Jessie Bingham. You did the right thing." Ned took in a lungful of air, and capped his speech by bending over and kissing the top of Jessie's head. She responded by laying her head on his shoulder.

"Thank you, Ned. You're such a good friend."

Ned tightened his gut as though he had received a blow. *A good friend? Ned, my boy, you have a long row to hoe,* he thought, resisting a sigh. Another thought came and brightened his attitude as he looked at their entwined hands. *Yes, and you're on a long, long journey. You have time to make her think different of you.*

Chapter 12

Several days later, Hannah cut flannel pieces to sew a man's shirt, then gathered the scraps to use during for her monthly. As she tucked them in a dresser drawer, she stopped short, her hands suspended. *I haven't had my monthly since we left Virginia. I won't have it again for a long time. I've got this horrid lump of clay in me, this bastard baby.*

She backed away from the dresser, wringing her hands, and paced beside the bed. *I'm trapped here with the mending and sewing. How can I find someone to get rid of this curse?*

She sank on the bed, feeling wicked for letting the appalling thought come again. *I'm already dirty, and unworthy of my husband for letting that Yankee dog rape me,* she thought. *Now I'm sinful, as well.* She wanted to scream, to vent her outrage and her anguish, but the walls of the boardinghouse were too thin. It was bad enough that she dared cry when she was alone. She wouldn't even have that release soon. Robert said they would leave St. Louis the following week. They'd be out on the trail again. She'd have no privacy for weeping.

Hannah got up and shut the drawer. She went into the main room, picked up her needle and thread, and began to sew together the shirt. When she pricked her finger, she began to cry, pretending it was because the puncture hurt.

When Robert purchased a team of mules and the canvas-topped wagon he'd been eyeing for weeks, Mr. Grant's broad face beamed with delight. Although the conveyance was not new, it had proved its worth on the trail to Kansas several times.

"You'll make better time with this vehicle and the mules than with that tumble-down farm wagon you folks brought with you," Mr. Grant said.

"Oh, we're still taking the old wagon, and another, as well," Robert said. "We've laid in a store of food sufficient for the journey, and we'll need every inch of space."

"Your brother-in-law bought a wagon?" the man asked.

"He found one to his liking down yonder," Robert answered, nodding toward another business. "He thinks there's enough grass on the plains, so he's using horses. Big ones."

Mr. Grant shrugged. "They pull strong, but they eat a lot. You'd best be taking grain along."

"Grain?"

"Yep. You're bound to come to places along the trail where the grass is eaten down. When you do, you'll have something to nourish your animals. That's the thing to keep in mind. Always look out for your animals."

"Hmm," Robert said. "I thought we'd simply be letting them graze."

"A couple hundred pounds of grain is a good thing to have along, just in case. You might even run into a big spot where a prairie fire's gone through. You'll need grain."

"Thanks for the advice. We'll buy grain." Robert shook the man's hand and climbed to the plank seat. He gathered the lines, took up a whip, and yelled, "Get up there," to his team. When the mules lurched against the collars and put the wagon into lumbering motion, Robert grinned broadly. At last he possessed his own means of transportation. Just as he predicted, they'd be on their way in two weeks.

One night, soon after their departure from St. Louis, Robert accompanied his wife into a wooded area to gather kindling and fuel for their campfires. When they were well hidden from the others, he took her shoulders in his hands and drew her to his chest. She went stiff in his embrace, and he lightened his touch on her arms.

"Hannah love," he whispered in her ear. "Calm yourself." His voice was very low, almost inaudible, but he deliberately made it gentle. "You went through a horrible time. I only want to hold you in my arms for a little while. Won't you let me smell your hair?"

"My hair is filthy," she muttered.

"Your hair is beautiful, like you are. Beautiful and soft and sweet."

"No!" Hannah tried to pull free, but Robert held her tight. She struggled against him for a moment and then gave up, her shoulders tensed. "My hair is filthy. My skin is filthy. My female parts are filthy. My womb is filthy, because it carries a filthy child. A dirty, rotten, misbegotten Yankee child. I'm filthy through and through!" She was almost screaming at him, and he shushed her with his hand over her mouth. "Don't. Do. That," she gasped, wrenching herself from his grasp.

He grabbed her before she ran away, and pulled her to him, his mind whirling. *A child!* "We're having a child?"

"No! I'm having a child. It has nothing to do with you."

"Hannah. It's my child."

She averted her eyes and sobbed out, "You don't know that."

Robert looked over Hannah's head into the deep woods, struggling with his conflicting feelings of joy and dismay. He kissed the top of her head. "Hannah, I'm your husband. It's my child."

"Robert. Don't." She took a deep gulp of breath. "It's a Yankee bastard."

He stopped her with two fingers lightly pressed against her lips, and bent down to look at her. "Don't say that. The only

Yankee bastard is the one we left in that barn. The vile . . ." He had to stop to get air and calm himself. After a moment, he said, "That child is most likely mine. I've been a husband to you all along."

"We'd been wed six months with no sign of an infant coming!"

"But this spring" He ran the back of his knuckles along her arm. "Don't you remember how sweet it was to be in our own home at last? Not have to share a house with your mother?"

Hannah stood still, rubbing her arm where Robert had touched her. "How do you know we created the child? How do you know this babe isn't from that Yankee's depraved, foul, revolting seed? He debased me." Sobs raked her body. "Why do I feel so soiled?"

Robert dropped his hands and released her. He chose his words carefully. "I can't pretend to know your reason for thinking that way. Perhaps a doctor could explain it. Or your mother."

"Don't you talk to my mother," she cried out. "Don't you dare." She pounded on his chest with her fists. "She can't know about this evil, wicked baby, this sin I've done against you."

"Hannah." He captured her fists in his hands. "Your mother will know about the baby. Everyone will know about the child coming as time goes by. Scarves and such only conceal for a while."

"Rip it from me! Tear me asunder!" She wept into his chest.

Robert felt the blood drain from his face. He swallowed and straightened his shoulders. "Hannah," he barked. "Hannah, come back to your senses." He softened his voice. "Hannah, you are very dear to me, every part of you is dear to me." He struggled to say something to touch her soul. "Can I cherish you more than I do now? My heart is knit to yours. Any child you bring forth will be sweet and clean. I will love it with all my being. We two are one, and the acts of a despicable man have no bearing on our union."

Hannah burrowed against Robert, sobbing. "I want to believe that. I want to." She began to shiver. "I cannot fathom such a thing."

He squeezed her hands. "I must consider that in time, you will believe me." He turned one palm upward and kissed the center of it. "There, I have cleaned a little part of you with my love. Trust in it. Feel it. Let it grow."

"Oh, Robert," she moaned. "You have no sense to be so good to me." Her body went slack against his, and he caught her before she fell.

He held close her for a long time, until her breathing slowed and she was restored to a state of calm. Then he released her with a sigh, bent down, and picked up a fallen branch.

"We'd better get on with our job. They'll be wondering where the wood is."

Chapter 13

After a matter of weeks, the party made camp near a spot where the westward trails divided. The northern branch led to Utah and California and Oregon. The southern track was still renowned as the Santa Fe Trail, which connected to old Spanish trails that continued through New Mexico Territory all the way to California, following a wagon road pioneered by a party of Mormon volunteers during the War with Mexico in the '40s.

Jessie stood over an iron skillet, frying bacon. She looked up from her task when Ned stepped into the firelight.

"Good evening, Jessie," he began.

"Hello, Ned." She tucked a lock of hair behind her ear. "Ma's not nearby, so I can call you that."

Ned smiled and nodded. "You look very nice tonight," he said. "Do you mind if I sit a spell?"

Jessie rolled her eyes in mild annoyance and said, "Suit yourself." She turned the bacon with a fork.

"Thanks." He found a box and lowered himself onto it. "Lovely night. Stars out and a full moon."

"Uh-huh," she said, laying down the fork and lifting the lid on a pot of beans. It needed stirring, so she picked up a wooden spoon and thrust it into the savory mixture.

Ned shuffled his feet

At the sound, Jessie looked up to see him gazing at George and Heppie, who were teasing each other near their wagon.

Ned cleared his throat, then spoke. "Married life seems to suit my brother and your sister."

"They do seem over the moon."

"Have you thought about getting married?"

Jessie cast her eyes down to her work. She hadn't given the topic much thought since . . . since she'd been left behind when James went west. She bit her lip. It didn't help. Her heart still hurt more. Slowly she looked up. Ned was sitting there, waiting for her to answer. She shrugged her shoulders. "Not for a long time."

Ned bent over and fiddled with the top of his boot. "Do you know what double cousins are?"

Jessie frowned. *What a strange question!* "No."

"That's when two brothers marry two sisters, or a brother and sister marry a sister and brother. Their youngsters are double cousins."

Jessie stirred the beans so vigorously that they sloshed over the rim of the pot.

"Jessie." Ned paused, fiddling with the lacing on his boot. "I, that is, you, I mean . . ." His voice trailed off. "Oh, confound it," he said, rising to his feet. "Will you marry me? We'll run into a town sooner or later, and we can scare up a preacher or a mayor or a judge to say the words over us—"

"Mr. Heizer," Jessie interrupted.

"Please, Jessie, hear me out. We're good friends, that's a fact, but I've got strong feelings for you. I thought of you a good deal during the months that I was lyin' there in the hospital up north. When I got back to Mount Jackson and found out you were gone, it tore me up inside. I want to be with you now."

Jessie turned and faced him. "Mr. Heizer, Ned, I—"

"If you don't want to answer yet, I'll understand." He stepped forward and took her hand. "Take all the time you need."

Jessie looked at Ned's hand holding hers. She looked into his eyes. She looked away. "Ned, we're only friends. I've never thought of marrying you."

Ned dropped her hand and shuffled his feet. "I think friendship is a good start for marriage."

Jessie stared at him. "But what about love?"

"I've never loved anyone but you, Jessie."

Jessie smiled wryly. "That's on your side of the matter, Ned. Don't I need to love you too?" Her smile slipped away as Ned jerked upright, his throat working as he swallowed several times. "Being in love matters to a girl."

She turned to the bacon and poured the grease into the bean pot. She whacked at the crisp bacon. It shattered into pieces that she scooped into the pot. She looked up. Ned was staring at her, his face somber.

After a moment, he spoke. "Don't misunderstand me, Jessie. Naturally I want you to love me, but I'm sure that will come in time. For now, consider takin' a good, hard look at your feelings for me. See if they ain't sufficient for marriage."

Jessie laid down her spoon and moved to face Ned. She put her hand on his arm. "I been in love before," she whispered. "I don't feel the same about you."

Ned looked down at the ground, then up again. Finally he spoke, his voice dark. "James Owen?" he asked.

"Yes."

"Is he anywhere around?"

"No."

"Then marry me."

"I don't love you like that. You're my friend."

"It doesn't matter to me what kind of love you bear me now." Ned took her hand from his arm and brought it to his chest. His heart beat strong, hard. "I hope that will change in time. I care for you enough for both of us." He nodded sharply, only once, then added, "You think about what I've said."

Jessie lowered her eyes. Her heart thumped in her throat, matching the rhythm of Ned's. *Maybe I do love him*, she thought. *Maybe I should think about marrying him.* Slowly she nodded. "I'll give thought to your suggestion." She looked up.

Ned was watching her face. "It may take me some time to . . ." She swallowed, took her hand from Ned's chest, then said in a gush of air, "To think it through."

Ned's eyes looked like the depths of a deep pool. He gazed at her for a long time, not moving, frozen in place. Then he nodded, again only one time. "I'll wait."

He strode off, his long legs barely limping, and Jessie wondered how hard it was for him to damp down his pride and give her the time she needed.

Riding in the wagon several days later, Robert watched Hannah out of the corner of his eye. She seemed wilted, like a bunch of wildflowers plucked in the morning and set aside without water by a careless child. The wagon lurched, and she gave a little gasp.

"Have you told your ma about the baby?" he asked.

"No." Hannah's shoulders rose and fell with her sigh. "Has Mama been askin' nosy questions?"

"A few. I try to remember she's concerned for you, darlin'." Robert slapped the lines over the backs of the big mules.

"Are you?"

"Am I what?"

"Are you concerned for me?"

"Oh, darlin', how can you ask that?" He looked over at Hannah. Her hands lay gripped tightly together against the growing mound of her belly. "Mercy! Hannah love, you know what I did to that man when I came after you."

"I have nightmares nearly every night. Will they ever go away?" Her voice dropped. "Will you ever forgive me?"

Robert swore softly. Nothing he said or did seemed to make a difference to Hannah. He pulled the mules to a stop and wrapped the lines around the brake handle. He grabbed

Hannah's shoulders and kissed her, firmly, possessively.

He let her go, took up the lines again, and slapped them against the animals' rumps a little more forcefully than was necessary. When they were once again on the move, he looked over at her. Hannah stared back at him with wide eyes. "You're my wife," he said, softly. "I love you with all my heart and soul, and no matter what happened in that barn, no matter what happens in the future, nothing will change that."

"I want to believe you," Hannah said, beginning to sniffle. "I just— it's so hard."

A feeling of helplessness washing over him, Robert sat dumbly on the wagon seat. If only there were something more he could do to assure her of his love. Theirs was the last wagon of the bunch, and he didn't dare stop again for fear they would fall behind. How dearly he would have liked to halt the wagon, lift Hannah down from the seat, find a scrap of shade, and tenderly show her how much he loved and needed her.

He grabbed the whip, uncoiled it, and cracked it with vigor above the ears of the mules. *That'll have to wait*, he told himself. *She's not ready for me yet.*

Chapter 14

Heppie watched the sky all afternoon as she walked beside the wagon. White clouds built into towering giants, filling the horizon. They loomed there, first turning gray, dark and ominous, then becoming almost black as a wind pushed them toward her. Soon they would be overhead. Prickles of gooseflesh raised the hair on her arms under her sleeves. Would rain come to dowse them as they struggled west? Lightning slashed to earth several miles ahead of the travelers. Heppie cried out, even before the deafening thunderclap filled her head. *Dear God in Heaven*, she prayed. *Not a lightning storm!*

Rubbing her arms with her hands, she looked over at George. He was standing in the wagon, gripping the lines hard to keep the four big horses from bolting. His lips were drawn back from his teeth, and she couldn't tell if he was grinning or focusing on the task. *He's probably grinning because he faces life like an adventure.* She shook her head. *Will I ever be brave like him?*

Another bolt of lightning struck ahead of them. Heppie shivered, bracing herself for the thunder, biting her lower lip to keep herself quiet. She could see rain falling in the distance, sheets of it, accompanied by wind lashing the grass. The sun had gone into shelter behind the menacing clouds. It was probably time for her to seek shelter as well.

Pulling up her skirt so her feet wouldn't get caught in the hem, Heppie dashed toward the wagon. "George," she screamed above another rumble of thunder. "Stop and let me get up."

George turned his face toward her. She saw that he was battling with the horses. He yelled back, "Stay clear! They want to run."

Heppie stepped out of the way, thinking, *No! He'll be killed if they run off.* Her heart banged against her ribs. *George, hold on to them*, she pleaded silently, watching the wagon lurch along the trail, gathering speed, until the animals broke free of George's control.

Heppie cried out, a long gusty "No!" that the rising wind swallowed.

From behind, noise pounded on the prairie like another roll of thunder. Heppie looked over her shoulder. What new danger was upon them? A horse approached with Ned bent low over its neck, driving forward to catch up to the runaway wagon. He passed Heppie. Clods of earth fell around her, stirred up by the horse's hooves. A small chunk of sod hit her cheek, sticking in place, and she batted at it as if it were a bug. She had to see what was happening to George.

She realized she was running, half falling over the furrows of churned-up earth left behind by hooves and wheels. Her throat felt raw, filled with her high, keening cry. Her lungs burned as she filled them with air that seemed to have been singed by the lightning. The wagon was so far away!

Another horse blew by, whipping up a dust cloud, pressing the thick yellow air against her. Mr. Fletcher. Luke sprinted by, his arms pumping with effort. She squinted her eyes, trying to find the wagon. Trying to see George.

At last she broke out of the dust. Ahead of her, the wagon lay on its side at the end of a plowed-up rut in the earth, one wheel smashed, the other spinning crazily. Ned Heizer and Robert Fletcher were off their mounts, struggling with horses thrashing on the ground. Luke ran toward them. Where was George?

Raindrops began to pelt her—needles on her flesh—but she kept running. Was George under the wagon? Her head seemed to reel as the storm grew in ferocity. Someone was screaming, "George!" over and over. She finally recognized her own voice.

The sky closed in, black and threatening. Sunlight had gone, fleeing from the violent flashes of lightning. A dark figure rose from the prairie floor and caught at her as she passed it.

"Heppie!"

She whirled around, screaming her husband's name, clutching at his arm.

Blood slid down George's cheek from a gash above his eye. It mixed with the rain to become a pink flow. He moved cautiously, as though he were checking his body for injury. His arms wrapped around Heppie, and she nuzzled against him, drawing in great panting breaths of air.

"Are you hurt?" she asked.

Heppie sensed George shaking his head. His body trembled, and she burrowed into his chest, trying to buoy him up.

"I have to see to the horses," he said in a tight voice. "And the wagon."

The tremors of his body frightened her. "Hold me a minute, then you can go," she said, still panting, willing him to stop shaking. After a moment, she turned him loose and watched him limp toward the overturned wagon. He bent to retrieve his hat, but the bending was slow and awkward. *Oh George,* she thought, *are you hurt in your innards?*

Lightning struck, much closer this time. A great roll of thunder followed.

Heppie jumped, stifling a shriek, wiping rain out of her eyes so she could see. She pressed her lips together, trying to settle her nerves. *Hepzibah Heizer, you stop that,* she told herself, making her inner voice as firm as she could manage. *George needs you.* She began to walk toward the group of men gathered around the horses. *This storm will pass. Sooner or later, they'll fix that wheel and set the wagon upright. After that, George will expect you to put our things to rights inside.*

~*~*~

Favoring his right leg, George trudged along the water-filled ruts toward the wagon. The leg didn't seem broken. Probably got bruised when he landed so hard. His side burned something fierce, though, so he sent his fingers to explore. Maybe he'd busted a rib or two. *Holy Nellie!* he swore, at the thought of going through that botheration and discomfort again.

Ahead, the wagon wheel on the rear axle still spun. Just like his head. The cut on his forehead smarted, but he figured the rain would wash it clean. He shut his eyes briefly, still walking, and tripped on an upturned ridge of earth. He didn't go down, catching his balance, knowing that Heppie was following behind, probably wide-eyed and breathless with fear for him.

A smile twitched at the corner of his mouth. Heppie. She was certainly grabbing hold of the spirit of being married. The previous evening she'd teased the tiredness out of him. His smile widened. It had been a good night.

Ahead of him, Robert and Ned had succeeded in quieting the team, despite continuous flashes of lightning that made the air sizzle and cracks of thunder that seemed to rip the sky from stem to stern. Luke knelt on one knee, bending forward. He got to his feet and stepped aside.

Three of George's horses were on their feet, but one lay on the ground, struggling weakly, flailing a leg that was clearly broken.

His mouth went slack and he began to run, his feet splashing into pools of water standing on the prairie.

Robert heard him coming and looked up. He rubbed his jaw and shook his head.

George uttered a curse. They'd barely started their journey across the Great Plains, and here he had a horse down. If that leg was busted, there was no hope. He'd have to shoot the animal.

When he reached the back of the wagon, he stopped running

and walked the last few feet with lead in his chest. Heppie was depending on him to get her safely to Albuquerque. How was he going to do that with three horses in a four-horse harness? Maybe they'd have to limp to the next settlement and plant themselves there.

No, that would never do. Heppie set a lot of store by her family. She was determined to get to New Mexico Territory. *It's my job to see that she does*, he thought. *Come hell or high water.* He set his jaw. *We've been through hell just getting out of Virginia. I reckon we can survive high water too. Just so long as them three other horses stay sound.*

Ned looked at George and said, "The leg's broke. Do you want to shoot the horse, or shall I?"

"Hold on. I want to see what's what first."

"The rifle's yonder, when you're ready." Ned nodded at his horse.

George looked over his team. Someone, probably Luke, had cut the harness from the wounded horse. He wondered if he could repair it. *I'll probably have to realign it, put the odd horse between the other two. Or maybe in front, in the center of the rigging. That'll be a job of work. We're going to be here for a while.*

"Well, let's unhitch them other horses from the wagon. I reckon we should move them off a piece so they don't take fright again when I shoot this one." Bitter regret washed over George. He hated to see a good animal lose its life, especially because of an accident like this one, right out of the blue. Rain drummed on his hat, matching his bleak mood.

Ned went for the rifle while the others took the sound horses away. Ned gave the gun to George.

George looked over Ned's shoulder. Heppie stood at the rear of the wagon, one hand resting on the wheel that had been whirling. He wondered if she had stopped it. She looked down at her shoes.

Behind him, the injured horse breathed with a whistle.

George shut his eyes. When he opened them again, Heppie was looking at him. He couldn't tell if the water coursing down her cheeks was from the rain or from her tears.

"Cover your ears," he said, his words sounding thick.

She nodded and whirled, bringing her hands up to do so.

George turned to the horse. Ned moved away and George took a breath, bringing the rifle to his shoulder. "Damnation," he said into a lightning flash, and squeezed the trigger. The sound of the shot was swallowed in the next thunderclap.

Heppie sat under Hannah's wagon, out of the storm, watching George and the other men as they struggled with the smashed wheel, trying to get it loose from the axle. George didn't want anyone to climb on the sides of the wagon lest they snap the bows with their weight. This left the wheel up in the air, the pin almost unreachable, making their task more difficult than it had to be. Robert and Ned had both argued with him about it, but he couldn't be persuaded.

Although it was only about five o'clock, the clouds were so dark and the rain so fierce that they'd had to light a lamp to continue working.

Why don't they wait until tomorrow? she wondered, shivering in the cold wind. *They're going to be struck by lightning if they don't stop.*

Luke held a broken spoke of the wheel to steady it. George sat on Ned's and Robert's shoulders, a mallet in his hand, banging on the end of the pin.

Heppie let out an exasperated sigh. *Is he daring the lightning to hit him? Luke weighs less. He should be up there, if anybody has to do this foolish job tonight.*

Lightning ripped through the clouds, hitting the ground a

hundred yards away. George was swinging the mallet when it struck. The men below him must have shifted, or jumped at the sudden explosion of energy released so close at hand, for he tumbled to the ground, landing with a splash in a rivulet of storm water. Robert leaned over to help him up.

"We're done for tonight," Ned said, grabbing the lantern and moving toward the Bingham's wagon. Luke followed him, and Robert came toward his own vehicle.

George threw the mallet to the ground beside the wagon and stalked away, stamping his feet on the wet ground.

"George!" Heppie called to him. "Come here!" More lightning banged into the ground. The roar of thunder followed almost instantly, the concussion in the air hurting her ears. George winced, then turned and hurried toward her. When he arrived, he bent down and slid under the wagon, grumbling to himself.

"You can't do more until the storm lets up," she said, laying her hand on his mud-caked arm.

"I wanted to get that wheel changed."

"Not tonight."

"I know," he said, and added a curse word.

"George!"

"I'm sorry, Heppie. I'm tired and sore and wet and muddy, and my wagon is tipped over with who knows how much damage besides the wheel." He slapped mud off his hat. "And I had to kill a perfectly good horse." His voice had dropped to a rough whisper.

"A horse with a broken leg," she said, wondering at how clearly her mind was working amidst the chaos.

"Yeah," George said, releasing a gusty sigh. "Yeah, broken."

"We'll be all right," she said, patting his arm. "I know you'll get us to Albuquerque, somehow."

George turned his head. Heppie met his gaze.

"Somehow," he repeated.

Chapter 15

Several days later, the Bingham party got underway again. In the meantime, George had butchered the dead horse, saying it was a shame to leave the meat to rot when they could use the flesh in their diet. Heppie balked at first, but finally helped salt the meat and pack it into a barrel. At last the men had changed the wheel and put the wagon upright, Heppie had straightened up the goods and gear inside it, and George had mended the harness. The rain clouds, along with the lightning and thunder, had moved east across the prairie, leaving sunshine and a mild breeze.

On the morning they left their forced camp, Mrs. Bingham chose to walk. She and her daughters set off in a group, but soon Heppie and Jessie lagged behind, gathering wild flowers. Hannah stared straight ahead, answering Mrs. Bingham's attempts at conversation in single syllables.

Mrs. Bingham pointed to the sky. "Look at that hawk, Hannah. Did you ever see such a wide wingspan?"

Hannah glanced up, then down again. "No."

"These plains birds are so much bigger than the ones at home."

Hannah shook her head slightly. "Home?"

"Well, I mean the Valley. You know that."

"Yes." Hannah's word came out sharp and breathy.

Mrs. Bingham said, "I reckon home is the wagon while we're traveling."

Hannah didn't reply.

Mrs. Bingham was looking at Hannah when a strong gust of air cooled her face and tightened Hannah's skirt against her abdomen. Mrs. Bingham took in a quick breath. *Oh lordy, lordy!* she thought. *There's a baby in that belly!* She'd worried ever since they'd left Mount Jackson that the Yankee had planted a seed. She closed her eyes against the proof while waves of nausea roiled in her stomach. *Oh my dear Hannah.* She wanted to weep. They hadn't left all their troubles behind, as she had hoped. Hannah was carrying trouble with them in her body.

What will Mr. Fletcher do? she asked herself. *Surely he knows. Oh, what can I do? I can't let Hannah carry this burden alone.*

When Mrs. Bingham opened her eyes, Hannah was staring at her, hostility clear in her face. Mrs. Bingham looked away, clamping her lips against crying out. Hannah had read her expression.

"Ma!" Hannah barked. She had her hands splayed out on the top of the small lump, as though she would push it out of her.

Mrs. Bingham turned her head, feeling like she was twisting a stubborn stopper on a crock of sauerkraut. "Yes, daughter?" Her voice sounded strained, shaky, as though she'd been down in bed for a week with a fever.

"Don't say a word!"

The intensity in Hannah's voice made Mrs. Bingham take a step away from her.

Hannah spoke again. "I won't discuss it."

"No?"

"No! Now leave me be."

Mrs. Bingham stopped walking, and Hannah strode on, her head down and arms wrapped around herself.

Mrs. Bingham let out a ragged sigh. *I've got to speak with Robert Fletcher.*

~*~*~

Ned tethered his horse to the back of the Bingham wagon and strode in Jessie's direction. She was alone for the moment, walking along with a free stride, carrying a bunch of wild flowers in one hand. Her yellow hair hung loose, blowing a bit in the breeze. He wished he could twirl a tendril of it around his fingers. He snorted to himself. *Forget it, Ned. She ain't given you an answer yet.* He took two more steps. *Maybe today she will.*

He caught up. "Hi," he said, grinning down at her.

"Hi, yourself." Jessie smiled, bringing the flowers in front of her. She raised them to her nose and sniffed.

"Smell good?" he asked.

"Very good. Want a try?" Jessie thrust the bouquet at Ned.

He inhaled. "Pretty nice. Prairie smells. Like rain and fresh breezes."

Jessie made a face. "I've had enough rain for now." She ran her free hand along her neck under her hair, then tossed it. "I'm glad I can dry out."

"Me too." Ned grinned. "Your hair is pretty today. Kind of shiny. Bright too."

Jessie laughed and ducked her head. "Well, it's yellow. That's a bright color."

Ned chuckled. *Good. She's in a happy mood.* He matched his stride to hers. How could he bring the conversation from bright colors to marriage? He walked along, thinking.

"What's on your mind, Ned?"

Her question caught him off guard. "What do you mean?" he countered, stalling until his thoughts made sense.

Jessie laughed. "I can almost see your thoughts floating out behind your head, silly."

Silly? Uh-oh. "I was admiring the picture you made with your hair blowing," he said, choosing the honest approach.

"You were?" Jessie had dropped her smile, but seemed willing to let him talk.

"Actually, I was wondering if you have an answer for me."

Jessie's face went guarded, and Ned mentally kicked himself.

"No, Ned." Joy in the day had gone from her countenance. "I don't. I haven't decided yet."

"But you're giving it thought?" He hoped a little pressure wouldn't send her skittering off toward her sister.

She nodded. And swallowed. "I'm sorry it's taking me such a long time." Her voice came out muffled.

Ned's chest squeezed, tight bands choking off his air. He didn't want that unhappy look on her face. Not when she was contemplating marriage to him. That wasn't how he wanted her to feel. Thinking on marriage should bring her pleasure.

"Well, you take all the time you need." He stopped walking and Jessie passed by him. Then she stopped and looked at him, hesitating like she was going to speak. She faced forward, glanced back momentarily, then walked away.

Ned took in a breath. He let it out slowly. His thoughts ran rampant. *By now Jessie should welcome the chance to wed. She knows she'll never see James Owen again. I'm twice the man he is, even stove up like I am.* A bitter fluid rose through his throat and into his mouth. He spit it out and trudged toward his horse. *I'd never run off and leave her.*

Robert hobbled his mules to graze and bent to pick up the harness he'd stripped off them. He looked toward the wagons, wondering why Mrs. Bingham was walking out to him. She usually left Hannah and him to their own devices, but she approached, calling his name.

"Mr. Fletcher, I must talk to you."

"Ma'am?"

"Tonight, after supper."

"In private?"

"Yes, please." She twisted her apron in her hands. "I don't want Hannah to know."

"To know what, ma'am?"

"That we're talking together."

Robert tilted his head. "That might be difficult to arrange."

"Perhaps after she's gone to bed?"

Robert winced. How many others had noticed that he and Hannah shared the same place at night, but not the same schedule? These days he almost always gave her time to go to sleep before he went to lie beside her, yearning to reach over and touch her. Knowing she would reject his touch.

He nodded and agreed. "After she's gone to bed."

The camp was quiet when Mrs. Bingham sat down by Robert beside the fire, puffing a bit as she bent over.

Robert was grateful that the firelight had died down as the wood went from embers to ashes. He twirled a stick in his hands, waiting for Hannah's mother to speak, wondering if she blamed him for the harm that had come to her daughter.

When Mrs. Bingham began, it was in a voice so low that Robert had to lean toward her to hear. He shifted in his seat so that he was closer.

"Hannah," she said.

"Yes?" He could hear her breathing, sucking in gulps of air as though to fortify her body against a lack of it.

"Do you know . . . are you aware?" She stopped, raised her shoulders, and let them drop. "Hannah."

He waited.

"She's going to have a baby."

He waited again, time stretching thin between them. When she didn't go on, he said, "I know." The air seemed thin too, and he caught himself breathing as Mrs. Bingham had. He said, "I know," again, and lapsed into silence. Mrs. Bingham would talk when she was ready.

"Do you reckon it's the Yankee's?"

"I do not!" His denial felt forced, a little too strong, but he had to make it. For Hannah's sake.

Mrs. Bingham examined her hands, spreading her fingers and staring at them. She rubbed her palms together as though they were covered in glue. "How do you know?" she whispered.

"The baby's mine. No matter what Hannah bears, the child is mine."

"You will claim . . . " She paused. "Anything?"

"Hannah is my wife. Whatever happens, the child is mine," he repeated. "I will give it the love of a father."

"You're a decent man, Robert Fletcher."

"I love Hannah. She suffered much at that man's hands." He felt tears filling his eyes, but resisted swiping at them. Perhaps Mrs. Bingham couldn't see the tears in the fading light. "She fought him hard," he said, envisioning the terrible scratches on the man's face. He raked his nails down his own cheek. "She tore at his hair." He put a hand to his head, imagining the pain. "It must have hurt, but he deserved all she did to him," he added, and knew his mother-in-law would perceive the husky note in his voice.

Mrs. Bingham sniffed and put her apron to her nose.

"Then she . . . " He stopped talking, reconsidering what to tell about the battle in the stable. He loosened his shoulders. "When the fight was over, the man was dead."

"My poor Hannah." Mrs. Bingham wiped her face. "You're a saint."

"I'm her husband." He leaned over, resting his forehead on his hand, bracing his arm against his chest. He remained that way for a time, then straightened up and blurted out, "She's so angry!"

Mrs. Bingham inhaled sharply. "Not at you?"

"At the babe. She won't love it." He turned away, suddenly

needing to hide his expression. "That breaks my heart. She must love her child. Sometime."

"Oh, Mr. Fletcher! Someday she will. I will speak to her."

He said, "Hmmmm," and could feel the sound buzzing in his head. Would Hannah's heart be changed by a conversation with her mother? He doubted that would do the trick.

"Where there's life, there's hope, Mr. Fletcher," said Mrs. Bingham, getting to her feet.

"Ma'am," he said, rising as well. "I'm sure you can do some good." He could say that to comfort Mrs. Bingham, but he knew the burden in his heart belied his words.

Chapter 16

Two hard months of travel brought the Bingham party to Pueblo City, Colorado. They camped on the outskirts of town in a meadow surrounded by trees that were just starting to show a hint of color. Before night fell, a buggy drew up near the wagons.

"Hello, the camp," called a round little man with a top hat perched on his sandy hair. "May we visit?"

Robert walked forward from the fire. "Visitors are always welcome. Step down and sit a spell."

Three men exited the buggy and moved forward. "Thank you," said the man who had hailed them. He was accompanied by a tall man in a black coat and by a man of medium build wearing a patterned vest over his shirt.

"Come to the fire," Robert said, gesturing toward the half circle of three wagons. "Will you take supper with us?"

"No, no, we've already et," said the short spokesman. He doffed his hat and nodded to George and Ned. "We've come to give you welcome to our fair city and to inquire if you will be staying hereabouts. I'm the mayor, Abraham Louis, by name, and these two men are members of the city council." He motioned to his companions.

Robert escorted them to what seats were available, and answered Mayor Louis's question. "We're mighty pleased to be here, but we're only passing through, heading on south. If no one takes it ill, we'd like to rest our animals for a few days, and the ladies would like to do laundry."

"That's acceptable to us. There's a fine creek about a mile in that direction, if you want to remove there tomorrow."

"Thank you. That's mighty kind of you to suggest it."

During the conversation, the tall man had been staring at Robert. He spoke up, his voice mimicking Robert's drawl.

"Say, haven't I seen you before? I'd swear I know you."

Robert drew himself up. "Sir? I'm newly come to this place. I don't know where we could have met."

The man turned to Mrs. Bingham and held his pursed lips between his thumb and knuckles as he stared at her. At length he snapped his fingers. "You're Joseph Bingham's wife! Where is the man? I'd like to greet him."

Mrs. Bingham turned white. Robert moved to her side, and she grasped his sleeve. "Sir, why would you know my husband?"

"Hell's bells, begging your pardon, ma'am, don't you know me? You've been in my store many times."

"No sir, we've barely come here."

"I don't mean the store in Pueblo City." The mayor and the second man tugged on the speaker's coat, but he persisted and pointed at Robert. "You're the Fletcher boy, and aren't you the, hmmm, the Heizer lads?" He gestured at the brothers and snapped his fingers again. "I've sold both of you many a piece of penny candy."

Jessie gasped, and the men turned toward her. "It's Mr. Hilbrands. You must remember him. The storekeeper in Mount Jackson. They left with . . ." She let out her breath in a loud sigh. "He and his family . . . when the Owens left."

"Mr. Hilbrands," Mrs. Bingham said, looking him up and down. "You've done well for yourself, getting onto the city council in so short a time. To answer your question, my Joseph died shortly after you left."

Randolph Hilbrands shook his head mournfully. "I'm most sorry to hear that, ma'am. You better let Rod Owen know when you pass by. He set a lot of store by your husband."

"We'll pass by?" she asked.

"Yes, ma'am. He took up land south of here. He's raising cattle and grandchildren." Rand grinned and continued. "The Owen place is about two days' journey south of here, toward the mountains. Rod and his boys are building that big dream he always had."

Jessie took a breath and stepped forward. "His boys?" she asked.

"Yes. There's Rulon, of course, who wed my daughter Mary. They have two fine children, young Roddy and a little baby girl. And Carl and his wife Ellen, you know, the Bates girl? They're helping out. Clay and Albert are too young to marry yet, but they pull their weight." He winked at Robert.

Jessie looked at Heppie, then back at Mr. Hilbrands. "And James? You didn't mention him."

"Well now, James is away from home. Ellen Bates was supposed to marry him, but she chose Carl. James took it hard. After the wedding, he had a dustup with his pa and he left. He stayed with us for a couple of weeks, sorely wounded in the side from a shootout with some Irish fellow." Rand put his hand over his right side in illustration of the location of James's wound. "After he mended, he refused to stay on as my freight driver. He went back south, and that's the last I heard of him."

As Mr. Hilbrands told his story, Jessie hunched her shoulders in shock. Heppie placed a hand on her arm, but Jessie shrugged it off, making fists.

"Chester Bates and them are raising wheat down along the Apishapa." He snapped his fingers. "I recollect that I told James of a job, breaking colts for Angus Campbell. Maybe he's still there." He looked over at Jessie and cocked his head. "You might hear more about him from the folks south of here, if you're curious," Mr. Hilbrands said.

Jessie looked up. "No," she said. "I'm not curious in the least."

The mayor took control of the conversation, said good-bye, and gathered his companions into the buggy. The man in the vest had not said a word during the entire encounter.

After supper, Jessie left the firelight. Heppie followed and found her sitting some distance away on a hill of sand, two hands over her mouth.

"Jessie, Jessie," Heppie said, sitting down and patting Jessie's arm. "What a liar you are! Not curious in the least! I'm sorry you didn't get any more news of James than what Mr. Hilbrands gave you, but that's probably for the best. Don't cry."

Jessie dropped her hands from her mouth. "I'm not crying," she said in a firm voice. "I'm screaming. How dare he?"

"How dare who do what?" Heppie asked. "What do you mean?"

"James! How dare he ask Ellen Bates to marry him. He loved me!"

Heppie shifted, adjusting her dress under herself. What on earth could she answer to sooth Jessie's anger? It seemed justified. James had been so attentive back in Mount Jackson. Once he'd recovered from his war wound, he'd come into town every chance he got so he could pay court to Jessie. Jessie had whispered that James was mentioning marriage. Heppie felt the heat of anger rising in her chest on Jessie's behalf. How dare he, indeed!

Heppie patted Jessie's back. "It appears James got his comeuppance when Ellen married Carl instead of him. Don't think about him. You got over caring about him once, and it's best to stay that way."

Jessie raised her face. "That's my difficulty," she said. "I never did. I reckon that's why I've kept refusing Mr. Heizer."

"Ned? He asked you to marry him? I didn't know he cared for you."

"He's always been a good friend, and now he declares he loves me. A while ago he asked me to consider marrying him. I reckon I'm still considering."

"You should snatch him up, Jessie. If he's as good a man as George is, why, he'll treat you very well. I'm sure he'll make a good living for you, once we get settled."

"I suppose so."

Something in Jessie's voice made Heppie turn to look at her. Jessie's lips were quivering. Heppie straightened her back. "I reckon he can make you forget James Owen." Heppie pressed her own lips together and frowned. "James didn't treat you right, goin' off to the west, then fixin' to wed Ellen."

Jessie sniffed as if her nose were dripping. "That was probably his pa's doing. Making him ask Ellen."

"That's neither here nor there! He's gone, and Ned wants you."

Jessie sighed. "I suppose so." She looked up. "I don't feel affection for Ned, at least not the kind to want him for a husband."

Heppie shrugged. "Many girls marry a man without caring for him. You can do that."

"I'm not certain I can." Jessie tucked her chin into her chest, and her voice came out muffled. "I don't want to marry a man unless thinkin' about him makes my knees go weak. Thinkin' on James still does that to me."

Heppie shook Jessie's shoulder with one hand. "Mercy sakes, Jessie! You ought to consider Ned's offer real hard and forget that James." She dropped her hand and sighed. "Come on. It's nearly bedtime, and we have a wagonload of wash to do tomorrow."

"Oh, yes, that's a better subject to think on. Doing the wash." Jessie laughed as she got to her feet, but there was no mirth in her voice.

~*~*~

A week later they camped below the Wet Mountains. Crickets chirped in the distance. A soft breeze blew down the side of the hills, bringing with it a chilly touch of autumn.

Mrs. Bingham sat in the flickering light of the waning fire, forking up a last bite of beans. When she'd swallowed it, she put down her fork and looked to Hannah, who sat nearby. Her daughter played with her half-eaten food as though her thoughts were a million miles away.

Mrs. Bingham cleared her throat and asked, "Dearie, did you take enough to feed yourself right? That little babe needs good nourishment."

Hannah stirred in her seat. "Ma, I don't want to talk about this . . . " She paused. "This mound of flesh. I can't stop it from supping at my vitals, but I don't have to talk about it."

"Daughter," Mrs. Bingham remonstrated, getting to her feet and collecting plates and forks. "Don't be unnatural. You must count your blessings."

As others drifted off to do their chores, she carried the dinnerware to a dishpan near her wagon. She got boiling water from the fire, poured it over the dishes, and called out to Heppie, "It's your turn to wash."

"Yes, Ma." Heppie came up and dipped her hand into the water, pulled it out, and shook it. She blew on her fingers. "This water is still too hot, Ma."

Mrs. Bingham rounded the fire and sat beside Hannah. "It'll cool down soon enough," she called.

Hannah clutched her hands together, her head bent over the abandoned plate. Her body seemed to vibrate with tension.

Mrs. Bingham straightened her shoulders. "You have many blessings, Hannah. Chief among them, you didn't die at that wicked man's hand. Mr. Fletcher says you punished him gravely."

Hannah interrupted. "I scratched his face and pulled his hair. That's not so much."

"Your husband told me a tale of great bravery on your part, dear. I got him to talk about it one night, and he wept as he told how you struggled."

"Robert doesn't weep."

"Mr. Fletcher has very deep emotions about that day, Hannah. He grieves that you were hurt. He grieves that your heart is so hard toward your babe. He loves you. He swears he will love your child, no matter what."

"How good he is," Hannah said, scorn tingeing her words. "How noble. How fine."

"Hannah! You must not talk that way about your husband. He deserves your respect."

"He is not the one carrying this bastard child!" Hannah blurted out. "No one blames him. Everyone will praise him to the heavens for his forbearance toward me."

"Hannah." Mrs. Bingham's voice rose firmly. "Robert Fletcher is one of the greatest blessings in your life. Once upon a time you knew that, and cherished his love. You returned it. It grew into a fine, shining thing. Don't debase it because you had a misfortunate experience with a vile man."

Hannah's face went white. "I can't forget that day."

"You must try. You must turn your thoughts to your babe, to being a good mother and a good wife. Give thanks each day for your blessings and for your family."

The anger in Hannah's face crumbled away, and her hands flew up to hide her face. "Mama," she said in a little-girl voice. "Don't scold me so. I can't bear for you to hate me. I hate myself enough for all the world."

Mrs. Bingham got up and gathered her daughter into her arms. "There now, dearie," she crooned, as Hannah cried deep gulping sobs. "Leave go of hate. Where there is life, there is hope. Your dear Robert knows that. He has been strong enough to carry you through this terrible time. Bear him a grateful heart for his fortitude. Don't turn your back on that gift."

Hannah turned her stricken face to look up at Mrs. Bingham. "Oh, Mama, I've been a dreadful wife."

"Yes, you have." Mrs. Bingham stroked Hannah's back.

"How can I cure that?"

"If you open your heart, you will know what to do, and when the time is right, you will be knit together as one soul again."

Hannah sniffled. "Can that happen, Mama?"

Mrs. Bingham stood still for a moment, looking at the moon as it rose over the meadow. She turned back to Hannah and hugged her tight. "Your Robert is fixing a snug bed under yonder stand of trees. I am confident he will receive you with all his heart." She looked again at the moon. "There's good luck in that light, daughter. Don't let it go to waste."

Hannah sat up and got free of her mother's encircling arms. She took a deep breath and stood up. She seemed to stand taller. "Thank you, Mama. I won't."

Mrs. Bingham stepped back and made a shooing motion. "Go on with you," she said. As Hannah walked away, she whispered, "Good night. May God be with you."

Chapter 17

By the middle of November, the Bingham party had reached the valley of the Apishapa River below the Mexican town of Leones. They pressed onward, anxious to cross Raton Pass before snow came upon them.

Late one afternoon, they approached a neat farm with fallow fields, pastures, grazing horses, corrals, and outbuildings surrounding a sod house. A teenage boy sat on the top rail of a fence and watched as their caravan drew near. Tied inside the fence was a saddled mouse-colored mustang, its sides flecked with sweat from recent exercise.

"Hello," Robert called out to the boy as soon as they were in voice range. "Is your pa at home?"

"Yep," the boy replied. "He's over yonder in the stable. I'll go fetch him."

"Wait a moment," Robert said, pulled up his team, and wrapped the lines around the brake handle. He smiled at the boy, jumped from the seat to the ground, and walked up to the fence. "We're looking for a place to spend the night and heard that the Campbells live somewhere around here. I figure you can give us directions."

The boy said, "Well, I reckon you've found it without my help. I'm Andy Campbell. My pa's name is Angus." He grinned down at Robert. "You sound a mite familiar."

Robert took off his hat and brushed at the dust on the crown. "We come from Shenandoah County, Virginia, same as you. Is your pa nearby?"

Andy got off the fence and waved toward the barnyard. "I'll take you over there."

"No need, Andy. I'll find my way. Looks like you're working with that horse. Is he new broke?"

"James Owen worked him some, but he had to go south, so I'm finishing up the job." He took a deep breath and stood straight, his shoulders back.

"James Owen, huh?" Robert tilted his head, looked at the boy, and nodded. "It's a good thing to take pride in a job well done." George and Ned had joined Robert by this time, and they watched Andy climb the fence into the corral, mount the mustang, and gently kick it into a series of turns before they strode off toward the stable.

"Angus Campbell?" Robert asked as they entered the stable.

Angus turned his head at the sound of his name, rose from his seat, and extended his hand.

"Welcome, gentlemen. By your voices, I'd say you're from my old neck of the woods."

"We are. I'm Robert Fletcher, and these men are George and Ned Heizer."

"From Mount Jackson?"

Robert nodded. "I worked there in the bank. George and Ned had the dairy outside of town. We're traveling down to New Mexico Territory with Mrs. Bingham and her boy Luke. George and I married the twin daughters."

"Mrs. Bingham? Alone? I take it Joseph didn't survive his wounds?"

"No sir," Robert replied. "Mr. Bingham took sick and died soon after y'all left. Max Bingham went west before his pa died. He sent word to invite the family to join him."

"Your timing is off. Most folks come through here in the summertime."

George jumped into the conversation. "Well sir, we planned

to leave next spring, but things got hurried up a mite. The old town wasn't pleasant for us anymore."

Robert nodded, shifting his feet a bit.

Angus said, "It's getting on toward suppertime. Will you and your party take nourishment with us and stay the night?"

George grinned. "We was hoping to ask you for a place to camp tonight on your land."

"You'll have it." Angus hung up the harness he'd been mending and put away his tools. "Come with me. Molly will be glad for the company. We don't get enough to suit her, seems like." He started for the house.

Robert matched his pace. "Womenfolk like to be sociable. I know Mrs. Bingham has enjoyed seeing her old neighbors again as we've passed by."

Angus pulled the door open and paused before entering his house. "Come say hello to Molly, then drive your wagons into the dooryard and water your animals at the well. You can make a proper camp after we eat."

"We'll bring food to contribute," Robert said. "Mrs. Bingham likes us to add to the meals we're invited to."

Angus laughed. "Fair's fair, I reckon. Molly!" He ducked his head and strode through the doorway. "Molly, we have company."

Jessie's spirits lifted as she helped prepare the meal. Molly Campbell was a jolly woman who laughed and told jokes and shared news of all the people who had come west from the Shenandoah Valley with the Owen family. The laughter untied the knot that had cinched Jessie's innards since Randolph Hilbrands had spoken of James and Ellen. *Maybe I'll hear some news of James*, she thought. *Mr. Hilbrands said he came south.*

Since there were so many people, the men took seats at the

table first, while the women stood aside, serving the food and chattering to each other. Jessie was content to let the conversation roll over her.

Young Andy mentioned the horse he'd been training. "Pa, I think that mustang is about finished up. Do you want me to start on the horse that bucked James off?"

Jessie's ears pricked up at the mention of James's name. Finally some news.

Angus laughed. "You're sure eager to follow in his dust," he said.

"You have horses to break, Mr. Campbell?" George asked.

"I do. James Owen came through and he started them off, but he was in a hurry to get through the Pass, so I let him go on. He's supposed to come back and finish the task, but I need a horse gentled down right away for Molly to ride."

"That James Owen!" Molly said with a click of her tongue.

Jessie's ribs ached as she held her breath, waiting for more information, but Molly only put a pie on the table and stood back.

"I can gentle a horse for you," George said. "That is, if you don't mind."

"Pa," Andy protested, "I can finish the horses."

Angus held up his hands. "It don't matter to me who does the job, so long as it gets done." He cut into the pie and served himself a large piece before sliding it down the table. He turned to the boy. "I have plenty of other chores for you, Andy." Then he turned back to address George. "If you want to tackle working the kinks out of the colts, I can pay you in cash or supplies."

"We have use for both, if you're willing to split up the payment when I'm finished."

"The deal is done." Angus stuck his hand over the table and George shook it, then attacked his piece of pie.

Jessie felt like screaming. The men finished their dessert and vacated their seats so the women could eat. As they filed out the door, she tried to think of a way to bring the conversation back around to the topic of James. Molly had information, and she wanted to hear it.

The women sat. Molly launched into a story. Jessie passed her plate down the table for stew, then added a biscuit at the side when it came back to her.

When Molly finally finished her tale of the wedding of her brother, the blacksmith, Jessie asked, "Do you get many visitors here?"

"Not so many as I'd like, Jessie girl. There'll be even less as winter comes on." Molly spread a bit of jam on her biscuit and raised it to her mouth. She lowered it to say, "I reckon the last visitors we had were James Owen and that Mexican girl he had with him." She put the biscuit to her mouth again and took a bite.

The bottom dropped out of Jessie's stomach. She swallowed hard and asked, "Mexican girl?"

"Yes. He said he was taking her down to her folks in Santa Fe. She got stranded somehow at the church up in Leones." She paused to take food and chew it. Finally she continued. "I suspected there was more to it than that. Amparo—that was her name, Amparo—looked at him in a special way, like they had a secret he wasn't sharing with us. Later on, I got a letter from Muriel Bates. She said my brother Tom told her husband that James and the girl were married."

Molly must have kept on talking, for Jessie's ears buzzed. Her head felt hollow, but throbbed, as if it were expanding and contracting. White dots filled her vision, then black dots, and she knew she was going to throw up, if she didn't faint first.

She left her seat so suddenly that the chair overturned, but she couldn't stop to put it upright. She had to leave the kitchen. She had to escape the heat and the talk. James Owen had got married!

~*~*~

Jessie wiped her mouth on her apron. Getting rid of her supper had relieved the pain in her stomach, but the hurt in her heart remained. She couldn't stop sobbing. Even though the news of James's betrothal to Ellen Bates had cut into her soul like a hot knife, knowing that he was free and somewhere in this country had given her hope. Jessie shuddered. She couldn't think of James anymore.

She wiped her eyes and looked around. She'd been lucky when she left the kitchen. No one had been around. Just then, two men came out of the stable, laughing and talking. George and . . . Ned.

Ned! Ned wants me. James doesn't. Ned does. He'll take care of me, and I'll never have to think about James Owen again.

She ran toward Ned, forcing a smile. *He'll be happy. I've got to be happy.* "Ned," she called.

"Jessie?" He smiled at her, and left George, taking long strides to meet her. "What is it?"

Jessie halted and let Ned approach. *He says he loves me. He'll never leave me.* She grabbed her upper arm with the other hand and waited. *He'll make me happy.*

Ned smiled down at her, and she lifted her head. "I'll marry you," she said.

Ned's smile widened to a grin. "You mean it?"

"Yes." She waited, her fingers gripping her arm. She'd be safe with Ned.

Ned picked her up by the waist and swung her around. She clutched his shoulders to keep her balance.

"Jessie, I'm the happiest man in the world. We can get married at the next town." He put her on her feet.

Married? So soon? She hadn't thought beyond her acceptance of Ned's offer. *What if I get pregnant?* She thought of Hannah, and the physical discomfort she was going through in carrying her child. "I think we should wait until we get to Albuquerque to wed. We have so far to go. I don't want to be like Hannah is." She watched disappointment mask Ned's eyes. Then he accepted her condition, though his shoulders sank a bit.

"I reckon you're right, honeybunch. I wouldn't want you to be burdened by—" He pressed his lips together, sighed, and nodded. "We'll wait."

Chapter 18

It took George a while longer than he'd bargained for to gentle all the horses to Angus's liking, so it was already far into December when the Bingham party got on its way again.

A few days into their renewed journey, Hannah asked Robert to stop the wagon so she could walk for a while.

"I can't stand the jostling for a minute more!" she exclaimed when Robert protested, so he put her off the wagon on the side of the trail and climbed up to the seat again.

"You're sure?" he asked her again.

"Yes!" She began to walk, or rather to lumber, beside the wagon. After a while, George rode up with a long stick that he offered her.

"Miss Hannah, this might make it easier to walk."

Hannah accepted the stick and laughed. "I reckon I make a comical sight."

George grinned. "Your sister worried you might fall and lay beside the track for hours before you could get up."

"You tell Heppie that I'm going to laugh at her when she's as round as a tub and can barely walk."

"What?" George's face went slack.

"She is bound to be in my state someday, and I'll tease her back. You tell her I said so."

George smiled, tipped his hat, and rode away toward the front of the wagons.

Although Hannah struggled to walk, being on her feet for a while was preferable to enduring the jarring motion of the wagon. She stopped to rest from time to time, leaning on the stick, and eventually the three wagons pulled ahead of her.

During one rest, Hannah rubbed the top of her belly after the baby inside kicked her. *Robert will love you*, she said to the child. *No matter who you are, he will provide for you and treat you as his own. You are my flesh, and that is good enough for him.*

She looked ahead, and saw one wagon pulling off the road. A figure descended from the wagon seat and came toward her. She stood and watched him for a while, a smile playing with her mouth, and then she started toward him, swinging the stick in time with her steps. He began to lope. She continued her clumsy gait. She could see his face, and he was grinning broadly. She stopped, and he broke into a run. She waited.

Robert skidded to a halt and stood in front of her, his breath coming in great heaves. "If you can't ride, I won't either," he gasped.

She put her hand on his bearded cheek and sighed. "You are impossible."

He took her hand and kissed it. "I'm impossibly in love with you, and I miss you."

She laughed. "I haven't been off that seat more than an hour."

"The longest hour of my life," he said, and enveloped her in his arms. "Come, walk with me."

She laughed again, shrugged out of his embrace, and dug her stick into the ground. "You came to walk with me!" She started toward the wagons.

He hustled to catch up and laid his hand on top of her belly. "Baby, you have the most obstinate mother in the world."

"Robert," she said, pushing his hand away, "don't do that. Somebody might see you."

He looked around, then up in the sky. "Who? That hawk circling up there?" He pointed. "I doubt it cares."

She giggled. "I care." She tripped a bit on a stone she couldn't see, and he steadied her.

"See how you need me around?" He put his face close to her stomach. "Mama needs me, little one."

She stopped and turned her glowing face toward him. "Yes, I need you. I think I've walked enough. Carry me to the wagon."

"It's just over there!"

She bent over, breathing heavily. "I know it, but I can't go any farther on my own."

"You're a caution, Hannah Fletcher," he said, and scooped her up. He carried her the five yards to the wagon, and helped her onto the seat, laughing all the time. He hauled himself up, took the lines in his hands, and looked at Hannah. "You are so very dear to me." He yelled at the mules and got them into motion.

Chapter 19

Jessie rode on the wagon seat beside Luke as they approached the next town on the trail. The weather had steadily grown colder, and she clasped a shawl around her shoulders. The sunbonnet she wore was for warmth as much as for shade, and she shivered as they crossed the stream that lay in their path.

Ahead of them, a long street meandered under the shadow of a stair-step mountain. They were the last wagon in the little train and the dust had been bothersome, so Jessie was glad they would soon stop for the evening. George had mentioned something about spending some of his cash on rooms in a hotel. Perhaps that was too wasteful of him, using his hard-earned money on hotel rooms. However, the closer they got to their destination, the more excited she grew at the thought of sleeping in a real bed. Of course, she would have to share it. Probably not only with Ma, but with her sisters, if the room only had one bed. The women would have one room, and the men another. She laughed at her mental picture of all of them jumbled together. The bed better be soft!

When Luke pulled up their horses at last, Jessie waited for the wagon to stop lurching, shook dust from her shawl, and climbed down from the seat. She pushed back her sunbonnet with one wrist and let the sunlight warm her hair. As she looked around, she saw a worn-looking, bearded man on a black mare across the street. He sat with his head bowed, his hat shadowing his face, and clutched a rope that extended back to the mounts of four other men.

"Luke," she said as her brother got down from the wagon. "Look at that. Those men are tied on their horses. Do you suppose they are outlaws?" She whispered the last word, cupping her mouth between her hands.

"Maybe," Luke said. "Do you figure that man is the sheriff?"

She shrugged her shoulders. "Why is he just sitting there?"

"He looks played out to me. Could be he's afraid he'll fall off his horse if he moves."

The man shifted in his saddle, and Jessie saw his face. She hugged herself, taking in a great gasp of air. Before she could help herself, she let it out in an explosive, "James!" Her hands flew to her mouth as he turned toward her. "James," she said his name again, calling out this time. "I thought I'd never see you again!" As a great rolling joy enveloped her, she bit her lip and started across the street.

She heard a strange, guttural cry, and realized it came from his mouth. Moisture slid down his cheeks. She watched him struggle, trying to catch his breath, and finally, he inhaled.

She reached his side, and he looked down at her from his seat atop the mare. After a moment, he extended his left hand, exhaled, took another breath, and held it a moment before he expelled it softly.

"Jessica."

Jessie looked at James's face for a moment. He looked as used up as though someone had hit him on the head with a shovel, then beaten him into the ground. Her gaze shifted, and she stared at the hand he held out to her, red and work roughened. The joy sank from her heart and drained from her body, leaving her cold and desolate. That hand had probably held Ellen Bates's hand. It had most certainly led his wife to their marriage bed. It was the hand of a married man, not the carefree James from her past.

"Jessica," James repeated, whispering. "Jessie Bingham."

Jessie watched James struggle. What was wrong with him? He should be happy, with a new wife and all his life in front of him. She looked around, fearing his wife would come out of one of the doors that lined the street. How could she bear to meet the girl named Amparo?

"Jessie," he said again, dropping his hand to his thigh. "Miss Jessie," he amended formally. "I left you in Virginia." He closed his eyes and shivered. "How did you get to Trinidad?"

Jessie started to speak, but broke off as a large man with a closely trimmed black moustache appeared in the doorway of the sheriff's office. She stared at the badge on the man's vest. She looked up at his face. His skin was brown, darker than the leather of his vest. *This man is the sheriff?* She wasn't sure she was interpreting what she saw correctly. What sort of place had brown-skinned people in authority?

The sheriff looked over James's train of captives. "What is this, young man?" he asked, his accent thick, nearly unintelligible. "Who are these *hombres*?"

"They're the men who escaped the hotel shootout, Sheriff. I tracked them down. Yonder is your escaped prisoner, Frank Blue." James motioned to one of the men. "I brung him back for justice," he said. Jessie hunched her shoulders at the flatness of his voice.

"I must thank you, *joven*." The sheriff removed his hat and held it over his heart. "Please receive my condolences on the loss of your wife."

Jessie furrowed her brow, unsure of what the sheriff had said in his heavily accented English. *Did I hear right? Did he say "loss of your wife?"* She put a hand to her abdomen, rubbing a bit at the lump of dread growing there. She looked from the sheriff to James.

He was nodding, his eyes glazed. He dismounted from the black mare with great caution, took careful steps toward the sheriff, and handed him the lead rope. A brown dog trotted up and thrust its nose into James's dangling hand. Next it sniffed at Jessie's skirt before it caught a new scent and followed it around the building.

"Can someone tend to my animals?" James asked the sheriff. "This mare and that there sorrel are mine, and the pack mule too." He rubbed his forehead, eyes closed. "They took the other three horses from the town."

"Sí, joven." The sheriff nodded, looking closely at James. "You have not slept, *no*?"

"No." James shook his head and tethered his horse. "If you need me, I'm going to see Philo about a room."

"*Está bien*," the sheriff said, and went to see to his prisoners.

"James," Jessie began. She stopped speaking to glance over him again. *He looks so tuckered out*, she thought. *He's worn down to a frazzle. Something mighty bad has happened to him.* Her stomach clenched.

As Jessie paused, James ducked under the reins to the other side of the horse, untied a worn satchel resting behind the cantle of his saddle, slid his rifle from the boot, and turned to face her.

She almost cried out at the pain in his eyes, but stopped herself, her insides churning around her own pain. She blurted out, "James, that brown-skinned man, that sheriff. Did he say something about your . . . wife? A loss?"

A look that terrified her flickered across his face, but was gone in an instant. "Yes, he did," James said. "She's dead, about a week past."

"Dead," Jessie echoed. Her heart quaked, and she felt herself shaking. She needed to say something, some word of condolence, of comfort, but the only thing she could think to say was, "How horrid!"

James looked away, out into the street. Jessie wondered what he was looking at so intently. Then he spoke in a hollow voice, stretching out the words as though to the rhythm of a slow heartbeat: "It . . . ain't . . . been . . . pleasurable."

Jessie heard footsteps behind her, a man clearing his throat. Ned.

She had told Ned she would marry him.

Ned's hand came down on her shoulder. His grip felt like a trap snapping on her flesh.

"James," she said, her voice shaking, pitched low. Ned's hand on her shoulder must have weighed a hundred pounds. "James," she started again. "Do you remember Ned Heizer?"

James nodded his head one time. "Heizer." Once more, his voice had no inflection.

"My family is traveling to join my brother Max in New Mexico Territory." She hesitated, then took a steadying breath and said, "I have agreed to marry Mr. Heizer when we get to Albuquerque."

James flung his "war bag" satchel onto his shoulder. "I reckon manners say I should stop and chat, but I need to catch up on my sleep. Y'all will excuse me?" He started across the street, feeling Heizer's eyes boring holes in his back.

Jessie Bingham. She was the last person he'd expected to see in Trinidad. She'd said her family was here too. That meant he had to talk to folks from his past, folks he'd left behind like ghosts. He wondered if Mr. Bingham was strong enough to horsewhip him for the shameful way he'd gone off and left Jessie behind in Virginia. Maybe a whipping would get rid of the agony that was consuming his soul.

"Amparo!" he whispered. Grief overcame him, and he stumbled a bit as he walked between the first and second wagons of the three parked in front of the hotel, and gained the wooden sidewalk. Planks of wood crisscrossed the gap where a glass window had been broken out of the frame.

A woman stood in the hotel doorway, peering out into the street. Her face lit up and she called out, "Jessie, Mr. Heizer, there you are. Come inside." She stepped back as James approached. Then her face changed and she gasped, "Oh my! You're James Owen! What has happened to you? You look wrung out."

"Hello, Miz Bingham," he mumbled. "I been on the trail without much sleep for most of a week."

"You poor thing! Come inside and find a seat. I'll send for a nice cup of tea to revive you."

He shook his head. "No, ma'am, I only require sleep. Excuse me." James pushed past Mrs. Bingham and strode into the room filled with mercantile goods, his legs quivering like jelly.

"Philo," James greeted the proprietor standing behind the counter. "I'll take a room today." He put his rifle on the planks and set his war bag on the floor.

"My boy!" The balding man looked startled. "I didn't think I'd ever see you again. Welcome, welcome."

James grimaced. Philo meant well, but this place would never hold a welcome for James Owen. He wanted to finish his business and get out of town, back to the clean air of the trail . . . to somewhere else. Anywhere else. Just so it wasn't Trinidad.

James touched his rifle barrel. The cold steel seemed to burn his fingers, and he pulled them back and made a fist instead. Maybe that would help him keep a rein on his feelings for a few moments more.

"I brought them four escapees back to the sheriff," he said at last. He shook his head. "I don't know which one of those jackals shot Amparo. Maybe a jury can figure it out." He put both hands flat on the counter and leaned on them, his arms shaking. "I know I swore an oath of vengeance against them all, but in the end, I couldn't kill 'em."

Philo nodded. "You did right, my boy."

"I know." James's voice was no more than a whisper. "She approved."

Philo raised an eyebrow. "She did?"

James tapped his chest over his heart. "Yes. I can feel it here."

Philo stood in silence for a moment, then said, "Take the last room on the right, end of the corridor." He clapped James on the shoulder. "I already filled up the front two rooms with those folks." He gestured toward Mrs. Bingham.

"Thank you, Philo. I'm falling-down weary."

"You look it, my boy." Philo leaned across the counter separating them and whispered in James's ear. "The room is yours as long as you need it. My compliments."

"Thank you." James tapped his rifle. "Will you mind this for me?"

"Of course, my boy."

James started toward the corridor, then looked back at Jessie. She was talking to her mother. Heizer was nowhere in sight.

Ned Heizer, he thought bitterly. *The turncoat.* He shook his head, wondering why it mattered to him who Jessie Bingham married.

Jessie watched James cross the street. His gait reminded her of an old man, struggling for each step. Her thoughts whirled. She could feel Ned's breath on the back of her head, stirring her hair. *I'm going to marry Ned*, she reminded herself. *James means no more to me than a rock on the trail.* She swallowed, wondering why her mouth was so dry. *We'll be gone tomorrow, and James will go . . . wherever he's bound.*

Ned's grip on her shoulder hurt, and she turned to look at him. His face was set, jaws clamped so tightly that corded veins stood out in his neck. His breath rasped in his throat. She touched his clawed hand. "Ned?"

He expelled his breath in a short "Hah!" then loosened his fingers and dropped his hand. After a moment, he said in a hard voice, "I reckon I didn't figure to see him again."

I didn't either, Jessie thought. *I didn't want to. Now here he is, disturbing my peace.* She frowned. *He shouldn't be able to do that. I've settled on Ned. I'm going to marry him. James can go take his ragged grief and . . .* And what? Did she wish him ill? *No. No. That's mean spirited of me.*

Despite her disgust at letting her encounter with James turn her emotions inside out, Jessie knew her peace was disturbed. *Am I angry? Yes! Feeling betrayed? Yes.* Agreeing to marry Ned should have put an end to this way of thinking. But it hadn't. Hearing about James had been a misery. Seeing him had tilted her world off beam.

Jessie heard her mother calling them, and looked toward the hotel. "Ma wants us," she said. She turned back to Ned. "If you don't want to see. . . . Maybe you should stay here."

Ned's face went grim. "I won't let the likes of James Owen keep me from goin' about my business."

Jessie's body recoiled at the vehemence in Ned's voice. She jerked up her chin and started across the road. She heard Ned coming along behind her, his limping walk accentuated by the quickness of his step. When she stopped at her mother's side, Ned passed her and entered the hotel. She gave her attention to her mother.

"Jessie," Mrs. Bingham said, clutching Jessie's arm. "Did you see him? It's James Owen!" She looked over her shoulder. "My, he looks done in. What do you reckon happened to him?"

Jessie's face burned. She licked her lips. What could she say to her mother? *"James Owen survived losing me, but looks like he's at death's door because he lost his wife?"* Anger stirred in her. She wasn't sure she could speak, but she finally found her voice and a few words. "His wife died."

Mrs. Bingham's eyes widened. "What?"

Jessie shrugged her shoulders. "You heard me, Ma. She died. The Mexican girl he married."

"Oh my! Oh my!" Mrs. Bingham seemed incapable of saying anything else. She squeezed her eyes shut and said, "So many people dyin'!"

"Ma!"

"How did it happen?"

"He didn't tell me. I heard him say to the sheriff that he'd brought back an escaped prisoner and men from a shootout here at the hotel." She gestured at the wood covering the window. "That must be why the glass is gone."

"That sounds real bad." Mrs. Bingham crossed her arms as though she were hugging herself. "Real bad." She rocked backward and forward for a while, and then said, "They weren't married long."

"Long enough that he mourns her."

"Jessica!"

The reprimand in her mother's voice snapped Jessie to attention, her back stiff.

Mrs. Bingham took a few quick breaths, her nostrils flaring. "I know you was hurt when James left. I reckon he was hurt too. That old reprobate Rod Owen had a lot to do with that, and James was just a boy. He's been a lone man out here, never thinking to see you again. Don't begrudge him a bit of happiness because it didn't include you."

Jessie didn't reply. Ma had had the last word, and Jessie felt sick at her own ill will. *What's wrong with me?* she asked. *Can't I leave it be?* She wished she could, and suddenly knew that the thing she wanted most to do in the world was to go and take James Owen into her arms and comfort him.

~*~*~

Robert came out of the hallway, passing a young bearded man on his way down the corridor. He seemed familiar, but his face bore such a look of anguish that Robert didn't stop him to strike up a conversation. Instead, he approached the proprietor. "Nice rooms," he said. "They'll do us fine."

"I'm glad you like them," the owner said.

"Say, that man." Robert hitched his head toward the hall. "I think I might be acquainted with him. Do you know his name?"

"That's my young friend, James Owen."

Robert nodded and smiled.

"Ah, I see the name rings a bell with you. From your manner of speaking, I believe you come from the same part of the country."

"Yes, we do. The Shenandoah Valley of Virginia. I'm a bit older than James, but we associated a fair amount."

"I knew it! I just knew it." Philo slapped his hand on the counter with a thud. An answering thud echoed from the hall, and he swung his head toward the sound. "I thought I heard something drop. Hold on. I'm coming back for some talk. I like to get to know my customers."

Robert nodded once more and looked around the room as Philo moved toward the corridor. Mrs. Bingham and Miss Jessie stood near the door, their conversation animated. Luke came out of the hall and went through the outside door. George followed a moment later. Philo came back, shaking his head.

"Your friend," he said. "He's had some real troublesome times of late. He and his new little bride was coming back from Santa Fe, intent on going home to his pa's place. We had a ruckus hereabouts, and the consequence of it all was the girl died of a gunshot. He's sure tore up about it. Wouldn't even use the cemetery to bury her." Philo expelled a gust of air and shook his head again. "I don't know if you saw them killers he tracked down and brought back to the sheriff. Bad *hombres*. That word, *hombres*, means 'men,' you know."

"I didn't." Robert felt his mouth quirk. Now he knew why James looked so bad. Losing his wife? He'd almost lost Hannah. Maybe tomorrow he could say a comforting word to James, give his condolences.

"He and I had conversation during the ruckus. He has mighty strong feelings for that girl. It's so sad to see him in this state."

"Why did you use that word, *hombres*?" Robert asked.

"Half our town is Mexican, including the sheriff, and I reckon I picked up a bit of their lingo in the natural course of life. You'll encounter a lot of Mexicans in this country. They owned it before we won the war with Mexico in '48. That was my war." Philo shrugged and wiped his nose with a knuckle. "But I forget myself. Is there anything I can do for you? Some comfort I've forgotten?"

Robert waved his hand negatively as he pushed himself off from where he'd been leaning against the counter. "No. I wanted to see if it truly was James Owen. Thank you for enlightening me."

Philo spread his hands. "No charge." He craned his neck toward the hallway. "I hope he'll get some sleep."

Jessie stood not far from the counter, her cheeks burning. She shivered as though she had a fever. If the dark-skinned sheriff was Mexican, that meant James's Mexican wife had been dark skinned too.

The memories that welled up as James walked down the corridor toward his room clogged his throat with nausea. Only a week past he had come to consciousness in the storeroom of this very hotel, finding himself bound and gagged.

Was that faint brown spot on the floor of the hallway the remnant of Amparo's blood? She had lain there with a grievous wound, the crimson life force staining her white blouse. *No!* his heart cried, riven with pain. *Not my Amparo!*

James stepped across the spot, stumbled, and fell to one knee, dropping his war bag. He gripped the nearest doorjamb and scrabbled his way to his feet.

Oh dear God in Heaven! This doorway led to the room where he had found his wife tied up, huddling on the bed in the dark. She was terror stricken and in pain from a beating she'd received at the hands of Frank Blue, whose cronies had invaded the hotel after they broke Frank out of the town's makeshift jail.

James untied Amparo, comforted her, and led her from the room into the dark hallway. They came so close to escaping from the dreadful experience of the sheriff's siege in which they'd been caught.

We only stopped in Trinidad to buy supplies, he thought. *If only them four men hadn't picked that same time to make their break for freedom!*

Memory crowded upon memory. Men hustling down the corridor toward the back door. The sound of the errant pistol shot that still rang in his ears. Amparo going limp in his arms. The lamp Philo had brought at his call. The wrenching sight of his wife's blood. Her final, whispered version of his name as she died: "Che-mes."

James covered his face with his hands and fled down the hall, bouncing against the wall in his blind flight. He bumped against the back door before he uncovered his face, found and turned the doorknob of the last room, and entered it: a room of which he had no memories to harrow up his soul.

James flung off his hat, unslung his revolver, sank onto a cot, and wrenched off his dusty boots. Philo knocked on the door, calling, "Here's your bag, my boy."

James said, "I'm obliged. Please leave it outside the door."

He couldn't bear to see the man's face.

"Do you want a candle?" the proprietor asked through the door.

"No. I want rest." His voice sounded gritty in his ears, but he repented of his brusqueness and went to the door to acknowledge Philo's kindness.

With the bag in the room, James shucked his clothes and left them in a heap. He turned down the blankets and lay on a bed for the first time in many weeks.

He could not sleep. His arms were empty. His body yearned for the gentle young woman who had been his wife in the last bed he had occupied, at the Inn of La Fonda in Santa Fe. That was the site of their *Noche de Bodas*, the real wedding night he had proclaimed once he acknowledged his love for Amparo.

"Oh my sweet girl," he groaned, his mind in torment. "I can't love you less because you died."

Thinking the cot was too soft since he'd become accustomed to sleeping on the hard ground, he tried pulling the blankets from the bed and wrapping them around himself on the wooden floor. Then the makeshift bedroll reminded him of the blankets and quilts he had shared with Amparo as they journeyed on the trail back toward his father's home. James shook with fatigue, but his mind would not let his body rest.

At length, he sat up, came to his knees against the side frame of the bed, bowed his head, and cried to heaven, "Oh God! Oh God, my ma says you love all your children. If you love me, let me have peace. Let me have rest!" He sobbed against his arms folded on the bed. "Dear God, I love her. She is my own soul. God in Heaven, when I die, let me be with my Amparo again."

His sobs gradually quieted, and he crawled onto the bed again, his body shaking with exhaustion.

Chapter 20

After the Bingham party ate dinner, Heppie kissed George good night and retired to the women's room with her mother and sisters. Giddy happiness surrounded her. Tonight she would sleep in a bed! She had to share it, but wonder of wonders, the room contained *two* beds, so she and Hannah would share the one shoved under the window, and Ma and Jessie would take the one by the door.

I wish it could be George instead of Hannah, she thought. Even in St. Louis, they hadn't shared a bed. They had lain together only on the trail, in blankets spread on top of rocks, small plants, and other discomfiting items on the cold, hard ground. The wide open sky had been their roof and the far horizons their walls.

Even though their privacy had been scant, George had not stinted in his matrimonial duties. Heppie wondered if a bedstead and four walls would make any difference in their lovemaking. *If I had my own house, I could yell all I wanted.* She smiled, unbuttoning her blouse. Being with George was almost always pleasurable, and that included wanting to yell out when he— *Well, not tonight*, she told herself. She asked aloud, "Hannah, which side of the bed do you want?"

"I think I need the outside," Hannah said. "This babe is taking up a lot of room, and I'm likely to use the chamber pot. You don't want me climbing over you to get to it."

Heppie laughed. "No, I surely do not."

Hannah patted her stomach, then winced.

"What ails you?"

"The child kicked me."

Heppie finished undressing and put on her nightgown. "Does it do that often?"

"Kick? Often enough. Hard too." She pressed her lips together and clasped her stomach. "I might have a bruise later. The little one is active tonight."

Heppie got under the covers and slid over to the wall side of the bed.

Hannah dropped her skirt and petticoats, revealing the extent of her stomach. It jutted out from her body, stretching against the fabric of her pantaloons.

"Oh my," Heppie said as Hannah's abdomen seemed to change shape. A knob stuck out, then receded. "What on earth?"

"That was probably a foot. Or maybe an elbow," Hannah said, grunting as she lay down. "I may not sleep well tonight."

"Will you let me feel your belly?" Heppie whispered.

Hannah sighed. After a moment, she said, "I reckon you won't quit asking until I let you. Give me your hand."

Heppie stuck it out and Hannah guided it to an area of activity. The baby rolled and flung out its appendages under Heppie's palm. "It's alive inside you."

Hannah sounded irritated as she answered, "Of course it is. Get some sense, Heppie."

"I never dreamed a baby would feel like that."

"You're only getting the half of it. It kicks inside too."

Heppie took back her hand and lay in silence for a long time. Was Hannah annoyed because she had asked to feel the baby? Did her anger come from not knowing if this was Robert's baby or that horrible man's? Perhaps all pregnant women got bothered, just from their condition. *I hope not! Life can be disagreeable enough, without feeling out of sorts all the time.*

"Hannah?"

"Um?"

"I hope you won't get riled at me for asking you something. I really want to know about it, and I don't want to ask Ma." She paused, and finally asked in a rush, "How did you know you were with child?"

Heppie listened to Hannah taking in air in short, sharp puffs. Maybe she wouldn't answer, given the circumstances. Maybe she didn't want to remember that time. *Maybe I shouldn't have asked*, she thought.

Just when Heppie was about to turn over and go to sleep without an answer, Hannah spoke. "I threw up a lot. My breasts swelled and hurt. When I was . . . violated, I worried that I might get pregnant. When I missed the monthly, I knew for sure I was." Hannah paused. After a while, her voice came again, barely audible. "I didn't have a chance to find someone to help me in St. Louis."

"Help you?" Heppie stopped breathing.

Hannah's voice sounded hoarse. "It crossed my mind to destroy the baby. I knew it was a terrible sin to think about that, Heppie. I couldn't help it."

"Oh Hannah!" Heppie's heart lurched. She wanted to vomit. How could her sister even think about getting rid of her baby? Maybe her mind wandered that way because she thought the child was the spawn of that monster?

"Working on that awful mending and sewing, I didn't have time or energy to find someone. I didn't know how to find someone. Before I could do anything, we left St. Louis." Hannah fell silent.

Heppie didn't want to say anything. She'd told George she would go west to take care of Hannah, and she hadn't even known the terrible times her sister had been going through. Shame ran through her body like a torrent of hot blood.

Hannah surprised her by continuing.

"I wondered what roots or weeds I could eat to be rid of the baby. But when Robert found out I was pregnant, he insisted that it's his baby. What if it is, Heppie? I couldn't kill my husband's child!" Her quiet breaths went on for a time. At last, she said, "He's almost convinced me to love it."

"Even if—"

"Even if it's not truly flesh of his flesh. Whatever it is, half of it comes from me. I must love at least that half, he says."

Heppie lay beside Hannah, partly ashamed that she had no such quandary in her life. She touched her swollen breasts. She cupped her belly. Despite her sister's tumultuous situation, she let joy leap into her heart.

Chapter 21

Robert looked around the Ratón Café. It was a light and airy place, with the morning sun shining in through clean windows. Red checked oilcloth covered several tables arranged in rows. He patted Hannah's hand, which was tucked into the crook of his arm. "Judging by the appearance of this place, the food should be nourishing, at the least."

Hannah smiled, and Robert's heart lurched at the brilliance of it. "Do you suppose they can put tables together for all of us?"

"I'll find out," he said, and letting loose of her hand, he went in search of someone to ask. Nearby, he found a middle-aged waitress, who wore a gingham checked apron that matched the tablecloths. She smiled, and he said, "Good morning. We have eight people coming for breakfast. Can we move a couple of tables together to seat all of us?"

"That's easy enough done," she replied, and went toward two large tables in the back of the room. "These will set up against each other, sir." She looked up at Robert. "Would you mind lending a hand?"

"I don't mind at all," he said, and helped arrange the tables and chairs until the waitress was satisfied.

"There now," she said, standing back to view the place settings. "There's room for ten, but I can take away the extra chairs on the ends."

"We might have nine people, so leave them be," he said. "Thank you for your help."

"My pleasure." The waitress turned at the creak of the

front door opening. "Are these your people?"

Robert looked. "That's them." He beckoned to Mrs. Bingham and the others, and they all sat down.

When they had given their food orders, Robert stood up and spoke to the group.

"Most of you know James Owen is here in Trinidad."

Almost everyone nodded. Ned scowled.

"He's had some hard luck lately, but he used to be a neighbor." Robert paused to look at the faces around the table. He went on. "We should look out for him. I propose asking him to accompany us to Albuquerque."

Ned swore, and Heppie clicked her tongue at his indiscretion in mixed company. Robert held up a hand against the tumult of replies.

"He knows the trail from here to Santa Fe, so he'll be of use to us. He's also a good hunter, if I recollect rightly."

Mrs. Bingham said, "It's the Christian thing to do, to give him the comfort of our company."

"Does he want our company?" George asked, eying Ned.

"We'll have to ask him that." Robert looked down at Hannah, and up at the group again. "His wife died not long ago. We can at least offer him the chance of a new start in a new place."

"He'll be in the way," Ned muttered.

"He'll be an extra gun when we go through Indian country past Santa Fe," Robert replied. "Think on it, but don't take too long. When he comes to breakfast, I want to invite him to go with us."

After the food came, Robert polled the group. Almost everyone agreed readily. George looked at Ned again, but eventually nodded. Jessie whispered a reply that Robert chose to interpret as yes. Ned's objection was voted down. Robert grinned. He'd always liked James Owen, and the prospect of having him along for the rest of the journey warmed his soul.

~*~*~

The next thing James knew, he awoke—ravenously hungry—to light filtering through the window, and he knew God had answered his petition for rest.

The knowing lifted his spirits, and when he had washed up, he sought out the proprietor. Philo moved a broom about the floor of his store.

"Philo, where can I get breakfast?"

"Good morning, my boy. The only decent place is the Ratón Café down the street. It's clean, and the grub's good. Go out the door and bear left. You can't miss it."

"Is that where the Binghams . . . where the folks who came in last night went to eat?"

Philo nodded. "They're heading to Albuquerque, they told me. Joining a relative, I hear. Now then, have you made plans?"

James scratched his cheek. His week-old beard itched. "I only want to find a place that has work for me to do. Hard work will help ease me, I reckon."

"What can you do?

"Break horses. Work cattle. I'm a crack shot, rifle or pistol."

Philo resumed sweeping. "You ever think of becoming a lawman?"

"It hadn't crossed my mind."

"There are plenty of rough towns hereabouts. You could find work along those lines easy enough, my boy."

James's stomach growled. Loudly. He gave a rueful chuckle. "Thanks for the talk, Philo. I'd best find that café."

The man waved him out the door. James walked along the wooden planks that butted up to the storefronts, slowing slightly as he approached the café's sign. He tried to swallow, but his throat felt like sandpaper rasping together.

James, he told himself, *Mr. Bingham's in there, fixin' to set you straight for hurtin' Jessie.* He came to a stop and put a hand against the clapboard wall next to him. He leaned on it, his head drooping, shoulders bent. *Maybe now she's got herself pledged to Heizer, her pa will go easy on me.* He raised his head and stared into the distance toward the stair-step mountain, but his eyes refused to focus. It would be hard to eat a meal comfortably with the Bingham family in the same room. *I reckon I owe them the courtesy of tryin'*, he thought.

James got himself under control and entered the café. Half the tables were occupied. Two others had been put together to accommodate the Bingham party. Two chairs at the long table remained empty. Mr. Bingham was nowhere in sight.

Upon seeing James, Mrs. Bingham stood up and beckoned to him. "Come over, you dear young man. Sit with us."

He moved in that direction and put his hand on the back of one of the empty chairs. "I don't want to intrude on your kin, Miz Bingham."

"It's no intrusion, James Owen. What would your mama say if I let you sit apart, all alone, when I was here to make you welcome?" She looked around the room and took her seat. "No, indeed! You just set yourself down."

James hesitated, confused that neither empty place had silverware or food at it. He said, "I don't want to take Mr. Bingham's seat."

Mrs. Bingham's face went from smiles to a pinched look and back to a forced cordiality in a matter of seconds. James waited, uneasy at not knowing the cause.

Mrs. Bingham looked down at her lap, then up at James. "Mr. Bingham is no longer with us," she said in a low tone. "We miss him a great deal, but must go forward, doing him honor with our courage in continuing on."

The bottom seemed to drop out of James's stomach. Joseph Bingham, dead?

"You must sit down, young man. You look quite overcome."

James pulled out the chair with shaking fingers and sat, surrounded by the oppression of death. Would he never be free of it? He looked up. "I'm very sorry to hear it. Last thing I knew, Mr. Bingham was getting better."

Jessie cleared her throat, and James realized too late that he had sat down beside her.

She said, "He sickened shortly after you left. It was a blow to us all." A rattlesnake dripped less venom than Jessie's voice.

Mrs. Bingham glared at Jessie, but jumped back into the conversation. "James, I want to reacquaint you with my family. We have added several members." She gestured to Robert and Hannah. "You may remember my eldest daughter, Hannah. This is her husband, Mr. Robert Fletcher."

Robert grinned. "James and I are acquainted."

"Rob," James said, nodding.

Hannah, who was clearly expecting a child in the near future, wore a scarf draped along the front of her dress, but it did not successfully hide a prominent bulge. She murmured, "Hello, Mr. Owen."

James nodded again, saying, "Miz Fletcher."

Mrs. Bingham continued her introductions by motioning to the young woman next to Hannah. "You may recall my second daughter, Hepzibah, twin to Hannah. She is the wife of Mr. George Heizer."

George's mouth tightened as he pressed his lips together, but he gave a slight wave of his hand in James's direction.

James nodded to George. Blood was thicker than water. The man would back his brother Ned to the grave.

Mrs. Bingham gestured to the gangly youngster seated to her right. "Possibly you remember Lucas, although he kept to himself when you were . . . calling at the house."

James craned his neck to see the boy and said, "Luke."

"I don't know if you remember Mr. Ned Heizer. Jessie has recently accepted his proposal of marriage."

James growled his acknowledgement, "Heizer," but didn't

look at Ned. He didn't want to spoil his appetite, now that his stomach had returned to normal.

The waitress appeared at James's elbow and laid silverware, a cup, and a napkin before him. He gave her his order for eggs and a stack of pancakes. She poured him a cup of coffee, and he took an exploratory sip, surprised at the genuine aroma that arose from the blue enameled cup.

"I ain't had real coffee since, well, since the war." He brushed a drop of the hot liquid from his moustache. "It's been a long time," he said, and took another sip.

When the waitress had returned to the kitchen, Mrs. Bingham spoke again. "My son Maxwell left the Valley not long after you folks did. He established himself in a town in New Mexico Territory." She paused, fussing a bit with her food. "Some months ago we received a letter asking that my husband and family come to join him. He did not know his father had died."

James looked up from his coffee, but didn't reply.

"Life became hard to bear in the Valley. We worked to leave for some time, then matters were—" She stopped and looked fleetingly across the table at her daughter, Hannah, and took up her story again. "We left quite suddenly in our farm wagon, and have been taking on odd jobs as we traveled." She sighed and put her fingers to her forehead.

Since Mrs. Bingham seemed exhausted by the strain of her narration, Robert added, "I had a bit of trouble with the Yankees, and we thought it best for all of us to leave."

"You said you had one wagon?" James said. "I counted three when you drove into town. One of them has an odd setup with the team."

"Our luck changed in St. Louis," George said. "We worked jobs and earned enough cash to outfit ourselves." He shrugged. "That's my team with the odd rigging. I lost a horse on the prairie."

"That's lamentable," James replied. "Clever rigging, though.

Does it work?"

"It does the job so far."

Robert leaned forward. "James, I spoke with the family before you arrived for breakfast. I understand you know the trail to Santa Fe and where to find game. We've all agreed . . ." He stopped, looked at Ned, then backtracked. "We voted to invite you to go to Albuquerque with us."

The waitress appeared, and James waited while she put his food on the table. He took a bite of eggs, put down his fork, and chewed.

After he swallowed, he said, "I can't see my way clear to go with you. I have a job waiting for me back yonder, some colts I promised to finish breaking."

George gave half a smile, his left eyebrow pointing toward the tin ceiling. "Would that horse-breaking job be for Angus Campbell?"

James rubbed his mouth in surprise, then smoothed down his moustache. "It would."

"I'm sorry to take bread out of your mouth, Owen. When we passed through, Mr. Campbell mentioned the colts, and I said I could do that task for him. The job pushed our schedule back some, but we hope with fair weather we'll reach Albuquerque without mishap."

"Did you finish up the job to his satisfaction? All the colts are gentled?"

"Yes," George said. "He was a pretty hard taskmaster, checking on me all the while I was working."

"Does he think ill of me?"

"Doesn't seem to. Mr. Campbell figured you were delayed by storms. He was glad the job is done and his wife has a saddle horse to ride."

James speared the stack of pancakes with his fork and cut into it with his knife. While he worked at the food, he considered. *I have nothing to show Pa to make up for laying into him. Ma has plenty to keep her busy, and I'm not bringing her new kin after all.* His stomach clamped down on the grief that arose momentarily, and he took a steadying breath to clear his head.

When he let out the air, he laid down his knife and said, "It appears I'm at liberty. I reckon I can go with you to Albuquerque."

"George," Hepzibah whispered when they had finished the meal, "I need to do a little shopping."

"Didn't you get your dress goods yesterday?" he asked, sliding her chair back from the table.

"Yes, but I discovered I need some other things."

"Like what?"

"Not here," she whispered, squirming a little under his gaze. "I'll show you in the store."

George accompanied her back down the boardwalk to the mercantile area of Philo's hotel. "What do you have such a pressing need for, Mrs. Heizer?"

"Flannel."

"Flannel?"

"And muslin."

"Flannel and muslin?"

"And maybe some linsey-woolsey."

"I cannot guess what you have in mind, Heppie."

"Clothes. Special, tiny clothes."

"No!" George looked shocked.

"You're going to be a father!"

"No!" repeated George, and fainted.

Chapter 22

When James left the café, a small brown man rose from the boardwalk across the street and came toward him. He was attired in loose white trousers and a tunic-like shirt, covered with a brown, everyday serape for warmth. When he came up to James, he took off his wide-brimmed straw hat and gave a slight bow. James stopped and nodded to the man.

"*Señor*, please, *venga conmigo*." He pointed down the street.

James hesitated, not sure what the man wanted. He tried a word or two of Spanish, knowing it was poorly spoken. "*Quiere habla* with me?" He tapped his mouth and hoped for the best.

The man cracked a huge smile and nodded.

"*Venga conmigo, por favor*." The man beckoned James to follow him.

"*No . . . hablo . . . bien*," James said, but the man only tugged on his sleeve, smiling and gesturing. "I go with you?" he asked.

"*Sí, señor. Queremos hablar con usted.*" The man dropped James's sleeve to move both hands in quacking duck fashion.

"I'll come," James said. Somebody wanted to talk with him.

The man moved in front of James and led off toward the center part of town. Soon the bell tower of an adobe church came into view. A group of brown-skinned men were gathered in front of the church, watching his approach. A vague feeling of apprehension stirred in his belly, but it disappeared as beaming smiles appeared on the men's faces.

The sheriff was among the men, but he hung back, as though this wasn't his show. James nodded to him anyway.

"Sheriff."

He nodded back, most solemnly. "*Señor* Owen."

James recognized the priest who had come to give last rites to Amparo. The man gently pushed through the crowd and came to stand before James.

"*Señor* Owen," said the priest, "we praise you because you honored *una de la gente*, one of our people." His voice was hesitant around the vowels and consonants, but James understood his meaning. "We are talking much about your kindness to our little sister *en Cristo*, but we talk a very much lot of your bravery, your courage. You are Anglo, but you leave the town to capture the outlaw Anglo and his *amigos* . . . friends, I mean to say. You are a hero for us."

James shook his head. "She was my wife, my *mujer*. Church wed." He pointed toward the church.

"That is also a very brave thing, *Señor* Owen. In this town, Anglos do not marry our women. We praise you for your honor treatment to her."

James let out the breath he didn't remember holding. "You are fine people," he said, slowly, looking at all the faces turned toward him. "Good *henti*. Amparo teach me *mucho*." He felt a blush creeping up his face at the way he knew he was butchering the words, especially the one for "people." He put his hand on his heart and took in air. He continued, slowly, softly. "*Amo Amparo siempre*. I love Amparo forever."

"*Sabemos* . . ." The man stopped and began again. "We know you must soon travel, leave *nuestro pueblo*—our town—and we give you this *regalo*." The priest looked a question back at the sheriff.

The sheriff said, "Gift."

"Gift," the priest echoed.

The priest turned behind him, to a man who handed him a sack. He faced James and held it out to him.

"We have collect *moneda*, I mean, money, to help you, eh, travel to your home, to your people. In this way, we honor you. Please accept our offering to you."

James took the surprisingly hefty sack and stood silent for a time. He nodded and said, "Thank you. *Mucho gracias.*" The kindness of the men built a large lump in his throat that kept him from swallowing for a time. He remained as though he were rooted in the road until he could clear it out. Then he said, "You are good *henti.*"

At length, he turned and walked slowly back to the hotel, to the accompaniment of good wishes from the men. At least, that was what they sounded like to James, as he swiped at his eyes and cheeks to remove his tears.

Philo stood in the hotel passageway when James arrived. He held up a finger, called out, "My boy!" and ducked into the storeroom door. James waited until the man reappeared with a large parcel in his hands.

"This is for you," Philo said. "The town council is giving you a token of peace. And their thanks, of course, for bringing back those runaways. I'm left to make the presentation. They were too cowardly to do it themselves, seeing as how you don't like them much." He shoved the package into James's hands.

Unsuccessfully juggling both items, James dropped the money sack, which thunked solidly onto the wooden floor. Several coins spilled out of the mouth of the sack, spinning erratically on the worn surface.

"I'm sorry, my boy. What's that you have there, a treasure trove?"

James knelt, put the package on the floor and started to pick up the coins. The irony of the situation struck him. He'd received a gift of money, given with sincere gratitude, and very likely offered at great cost, from the brown-skinned people of the town. Here was a backhanded peace offering from the white town fathers, probably given more through guilt than appreciation. He began to laugh, feeling a bubbling relief of his tension. Dropping the coins, he sprawled out against the corridor wall and threw back his head, banging it hard enough to bring tears to his eyes. He whooped, rubbing his hands up and down the stubble on his cheeks. "Six little beans!" he said, letting his hands fall into his lap.

Philo reached for his broom and swept up the errant coins. He knelt on the floor and put them into the sack. When he had finished, he sat back on his heels and waited. "Will you explain the joke for an old man with a slow brain?"

After several false starts and renewed guffaws, James regained his composure.

"Philo, it seems I am the hero of the day. This cash money is from the Mexicans, in honor of my kindness to my wife and my bravery at bringing back those ruffians. You give me a mystery package from the council to cool my rage against their town. Do you know what's in it?"

"Yes I do. Alton come by a while ago to pick through my goods." Philo tapped the package. "He found this in the storeroom, and asked me to wrap it up for you. It's a small tent the Army put on the market a few years ago, after the doings, and all." He slapped his knee. "He actually paid me money for it."

James straightened his face. The time for laughing had passed with Philo's mention of the war. "Alton's hustling me out of town, isn't he? I had breakfast with the Bingham family. They asked me to accompany them on their travels." He touched the parcel. "A tent will come in handy enough on the road. I don't know if we'll come upon snow or sunshine, but shelter can't hurt." He gave a little grimace, remembering that Amparo's name meant "shelter."

"So you're going with them." Philo found a leverage point on the wall and got to his feet. "Give thought to what I said about taking up a career as a lawman, my boy. I think you'd do well as a sheriff or town marshal or the like."

"The dog did half the work of capturing those men," James said. "Mayhap he can get elected." A grin creased his face. "Give me a hand up, Philo. I've got to make a list of provisions."

When James had gathered the items on his list and paid Philo, he took the supplies to his room. The kindness of the Mexican people had brought him a thought that he should be kind and set his mother's mind at ease concerning his welfare. For that purpose, he had purchased a few sheets of writing paper and a pencil. These he brought out, and sitting at the small table, he began a letter to his mother.

"Dear Ma," he wrote, then put down the pencil. His head bent forward as his hands came up to hide his face. *Oh Ma! How do I say good-bye to you?*

He hadn't done it when he'd left home all those months ago. It pained him now that he'd likely caused Ma a deal of worry. He'd let his anger at Pa drive a wedge between him and his family, but when he acknowledged his love to Amparo, he pulled that wedge free, looking forward to taking her home with him. She was gone, and he now understood the heartache of not being able to say good-bye.

James bit his lip and took up the pencil. "I am well," he wrote, "although troublesome times have plagued me. I set off to dig out Uncle Jonathan's mine, but only made it as far north as Pueblo town. Ask Mr. Hilbrands for the particulars next time you go there for supplies.

"I traveled as far south as Santa Fe town, but arrived back here in the city of Trinidad, intending to return to the bosom of the family with my new wife. To our great misfortune, she met Death's grim fingers in this place.

"I own to having had good times, but they are presently overshadowed by the bad. I wager you won't see me again until time knocks the corners off my sorrow. Receive a kiss for yourself and my sisters, and an embrace for my brothers. Tell Pa I have learned much from his example.

"Your affectionate son, James Owen"

When he had folded the letter and addressed it, he left the hotel and put the note into the care of the sheriff, along with money to pay the next traveler north to deliver it.

Chapter 23

Although he had been invited to stow his gear and necessities among the wagons, James preferred to leave them on his mule. Not only were the wagons showing hard use, but the livestock—two teams of horses and one of mules—was wearing down. Surely George Heizer's team of three was under a handicap in the cut down harness. If he could spare the animals having to pull extra weight during the ascent ahead, he would do so. His grief also kept him apart from the other travelers, so he tied his mule and spare horse behind a wagon and rode alone, his coat collar turned up and hat pulled low over his ears in the cold wind.

This time when James climbed into Raton Pass, the dog trotting alongside his black horse, he felt empty, knowing Amparo's grave was ahead, knowing that unless some happenstance brought him this way again, he would soon see her final resting place for the last time. It wasn't likely he'd be back. His connection to his family had been cut by his leaving as surely as Amparo's life had been cut short by that bullet.

Robert rode up beside James in the late afternoon, on a mount with Union markings. James wondered how Robert had acquired it. *I'll ask him about it sometime*, he thought.

"Hey, James."

"Rob." He felt comfortable with Robert Fletcher. They'd crossed paths many times in Shenandoah County. There had been some memorable escapades. Boys had been boys.

Robert explained why he wasn't on his wagon box. "Luke's taking a turn driving the mules. That boy does like a challenge."

"Who's driving Mrs. Bingham's wagon?"

Robert turned, grinning. "Your old nemesis, Ned. He's trying to get in the good graces of my mother-in-law."

James frowned, rolling the new word around in his mouth. Finally he asked, "What's a nemesis?"

"That's a fancy word for an enemy."

"Huh," James retorted. "He was your enemy too. Not to mention George's. It's a wonder you never met in battle."

"God works in mysterious ways." Robert rode in silence for a moment, and then changed the subject. "Say, how many times have you been through this Pass?"

James counted off the occasions on his fingers. *Texas, down and back. Santa Fe . . . and chasing down Frank Blue and his lot.* "I reckon about six times, now. This will be my seventh trip over, if you count coming and going both."

Robert nodded. "That's quite a few for the amount of time you've been in the country. What's the most likely camping spot? We should set up in daylight, if that's possible." He looked around at the gathering clouds. "Looks like we're in for a storm."

"Yep. I reckon it's rain coming in. Not cold enough for snow." James remembered a meadow beyond Amparo's clearing that would hold the party, and his heartbeat quickened. "I'll ride ahead and see about a place I know."

"Good. Thanks." Robert nodded again and wheeled his horse.

James touched his spurs lightly to the flanks of the black mare. "Let's go take a look at that big meadow," he said to the dog, leaning forward to pat the horse on its neck. "It's close enough to . . . go visiting tonight."

A mile along the road, James slowed the horse to a walk. *Oh my sweet girl,* he thought, *you're lyin' all alone just around the bend. Thank God you got that warm cloak I bought you in Santa Fe.* Shudders swept through his body that had nothing to do with the cold wind that blew down the mountainside. He felt a strong impulse to guide the mare off the road and into the clearing ahead, but he resisted. *I can't stop now, but I'll come back tonight.*

The dog had no such control. It whined and crept off the trail, but James rode past it, and it crouched in the underbrush at the edge of the path, whimpering, until he whistled it back to his side.

Once he was past the turnoff to Amparo's gravesite, James put the horse into a lope, and they went on until a flat meadow opened out to his left. He turned into it and slowed again to a walk, circling the area to look for windfalls of dead branches. There was enough firewood for the party, but it would be a dry camp.

"It'll do for the night," he grunted. "Come on, dog. This should please Robert."

James turned his mare and went back to the wagons and reported.

"Good!" Robert said. "It doesn't matter about the water. We have enough in the barrels for tonight."

James untied his animals from the tailgate of the wagon where he had tethered them, then rode back to the meadow and dismounted. He unsaddled the mare, removed the pack from his mule, and watered the animals from a canvas bucket before hobbling them in an area of good grass. James found his lantern, made sure it was full of kerosene, and set it to one side, ready for nightfall.

By then, the wagons had pulled into the meadow, and the travelers made camp, the men seeing to the livestock while the women brought in wood for cooking fires. Night overtook them just before they settled down to supper, and the men lit the lanterns. When supper was finished, the women gathered up the plates and utensils and started to clean them, using as little water as possible.

James told the dog to stay put, took his lantern, and walked out to the road. He knew the light would draw attention, but hoped any curious soul would think he was following nature's call. He headed down the road, anxiously watching for the break in the trees that indicated the path he sought. The night fooled him once: he thought a wide space between two trees was the turnoff, but soon retreated to the road and walked on. The second spot was the true path, and at last, he stood over the grave of his wife, holding the lamp in front of him.

"*Amparo*," he said, using the Spanish way she had said her name. "*Amparo, te amo para siempre*. I love you forever."

The lamp sputtered in the wind, and James shifted it a bit to shelter the flame. He sighed as grief poured into his veins, icy, but not numbing. A muscle throbbed in his jaw, and he unclenched his teeth.

"Amparo, I'm movin' along, going to a new place called Albuquerque." James sighed and knelt on one knee at the head of the grave. "I'm going there with some folks I know. I reckon I won't come back this way to visit, but I will love you forever. Oh my girl, my sweet girl, I miss you sorely." His voice fell to a whisper. "I want to be with you when I die."

The mound of Amparo's grave had settled a bit more since James had last visited it. He rose and tidied the grave one last time, wishing he had a marker to place at the site. He said, "I don't even know how you spell '*Garcés*,' but you were 'Amparo Owen' when you died, and that's what matters."

A small explosive cough attracted his attention, and he turned toward the path from the road. A figure stood a few yards from the foot of Amparo's grave, and James held up the lamp to see who was there.

He groaned involuntarily. "Jess . . . Jessie!" he stammered, and took several steps in her direction. "You followed me. How long . . . ?" Anger welled in his chest, and he stopped talking to keep from lashing harsh words at her.

Jessie let her hand fall from before her mouth. She looked stricken, but stood her ground. "A few minutes. Is this . . . ?" She cleared her throat and began again. "This is your wife's resting place?"

James nodded. A clash of emotions made him weak—annoyance at being overheard in his deepest agony, relief that Ned Heizer was nowhere to be seen, and a very odd visceral reaction to the pain on Jessie Bingham's face—and he half staggered as he covered the rest of the distance to where the girl stood.

Jessie asked, "Her name was Amparo?" James watched the motion of her throat as she swallowed after speaking the unfamiliar name.

"It was." Why was Jessie biting her lip?

"You loved her? A Mexican girl?" Jessie's hands curled into fists that she brought up in front of her mouth.

James set down the lamp, then bending over it, fussed with it, giving himself time to find the right words, trying to quell his resentment. He never thought he'd have this conversation with Jessie. He never thought he'd see her again. Why was he so angry with her? He straightened up and said, "I loved her. I still do."

"A Mexican with black skin?" Jessie's face blanched, then began to redden.

James shook his head and his words spilled out in a rush. "Her skin wasn't black. It was brown. She put me in mind of a bay horse, with her black hair and—"

James broke off as Jessie flew at him and began to drum against his face and chest with her fists.

She cried out, "You left me. You said you loved me, but you

left me behind. You chose Ellen Bates over me. When she threw you over you married a nigra!"

His anger flared. "Don't say that," he grunted as she struck him on the shoulder. He struggled to capture her fists, but she fought him hard, her voice choking on her vehement words. Finally he trapped her flailing arms at her sides. His body shook at holding onto a woman he had once loved. Her sobs cut into his heart, and the anger drained away as he realized he *still* cared for her. The insight rocked him. After so long a time, and in spite of her flinging such an ugly word at Amparo, he still loved Jessie Bingham.

"You said you loved me," she managed to get through her tight-clamped teeth.

"I did," he murmured, letting the vagueness of his answer hang in the air. Reason cried out that he should explain: he did say it, and he did love her then. He concentrated instead on trying not to betray how her closeness affected him now. How could this be happening? Amparo lay in her grave not two steps behind him. Jessie stood here, crying her eyes out. He barely could keep from pulling her into a tight embrace. How could a man care for two women at the same time?

He ached to tell Jessie the truth. As much as he loved Amparo, he loved her too. He opened his mouth, but he couldn't force out the words.

Nothing he said would matter.

Jessie had promised to marry Ned Heizer.

A clap of thunder made them both jump, and rain began to pelt them. Lightning blazed in the sky. "Get back to camp," James shouted over another roll of thunder. "Take the light." He held the lantern out to her.

Jessie looked at him with desolate eyes, accepted the lamp, and with a final sob, bolted toward the road. James turned to Amparo's grave, the sky lit by intermittent flashes of lightning.

Confusion swept over him. "Amparo," he whispered, hanging his head at his easy betrayal of his newly buried wife. He stood there, silent for a long time, gazing at the recently dug earth with its adornment of rocks. He could hold his silence no longer and yelled her name into the storm. "Amparo! Forgive me! *Te amo! Te amo!*" He spread his arms out wide, then sank to his knees and prostrated himself on the rocks of the grave, sobbing with grief and frustration that she was dead and he had been disloyal to her memory.

Jessie stumbled into camp, her skirt muddy and her eyes wild. As she passed the tarpaulin that sheltered the members of the group, her mother put out a hand to stop her.

"Jessie! You're soppin' wet, girl. Where have you been?"

"Oh, Mama," she gasped, pulling her mother with her into the storm. "Oh, Mama, I've done something terrible."

"Terrible?" Mrs. Bingham exclaimed, slipping free of Jessie's grasp so she could yank her shawl up to cover her head. "Get in the wagon," she yelled over the din of the rain hitting the tarpaulin.

Jessie climbed up the spokes of the front wheel and put her hand down to help her mother ascend. The women ducked through the opening in the wagon cover. Jessie slumped against the goods piled on the floor of the vehicle.

"Tell me," Mrs. Bingham demanded. "What terrible thing did you do out there in the wind and the rain?"

Jessie was crying, tears choking her, but she managed to gulp out a few words at a time. "I followed James. He went to a grave. His wife's. He talked to her. Said her name. Oh, Mama!" She bent her head and hid her face in her hands.

"There, there. It was a bit indiscreet of you to follow him, but not terrible." Her mother patted Jessie's head.

"I beat on him. Hit him. Called her a name." Jessie snuffled. "I told Ned I would marry him."

"What?" Mrs. Bingham's hand stopped moving. "Not just now?"

Jessie shook her head. "In spite, in spite of all . . ." She couldn't seem to get her breath, so she raised her head and forced the sodden air deep into her lungs. "Mama, I still love James."

Mrs. Bingham said, "Well now. Mr. Ned Heizer will take that as ill news."

"Ned?" Jessie said in a low voice. "What of Ned?"

"You're to marry him, dearie."

"Oh. Yes." She paused to think. "No, I hate him!"

"What? You hate Ned? I'm confused, daughter."

"No, no, I hate James."

"Well now . . ." Mrs. Bingham began.

"Ned is reliable," Jessie said in a rush. "He's safe. He'll take care of me and won't leave me."

"Jessie girl," Mrs. Bingham said. "Hush." She sighed, stroking Jessie's hair. "Albuquerque's a long way off. You have time yet to sort it all out."

Chapter 24

James arose well before the sun to get himself together. Of all times of the day, he liked morning best. The hush and the soft air always drove away the demons of the night. As he tended to his animals, the twitter of the awakening birds soothed his soul, smoothing away the anguish of his encounter with Jessie. Last night's storm had left the air clean and crisp. The temperature had fallen, and the cold worked its way into his ungloved hands. James enjoyed seeing the mule's breath streaming out as it put its head down into the feedbag he held under its nose.

Soon, the rest of the travelers got up and began the day's work. Luke Bingham had a cook fire started by the time the four women had breakfast preparations underway. Ned fed the stock while Robert and George inspected the worn-down wagons. James walked over and joined the two men where they were looking at the loose iron rim of one wheel.

"Good morning," Robert said. George scowled, but nodded an acknowledgement of James's presence. "You figure that rim will stay on till we reach the next town?" Robert asked.

James ran his hand over the rim, wiggling it back and forth. "I don't reckon it will. You need to shim it until it's tight." He looked around the ground for a stick, and pulled his clasp knife from his pocket. As he worked with the wood, the other two men followed his example and whittled out several wedges that they shoved into the crevices.

"Nah," said James. "You need to space them out." He eased two or three of the wooden slivers out and gestured with his head, "Just lift up the wagon bed there a bit, and I'll put these in where they'll do the best job."

"The wagon jack's broke," George said, bending down to put his shoulder against the side of the wagon. "You take the front, Robert." The two men heaved together, and James turned the wheel, hammering the wooden shims into place.

"There. That ought to hold until you can get a blacksmith to tighten that tire. They should have one in the next town over the pass." James picked up another stick or two as the men let the wagon bed down. "Just the same, I'll whittle up a few more shims in case any of these work their way loose as we go along."

Robert wiped his hands on his trousers. "I'm pleased to have you along, James. You know a great deal more than I do." He tilted his head, gesturing toward the wagon. "The livery and the blacksmith took care of my vehicle problems back home, and clerking in the bank didn't fit me for all this outdoor work. I've learned plenty, but it's a comfort to have you along." He put out his hand, and when James extended his, he clasped it. "Thanks for coming with us."

James shrugged. "I don't have a home. Albuquerque is as good as any other place to light for a while."

George strode off to hitch up his team. Robert looked fidgety.

James asked, "What's bothering you, Rob?"

Robert took in some air. "You may have noticed my wife is carrying a child. The babe will be born soon. I'm not sure when. I reckon I'm wondering if the road through this pass is safe." He let out a short laugh. "That may seem foolish, but the thought of a runaway wagon makes my stomach hurt."

"You have dear ones to protect," James said, wishing his own stomach didn't ache as he thought of his loss. He no longer had anyone to protect.

Robert's voice shook a bit as he said, "Hannah means the world to me. And the babe." He paused, looking off into the distance. "I'm a mite anxious to see what we have. Whatever happens, I want to give Hannah and the baby a good life in a new land. A clean start."

"The road is good," James said, laying his hand on Robert's shoulder and squeezing it. "Steep in some places, but if we need to do it, we can chain logs on the back as extra brakes. Don't fret. We'll be fine."

James headed back to his animals, making sure he didn't cross paths with Jessie. After last night's experience, he thought avoiding her would be the best way to keep clear of any awkwardness.

Breakfast came and went, and the party got on the road, moving through the pass at a steady pace. James always took the forward position. He liked it there. Not only was there no dust, but he didn't have to talk to anyone, since the dog and the horse didn't make conversation. He could be alone with his thoughts.

The farther he got from Amparo's grave, the more he thought of her sweetness, her self-sacrifice, and her unconditional love for him. It was as though she had decided to love him from the moment he said he would marry her. Shame suffused his body as he recalled his intention to take her back to her home and abandon his vow of marriage. How could he have been so ignorant, so selfish? How could he know his marriage would last such a short time?

Grief hit him anew, grief so tangible that he rocked in the saddle from the blow. *Oh God*, he cried in his heart, *let me be with her again!* Fire seared through his limbs at the despairing thought of never being able to see Amparo again.

God, please, he prayed silently. *I love my dear little wife. How can I ever be happy on earth, if I can't have a mite of hope of having her by my side again? How can love end with death? Oh God, it don't! And it hurts so powerful much!*

Suddenly, he realized this love was like that his parents shared. Yes, Rod Owen was arrogant, overbearing, and brusque, and James would have fought him to a standstill if he had the chance, but Rod loved his Julia, and she loved him back. James recalled the exchanged glances, the occasional touches, the muffled laughter in the night. *How would Ma or Pa get along without the other?* The question had no answer.

At noon, James returned to the wagons and called a halt to rest the teams and get a bit of dinner. Soon the trail would dip downward, and they would be in New Mexico Territory. An ache started as he remembered all the joy and pleasure he had known with Amparo in that part of the land.

He dismounted and took care of the black mare. Then he went to the mule and dug around in the pack until he found the bean pot. He didn't bother with a fire, but stood by the mule as he spooned up and ate a few cold mouthfuls of beans. The dog had hunted down and killed his own lunch, and lay nearby, chewing on bones.

Back in the saddle, James made circles with his shoulders, loosening his clenched muscles, and put his spurs gently to the black's flanks. The wagons creaked behind him as they got underway.

"James," floated out to him, but he disregarded Jessie's call and continued to ride in front of the wagons. As she called his name again, he recognized the desperate tone of her voice. It was the same one he used when he called on God.

"Jessie," he muttered through clenched teeth, "I don't have room for you now." Shame flowed over him once more. "Maybe God don't have room for *me*," he said under his breath, and a guttural groan escaped his lips. He squeezed his eyes closed, and then opened them and turned the black mare back toward the wagons. The dog bounded up to James.

Jessie walked alongside the Bingham's old farm wagon, so James maneuvered the horse in a circle that brought him up beside her.

"You called me?" James strove mightily to keep a blank expression as Jessie halted beside his mount.

The dog put out his paw, and Jessie took it in her hand. She shook it, then peered up at James. Her face looked pinched and hollow. She took a deep breath and held it for a moment. Finally she spoke. "I'm sorry for what I called your wife."

James must have clenched the muscles of his legs, because the black danced sideways, almost tangling legs with the dog. James was obliged to bring the horse back beside Jessie before he spoke. "Six little beans! I got feelings I can't get shed of, Jessie. It pained me to hear you pin that name on somebody I hold so dear." He laid his free hand on his thigh and rubbed up and down its length, working out a cramp.

Jessie was silent for a moment. When she spoke again, her voice was so low and anguished that James had to lean forward to hear her. "I'm sorry. It was almighty rude of me. Can you forgive me? Forget what I said?" The dog perked its ears, came up to Jessie, and licked her hand for a long moment before it loped away down the trail.

James nodded acceptance of her apology, holding his emotions in tight rein. "Hush," he breathed to himself, put his spurs against the black's sides, and rode out to join the dog at the front of the company.

As the afternoon wore on, the trail began its descent out of the pass down onto the flats. James passed the point where he had stood with Amparo, gazing down over the plains of New Mexico, making plans to see his family again, to start a family of his own. He gritted his teeth and rode on, through juniper and stunted oak trees bordering the trail.

A small bird whirred out of a juniper bush and flew toward the east. It startled the black and caused the dog to bark after it, but James soothed his mount, patting and rubbing it on the neck. "Whoa, there. Easy, easy. *Cállate*, old dog. Quiet down!"

Soon James rode on a flat trail. A creek on the right burbled through rocks as it wound its way south.

I turned off about here.

James touched his forehead as though his head had begun aching. His thoughts continued about the hours he'd spent tracking the men who had killed his wife. He squeezed his eyes shut to blank them out. *Mule tails! Am I goin' to remember everything that happened to me all along this trail?* Some of the memories would be sweet, he considered. *Amparo made my life sweet. We were happy. She was a shelter place to me, just like her name means.* He sighed, remembering her playfulness in their camp on the prairie that lay spread out far before him. *Oh, Amparo*, he thought, feeling the hole in his soul that her absence left.

He realized that yes, he would remember every occurrence that had burned into his memory during their journeys together, every happening along the trail's twists and turns. As he covered the same miles again, he would remember it all, the apprehension, the joy, the guilt, the laughter, the struggle to communicate without a common language.

He clenched his fists in an attempt to get rid of the longing to touch her hair, the hunger to run his fingers through the black strands framing her little brown face. He closed his eyes and swallowed hard as remembrance of the feeling of her smooth skin beneath his hands swept over him. His body ached as he recalled the desire, the relief, the joy of being with her as a committed husband, rather than as a reluctant bridegroom.

"Oh God," he cried out to Heaven. "She's gone!" Unashamed, he wept in the middle of the trail, bereft at her loss. Without his Amparo, life had no purpose. He had nothing to do except take some folks to the end of their trek because they were people he knew.

Chapter 25

Early in the afternoon of the next day the travelers came into Raton and found the blacksmith shop. The burly smith took off the wheel with the loose rim and left the wagon jacked up while he began his work, saying it would take him all afternoon to tighten the tire, and they might as well park their vehicles on the flats by the creek overnight.

George and Robert drove the other two wagons out of town and, with Ned, began to make camp. James prepared his own campsite a little apart from the main one. It being too early to start dinner, the women pulled up seats and rested, after finding mending that could be done as they sat.

Jessie, who had decided to explore the town, got her mother's permission to go, if someone went with her, and set about persuading Luke to accompany her. "Come on, Lukie, you really want to see the sights, don't you?" she said, tilting her head to one side.

"Ain't no sights here, Sis," he muttered. "Just another little town on the road."

"Please," she said, looking up at her younger brother, who had grown a couple of inches since they'd left St. Louis.

"Ain't nothin' else to do," he said, agreeing to join her in her ramble.

They set off down a road so dry that puffs of dust rose from each step they took.

"I hope Ma's planning to cook something fillin' for dinner," Luke said as they walked along. "My belly's fixin' to whine, it's been so long since I last ate."

Jessie gave him a little shove as they entered the main street. "You're always hungry, Luke."

"Am not."

"Are so."

"Only at meal times."

Jessie laughed. "All day long!" She looked sidelong at him. "Who was asking Ma this morning if she had any extra biscuits tucked away in the wagon?"

Luke made a face. "You heard me?"

"I have good ears."

"What you have are long ears, great big hanging donkey ears."

"Do not!"

"Do too."

"Do not."

"No, you don't," said James, passing them by with long strides. The dog followed behind, its tongue lolling out of its mouth.

Jessie took in a quick breath, feeling her body flush, and turned to Luke. "See? An impartial party disagrees with you."

"What's 'impartial' mean?"

Jessie stopped walking, waiting until James was out of earshot. Luke turned to her, folding his arms across his chest.

"Well?"

"'Impartial' describes someone who has no interest in a dispute or the parties involved. Judges are impartial." She continued softly, "James Owen is impartial." She watched him as he strode away.

Luke shrugged. "That may be. But your ears are still long."

He cuffed her gently on the arm, but Jessie's joy in the banter was gone. "Not now, Lukie," she said, and turned down a side street.

Luke followed, his stomach rumblings reaching Jessie's ears. Soon they found themselves in a narrow byway made up of connected whitewashed houses facing each other, with doors set flush to the street. When they had walked nearly to the next intersection, they saw an old, brown-skinned woman sitting in an open doorway. She wore a colorful shawl against the cold breeze that swept down the lane. Luke's stomach took that moment to complain. The woman looked up, grinned, and hailed them.

"*Jóvenes, vengan,*" she said, gesturing them to approach, and went back to what she had been doing, patting something white between her weathered brown hands.

Jessie put her hand on Luke's arm and clutched it tightly. At the same time, she drew him along toward the wrinkled woman, who wore her white hair in a braid wound around the top of her head. *That style's real pretty*, Jessie thought.

"*¿Tienen hambre?*" asked the woman, gesturing toward her mouth with her fingers close together.

Luke caught on right away. He mimicked her motion, saying, "Yes. I'm hungry." His stomach chose that moment to agree, loudly, and he hung his head. "Sorry!"

The woman laughed, and reached back into her home to lay down what she'd been working on. "*Tengo tortillas,*" she said, and brought her arm back, holding a plate covered with a cloth. She removed the cover, and revealed several round, flat, white patties, about six inches across. "Uuu eeet," she said in broken English, extending the plate toward the two, while making her eating movement with the other hand.

Luke grinned. "Thank you, ma'am," he said, and reached out to take one of the patties. "*Tengo tortillas?*" he asked, repeating the woman's words.

"Jes. *Tortillas,*" she answered. "Ver, very good eeet."

Luke ripped off a piece of the *tortilla* and put it in his mouth. He chewed, and his face brightened. "It's good, Sis," he said. "Try one." He turned back to the woman, and speaking around his next mouthful, thanked her again.

Jessie bit her lip, took a *tortilla*, and popped a piece into her mouth. It was warm and tasted of corn and lard. She smiled. "It's like corn pone, only different," she said to Luke. "Thank you, ma'am." She put another piece into her mouth and bobbed her head at the woman.

"*No hay de que*," the woman said, flipping her free hand above her shoulder in a self-deprecating gesture. "*Coman todos*," she said, indicating the rest of the *tortillas*.

"Oh, we couldn't eat them all," Jessie exclaimed. "I haven't got any money to pay you." She turned to her brother. "Luke, do you have any coins?"

He shook his head as he ate another *tortilla*.

"Luke! We have to pay her."

"I don't reckon she wants money, Sis," he answered. "She's bein' nice."

"Ma'am, you're very kind," Jessie said, as the woman pressed another *tortilla* into her hands. She took it and tore pieces off, wondering why a brown woman would share her food with two strangers. White strangers.

When Luke had eaten his way through the plateful of *tortillas*, he thanked the woman another time and she laughed, her eyes narrowing into massed crinkles.

"Uuu good boy," she said, and patted Luke's hand. "Uuu good girl." She looked at Jessie. "*Vayan con Dios*."

Jessie was quiet as she and Luke continued their exploration around the town. When they were nearly back to the wagons, she tugged on Luke's arm to stop him.

"Why did she feed us?" she asked him.

He shrugged. "There's no doubt she heard my gut rumbling. Likely she took pity on me. You were there, Sis, so she gave you food too." He grinned. "Just bein' polite, I reckon."

"But why did she feed us?" she asked again, emphasizing her words. "She as much as invited us into her home and gave us a meal. But she's a Mexican, and we're white."

"You worry on such things too much," Luke said, and turned away.

"Yes, I do," she muttered to herself, and immediately followed it with a thought: *Aren't Mexicans different from us?* She followed her brother back to camp, not sure she knew the answer anymore.

Chapter 26

During the next few days, Mrs. Bingham kept a close watch on Hannah. Robert had told her that his wife had been secluding herself in their wagon, hauling herself over the load to find bits and pieces of cloth and sack toweling and arranging a bed in an empty crate she'd insisted they not burn.

"She's nesting, just like a broody hen," Mrs. Bingham told him. "Her time is near, I reckon."

Robert drew his brows together. "What can I do to help?"

"Stay out of her way, Mr. Fletcher. Perhaps I need to sit on the seat tomorrow and see what she's about."

"I'll welcome your presence, ma'am," he said, sighing. "She's snappish with me."

Mrs. Bingham laughed. "I thought you'd be used to that by now. Hasn't she been off in her behavior during the whole journey?"

Robert blushed. He compressed his lips, and nodded his head positively. "Yes, up until lately. Then she . . ." His head motions went from side to side. "One night she . . ." His voice trailed off, and after a pause, he tried again. "Well, ma'am, matters between us got better. I'd have to say, they got much better." He nodded up and down once more.

Mrs. Bingham patted Robert on the arm and smiled. "I'll put my eye on her, my dear, and let you know what I think."

The next day, Mrs. Bingham sat on Robert's wagon seat, while Hannah fussed around in the bed, after her initial remonstrance against her mother's company went unheeded.

At the noon stop, Mrs. Bingham touched Robert on the arm and said, "She has only a few days left, Mr. Fletcher. If she complains of continuous pains, we'll need to pull up and make camp."

Robert let out a short gust of air. "Then the baby will come?"

"I figure so. See, she's carrying low now. Her time is near."

"Need I let her know?" Robert fidgeted with a thumbnail.

"I'll do you the service, if you don't mind."

"Please, go right ahead. I'd rather a woman tells her." He worried at the thumbnail with his teeth, and when he had got the rough edge torn off, he added, "I hear childbirth is mighty painful."

"It is that, Mr. Fletcher. Dangerous and painful. Ever since Mother Eve."

The company traveled on, striking southwest toward the town of Cimarron, where, a few days later, they crossed the river without incident. Having done so safely, James had no end of irritation when a day later the sorrel pitched him into the icy water as he crossed Rayado Creek.

"Damn horse," he muttered, along with all the other animal-related curses he could think of as he regained his feet and slogged through the water to the creek bank. The dog stood hunched down with stiff front legs, barking excitedly at him. Ned stood nearby, doubled over with laughter.

As Robert and George built a fire on the south side of the creek, Luke retrieved the sorrel, and asked if he could clean and reload James's rifle.

"I reckon," James sputtered, water coursing down his face from his wet hair. He reached to his side, loosened the thong holding his handgun in his holster, and gave it to Luke. "Thanks, Luke. Do my pistol too, will you?" he said, swiping water from his eyes.

Heppie brought James a blanket from his bedroll, which had

made it safely across on the back of the mule. "Come to the fire," she said, holding out the blanket.

"Hang on to that a moment," James said. "Let me get my boots off. They're full of water."

He sat near the newborn fire to remove and dump his boots, then, shivering, took the blanket from Heppie.

Robert came up to him, but waited to speak until Heppie had moved away. "You need to strip off, dry your clothes," he said.

James shook his head. "I don't want to hold up the party while there's daylight."

"We'll take the time to let you dry out. Don't you have a tent packed away? You can use that to preserve your modesty."

"I'd forgot. It's in the bundle on the offside of the mule."

Robert unpacked and set up the tent while James huddled near the fire. When they had finished, he hustled in to take off his clothes. The men outside strung a rope line across the fire and hung his coat, shirt, and pants over it as he handed them out.

"Let's have your underclothes, too!" Robert demanded, thrusting his hand into the door of the tent. "If everything ain't bone dry in this weather, you'll take sick."

James, teeth chattering, complied, and Robert draped the underwear over the line. "Tell the ladies to stay away from the fire," Robert said to George.

George laughed. "What's the use of that? They've all seen a man's small clothes, one time or another. If not on a body, at the least, hangin' on a line."

"These could use a good scrubbing with lye soap."

James stuck his head out of the tent flap, clasping the edges together, in time to see Jessie taking his underwear off the line.

"Rob, don't let her— Jessie! Don't you touch my things!"

"They want washing," she replied, wrinkling her nose. "They reek something fierce. I have a crock of soap, and I'll use a little creek water to—"

At that point, Robert kept her from getting any more clothes off the line, but she remained in possession of James's undergarments.

"Jessie! Hang those back on the line," James yelled at her as she turned around to depart. "Six little beans! You remind me of Rida O'Connor."

Jessie spun around. "Who's that?"

"The blacksmith's little girl in Leones. She stole my clothes when I was—" James stopped short, remembering the occasion had been his marriage day. Probably not the best thing to bring up with Jessie Bingham. "Never you mind. Leave me be." He pulled his head into the tent and sat on the ground, wrapped in the blanket.

The next thing he heard was Ned's angry voice. "What are you doing?"

Jessie replied, "A little laundry."

"His laundry. You don't do mine."

"You never asked."

"It's not fittin'!"

"What, washing a few things?"

"He didn't ask you to."

"Humph."

James could imagine Jessie shrugging her shoulders and turning her head away from Ned. That should have ended the quarrel, but Ned pressed on.

"He didn't ask, and you shouldn't have offered. You're spoken for." Clothes rustled. Jessie's skirts. Was Heizer fool enough to lay hands on her?

James almost got up, but reflected that he was not in a suitable state to go rescuing young women from their folly.

"Ned Heizer, get away from me." Jessie's voice was low, carrying a threat that a thinking man should take heed of.

After a long pause, Ned said, "Stay away from him, Jessie. He treated you poorly."

Looks like everyone shares that opinion of me. James waited for Jessie to counter Ned's statement.

When she did speak, her voice was low, but had a somber tone to it as she agreed, "Yes, he did."

Ned made a sound like wind rushing through aspen leaves, but he didn't say anything.

Jessie spoke again. "I begun this. Let me finish, Ned."

"Keep clear of him in future," he said. Ned's boots crunched on the gravel of the creek bank as he moved off.

James heard Jessie sigh. He pulled the newly learn word out of his mind. *Nemesis.*

Later, when the clothes were dry, Robert brought them to James, including the stolen—and washed—undergarments. "It's a pity you have to put this dirty shirt on over such sweet-smelling small clothes," he said. "Maybe I shouldn't have stopped the young lady." He turned away.

James glared at Robert's departing back. "They'll be dirty enough when the week's out," he said, and began to dress.

Robert kept his eye on Hannah during the forced halt. She couldn't seem to light and sit down, but roamed around the wagons, twisting a loose rope end here, patting a horse there. Sure she would tire herself out, he approached her.

"Hannah love. You must sit down and rest. We'll be on our way soon, and you'll miss your chance." He caught her hands, gently holding them still. "Come over here. Sit yourself down."

"I'm restless," she said, glancing around the temporary camp. "Ma said I'm about due to, well, she said, my time's nearly up for, you know . . ." Her voice trailed off as she finally looked at Robert.

"She told me the baby would come soon," he said.

Hannah's mouth twisted. "I'm frightened," she whispered.

Robert drew her toward him. "Don't you be," he said to sooth her. "I'm here. Whatever happens, I love you. I love our babe."

"Even if . . ."

His firm statement cut her off. "No matter what happens." He tugged her toward a barrel.

"I've been having pain," she admitted when she had sat down.

Robert knelt beside her. "What kind of pain?"

"Cramping. Here." She laid her hand on her abdomen. "Oh!" She tensed up and moaned. "Like that one."

"Do they keep coming, love?"

"They have since morning."

"That long?"

"I didn't want to trouble you. They weren't much at first."

"But now?" Robert got to his feet.

"Now I reckon I'm troublesome."

"Mrs. Bingham," Robert called out. He caught George's eye. "Make camp. The baby is on its way!"

The mad scramble that Robert's words brought on would have been amusing to him, except that Hannah had doubled over, and her initial moan had turned to a keen that ripped through his heart.

James came striding up, a look of concern on his face. "Use the tent," he said, and was gone so fast that Robert doubted whether he had been there at all.

"Luke! Find our bedding and take it to Mr. Owen's tent," Robert barked. He didn't want to move Hannah while the pain was upon her, but he figured she should get settled into a private place for her laboring. James's tent seemed the ideal location.

"Heppie," Mrs. Bingham called. "I need your assistance. Jessie, set a kettle on the fire. We'll need wash water by and by."

Robert felt his innards quake at the sounds that came from Hannah's throat. She was counting on him to be strong for her.

Could he do that? *Will I let her down at the last moment?* he wondered. *I've been saying I'll love the baby, even if that brute was its father. Can I actually manage it? Or did I say that only for Hannah's sake?* He let out a long sigh, just as Hannah straightened up, her face shiny with sweat. "Can you walk?" he asked.

"I don't know," she said, wiping her eyes. "I'll try."

Robert got her to her feet, his arms supporting her, and they took a few steps.

"Don't leave me," Hannah said in a throaty growl. "Ma will try to make you go. Stay with me! Uh!" She bent over, and Robert stopped walking her along, waiting for her pain to pass.

"I won't go," he said, rubbing her back in small circles.

"Lower," she grunted.

"Not out here," he replied. "Let's get you into the tent. I'll do whatever you say, once we're sheltered."

"I don't care," she moaned. "Rub lower!"

Robert looked around, shrugged his shoulders, and furtively moved his hand lower on his wife's back.

"Yeees," Hannah said on a long outward breath. Then she stood upright and asked, "Where's the tent? Get me to it."

Robert half stumbled, half walked with Hannah to the tent and through the open flap. Luke had brought the bedding—*blessed boy*—and arranged it on the ground.

Mrs. Bingham came through the tent door, Heppie in her wake. "Thank you, Mr. Fletcher," she said as Robert helped Hannah get situated on the quilt. "You can leave now."

"I'm stayin'," he said.

"But you can't," said Mrs. Bingham. "This is women's work."

"She told me to stay," Robert said.

"At least be useful. Help me take off her clothing." Mrs. Bingham looked over her shoulder. "Take off her shoes," she told Heppie, whose face had paled since she had come into the tent.

Robert began unbuttoning Hannah's blouse. Mrs. Bingham

untied her skirt, and Heppie attacked her shoes. Between them, they removed her outer garments.

Hannah cried out. Mrs. Bingham felt her belly under her petticoat. "That's a hard cramp. Breathe, dear. You need air. There, that's right." She looked at Robert. "I need to take a look at her, Mr. Fletcher. Please turn your head." He gave half a smile, but acquiesced and looked away.

Mrs. Bingham lifted Hannah's petticoat and examined her. "You have a ways to go, dear, but you're doing fine." She covered Hannah with a blanket. "Keep breathing between the pains. I have to fetch some things from the wagon, but I'll return shortly. Heppie, come with me." The two women left the tent.

Robert stroked Hannah's hair. "What can I do to help?" he asked.

"Get behind and hold me up. Rub my shoulders," she gasped out in a small voice.

Robert raised her torso and sat behind her on the quilt, his legs extending on either side of her body. "Like this?" he whispered as he massaged her neck and shoulders.

"Oh yes," she said, then screamed and curled forward.

Robert ran his hands down Hannah's arms and touched her belly. "It's hard as rock, love. No wonder you're screamin'." He rubbed her stomach.

"Oh, don't touch me, not now. Later," Hannah said, catching her breath and pushing his hands away. "It hurts so much." After a moment she leaned back against his chest, panting.

"It can't go on much longer," he murmured.

"Hours and hours," she said, bending forward and clutching at his hands.

In a few moments, Mrs. Bingham returned with Heppie and an armful of supplies. Hannah was in the throes of another pain, doubled forward. She caught her breath and screamed.

Heppie gagged. "Ma, I can't help you," she choked out as she fled the tent.

"Send Jessie," Mrs. Bingham flung over her shoulder. "There's no help for it. I need someone here," she grumbled to herself as she sat down and arranged the supplies.

"What can I do to assist, ma'am?" Robert asked.

"Now, you keep right where you are," Mrs. Bingham said, motioning him to stay put with her hands. "You're doin' fine right there."

Robert chuckled. "You want me out of the way."

"Yes sir, I do," Mrs. Bingham said. "This here will always be woman's work." She turned her head and hollered out the door of the tent. "Jessie! Where are you, girl?"

Jessie came reluctantly into the tent. Not only was Robert Fletcher in there, but Ma was likely to raise up Hannah's skirt, and that was a sight she wasn't prepared to gaze upon. *There's going to be blood. I know it!* Hannah was panting, and Jessie turned her head, ashamed of the revulsion that swept over her.

She had little concrete idea of how babies came into the world, except that it involved a woman's secret parts. She'd been too young to learn much when Luke came along. As far as the process for making a baby went, she'd seen the occasional dog and chicken matings, but gave little credence to the notion that humans did the same thing as the lower animals. Ma's warnings about kissing boys had not prepared her with actual useful information about what came afterward between a man and a woman. Even James's persistent kisses, which had stirred her to the core, had done nothing to reveal the mystery. All she knew was that babies came after couples did something together that had to do with lust.

She'd visited the Owen farm, years ago, where she and Marie

had spent a lazy afternoon lying on the side of a stack of hay as they chatted. When she heard loud whinnies and snorts coming from a small corral, she'd climbed up to the top of the hay to see what the commotion was about. She barely caught sight of a stallion mounting a mare when Marie pulled her back down the slippery stack, saying, "I forgot Pa was breeding the mares today. You don't want to see that."

"Don't I?" she asked.

"No. It'll spoil your weddin' day, worrying about that big long thing coming at you." Teasing was one of Marie's great pleasures in life.

The size of the stallion's "thing" had been truly impressive, but Jessie hadn't thought much about it through the years. The only time she'd seen the result of such an encounter was when a pregnant cat had sped into the house through a carelessly opened door and given birth to its kittens behind the stove. She'd watched the cat's convulsive expulsions of slimy sacs, one by one, each followed by a barbaric eating of that kitten's protective coating. She shuddered at the remembrance. Surely a human birth was more, well, humane?

Jessie sat down to one side of Hannah. What did Ma want her to do? Was this baby going to have red hair and a grizzled, bearded chin, dripping tobacco juice? A feeling of dread settled on her. Would Hannah turn away from such a baby and let it languish from neglect? Surely Robert wouldn't allow that.

Jessie looked at Robert, tucked away behind Hannah, supporting her body with his own. *What's goin' through his mind? He's said over and over how this baby is his own, no matter what. Will he be able to follow through on his talk? I hope so. He's a good man. Hannah's been lucky to have him. Steadfast, that's what he is. Would James be steadfast, stand by me if I was in such a fix? No, I mean Ned. Would Ned do that?*

"Jessie, hold this towel." Mrs. Bingham's demand cut through Jessie's thoughts.

She took the piece of flour sack and let it dangle between her hands. Her sister was doubled over again, cupping her belly with white hands, gritting her teeth and grunting. *Is this why they call it labor? She's doin' a lot of work.* Ma had her hands down by Hannah's private place, mopping at something. *Ah! That's blood!* Waves of nausea hammered at Jessie's body, threatening her consciousness, but she kept above the black pool by wrapping the cloth tightly around one hand and biting her lip.

What is Ma doing now? Jessie quit biting herself and craned her neck. It looked like Ma was holding a head, a tiny head covered with blood and a white gooey substance.

"Now push!" Ma said to Hannah.

Hannah took three quick breaths and bore down, her face turning from white to crimson with her effort. Jessie watched in amazement as Ma's hands suddenly contained not only the wee head, but a baby's body, followed by a long twisted cord that seemed still attached to Hannah's nether regions.

"I need more hands," Mrs. Bingham said in a grumbling voice. "Jessie, that towel!"

Jessie leaned forward and gave the cloth to Ma, who wiped up the blood on the baby's face, scooped something out of its mouth, and tapped it on the chest.

The infant let out a squall that filled the tent. It continued crying as Mrs. Bingham fired instructions at Robert and Jessie.

"The string, Mr. Fletcher. Here and here." Robert tied twine around the cord in two places, pulling it tight at Mrs. Bingham's direction. Then he picked up a pair of scissors.

"Now?"

"Yes, cut."

Jessie turned away, bile rising in her throat.

"Give me that blanket beside you, girl."

Jessie fought down the acrid gall and found the blanket.

Ma wrapped the child, swiping at its little face once again. She held out the bundle to Robert. "He is your true son, Mr. Fletcher. See how his hair grows?" She touched the infant's forehead tenderly. "Now Hannah, you have a bit more work to do."

A few moments later, the afterbirth came, and Ma started tidying up.

"Can I go, Ma?" Jessie asked, and without waiting for an answer, got up and flung herself through the tent flaps and into the sweet, cold air of the late afternoon.

Chapter 27

James looked up as Jessie stumbled out of the tent door, her face white and drawn. *What's amiss?* he wondered, and caught up to her in three strides. Hannah had stopped screaming, and he was sure he'd heard a baby cry. "Jessie?" he asked, touching her arm.

She shook him off, rushing toward a circle of trees, when she bent double and wretched. James dug out his handkerchief and pressed it into her hand. "Does your sister live?" he asked. "Is the babe well?"

"The blood," Jessie choked out. "It unnerves me." She paused to wretch again, and James held her arm to keep her from falling.

"All is well?"

She heaved, and vomit splattered the ground. After a moment, she spit out, "Do I look well?"

"With the birth, I mean." James stifled a chuckle at Jessie's heated tone. She looked pathetic, but he wasn't going to mention that fact. That was Ned's concern.

Jessie took a breath and mopped her mouth. "The boy is born. Hannah lives."

"Thank God," James said, just as the hand he'd been expecting clamped down on his shoulder.

"Turn her loose," Ned growled.

James did so, and Jessie staggered a step away. He turned to Ned, making his face into a bland mask.

"Why were you touching her?" Ned barked.

"She would have fallen," James answered. "A man doesn't like to see that happen."

"That's my lookout."

"You weren't looking out for her." James felt a churning in his gut. *Nemesis!*

"You got in the way."

"You weren't around."

At that jibe, Ned swung, hitting James on the cheekbone and knocking him backward. "Leave her be!" he shouted. "She's my girl."

James shook his head to clear away the ringing. He'd known Ned was spoiling for a fight. He shouldn't have pushed him toward it, even accidentally. But Ned had thrown the first punch, and *hush!* James was ready to oblige him. He put his head down and charged, butting Ned in the stomach. They both went down, rolling on the ground, fists flying. Jessie shrieked.

Mrs. Bingham laughed, a great trilling sound that filled Hannah's senses with relief. "All our worry was for naught, Hannah. He's a splendid boy, the spitting image of his papa." She gathered up the soiled cloths. "You had a short delivery, for a first-time birth," she added. "That's another blessing to give thanks for. God's compensation, I'll warrant." She got to her feet and went to the doorway. "What's that row?" she asked, and turned back with a shake of her finger and a word of command, "Rest!"

"Robert!" Hannah exclaimed as her mother left the tent. "Show me the baby."

He touched the child on the tip of its nose, then handed the bundle to Hannah, who took the infant into her arms. "Oh!" she said, wonder filling her breast. "Oh, he's so tiny." She looked at his hands, made sure five fingers sprouted on each one; inspected his feet, his legs, his obviously male parts. "He's a boy." She glanced at Robert, blinking away tears.

"Yes."

"And look at his hair. There's so much of it. Just like yours. Oh, Robert! He does look like you."

Robert stroked the baby's forehead where the hair grew in a point like his own widow's peak. He nuzzled Hannah's neck and whispered in her ear. "I am the father of our babe. There is no doubt."

Hannah looked sideways at him and nodded, joy leaping in her soul. She turned her attention to the wiggling infant. "What shall I do with this howling boy?" she asked. The feelings of her heart expanded to enclose the three of them in a soft cocoon of love. Then her body shook as great peals of relieved laughter came from her throat.

"Feed him," Robert said, and chuckled. "You know he's hungry."

"Poacher!" Ned shouted, his fists flailing at James.

"Turncoat!" James replied, catching Ned on the ear.

"Get up!" Jessie screamed. "Stop it this minute!"

James got to his feet, dragging Ned up from the ground. He punched him again, and Ned reeled backward. James followed, ready to pound him with another well-placed fist, when Mrs. Bingham shoved between them. Her stiff arm stopped James in his tracks.

He pawed the dust out of his eyes and watched Ned come to a halt, his face wary.

"You men!" Mrs. Bingham's voice sounded like a clap of thunder. "Acting like little boys, rolling in the dust, fighting each other like heathens! You will stop it this instant. There's a baby to think about, and y'all are causing nothin' but turmoil."

James winced at the vitriolic burn of her words. Of course she was right. He hadn't meant to lose his temper. There was just something about Ned that rubbed his fur the wrong way.

"Shake hands, now. There'll be no more antics like these," Mrs. Bingham scolded.

James held out his hand. Ned briefly touched it, his eyes challenging James against gripping it in amity. James shrugged and turned away. *Ned's bad humor is Jessie's concern now, not mine*, he reflected as he walked toward his horses. Even so, his stomach churned at the thought of Jessie's having to placate an angry man.

"Do you feel anything growing?" George whispered, his hand caressing Heppie's stomach. He lay on his side in their bed under the wagon, propping himself up on one elbow.

"I just feel sick," she said, snuggling beside him. "Not now, but sometimes."

"Did your sister feel sick?"

"Oh, all the time," she answered. "She tried to hide it, but she did, and she had this . . . smell. I hope I don't get like that."

"We're all smelly," he said, kissing her ear. "We can't help it much."

"George! Do I smell?"

He chuckled. "Don't I?"

"Well, yes, now that you speak of it."

"Think of this. Every day we travel, we get closer to a bathtub. And regular weekly baths." He kissed her nose.

"That tickles."

"Does this tickle?"

She took a quick breath.

"How about this?"

She moaned. "I don't think . . . you're supposed . . . to do that!"

"Why not?"

"I don't want to faint."

George drew back. "You're cruel to bring that to mind, Heppie. I didn't faint on purpose!"

Heppie let out her breath in a short puff. "I wasn't thinkin' of that, George, but you were such a sight, topplin' over like a great felled tree. Good thing you landed on the dry goods." She giggled.

George lay back. Heppie cuddled up to him.

"You stopped," she whispered.

"Yep."

"Don't."

He said nothing.

She poked his chest. "George."

He turned his head. "What?"

"Don't stop."

George sighed. "I can't do nothing now, Heppie."

"You can't?"

"Nothing takes the air out of a man's sails like knowing his wife is makin' fun of him."

"I wasn't, George."

"Sounded like it."

"I wasn't even thinking about that time. When you tickled me like that, it took my breath away." She curled closer to him, and her voice sank to a murmur. "I felt like I was up in the trees, floatin', kinda hangin' there, breathless and all quiverin' and losing control of myself. George, don't stop. Even if I faint, don't stop takin' me up to that place in the trees, where—"

He turned and kissed her, impeding the movement of her lips. After a moment, he whispered, "You like that?"

"More. Do more."

George chuckled. "You won't talk about fainting?"

"Don't stop."

"I don't reckon I will."

Chapter 28

Several days later, James was leading the Bingham party down the road when, ahead, he saw a train of wagons winding its way along the trail toward him.

"That's odd," he said aloud to the dog. "We ain't met other travelers for a long while."

James looked to the south. Off in the distance a hawk soared in an afternoon updraft, looking for a meal. To the north, snow-covered peaks loomed on the horizon.

When he looked west again, James could see that the party coming toward them wasn't making any progress. A few minutes later, he realized that one of the wagons in the band lay toppled on its side. He turned his horse and bellowed toward the wagons. "Robert, George, Ned! Come quick!" He put the black mare into a canter down the road.

As he drew near, James saw several men working to pull the wagon upright. They had unhitched the team, tied ropes to the side of the wagon, and were using the animals to haul on the ropes to get it back on its wheels. Although the animals strained at the lines, the vehicle didn't budge.

James rode on to offer his assistance. He could see several women standing to the side, small children hanging on their skirts or aprons. Older children stood around in knots or helped with the upset wagon. Arriving in earshot, he heard screams coming from the vicinity of the wagon. Someone was caught underneath. James reined in the mare, got down, and led the horse to where the animals were sweating and straining to right the wagon.

"Add my horse," he said to one of the men. "She's strong."

"Thank you. We're obliged," a man said, and took over the task. James strode around to the other side of the wreck to see if he could help in the lifting effort. A woman knelt there, tears streaming down her cheeks as she crooned to the young woman caught under the wagon.

"Laurie Sue," she said over and over. "Laurie Sue, we'll get you out. Please, don't scream, Laurie Sue. Think of Zion. Praise God for your blessings. Laurie Sue, don't cry."

James found a place among three other men and put his shoulder under the wagon box. "Push," cried a man, and James heaved with all his strength. He was aware that Robert and George had joined them. They all gave a second mighty heave, and the wagon tilted skyward. With a great rattle and a cloud of dust, it settled back on its wheels.

Laurie Sue had stopped screaming, and the woman on her knees wailed, "She's gone. Lord have mercy, she's gone to Jesus."

James bent to raise the woman up, but she struggled until another man came and took her in his arms. "Eliza, hush. Hush your cryin', honey. We'll join her to us in Zion." Tears muddied the man's cheeks.

What does he mean, "join her to us?" James wondered. He retrieved his horse, whistled for the dog, and would have mounted and left, but another man hailed him.

"Stranger, wait up, there." A tall thin man with high cheekbones and a wan smile approached James. His black hair was worn slicked back from his forehead, and he smoothed it down before he put on his hat. He offered James his hand. "I'm Jeffrey Julander, leader of this company. We're obliged for your help, and that of your friends." He nodded toward Robert and the Heizer brothers, who had come over to stand near James. "Will you stay and partake of supper with us tonight? It appears we're obliged to camp until we can have a service for our sister and bury her."

"My condolences about your sister." James blew out his breath, and turned to the other men of his party. "What do you say, Robert? Are we ready to camp? We've come a goodly lot of miles today."

Robert nodded. "We have. Is there water nearby? We need to fill our barrels."

Mr. Julander answered. "We've been following a river up from the south. It runs alongside the trail over there." He gestured toward a thin ribbon of water.

Robert nodded, satisfied. "I reckon we can join you for supper, Mr. Julander. I'm also sorry for the loss of your sister."

Mr. Julander pumped the hands of all the men, and said, "Laurie Sue isn't my blood sister. She's my sister in the gospel. We all belong to the same church, and we call each other Brother and Sister. You can call me Brother Jeff, if you've a mind to."

James shrugged. "If that's what you'd rather we name you, I can get my mouth around it." He looked back toward the river. "There's a flat piece just along there, if you want to pull your wagons off the road. We'll camp the other side of you." James made as though to leave, then turned back to the man. "You'd better check that wagon for damage before you try to move it. It might fall into a wreck and block the whole road."

"We'll do that. See you at supper."

James rode behind the Heizer brothers and Robert to the Bingham's halted wagons. When Mrs. Bingham saw them coming, she inquired about what was going on.

George said, "The party coming this way had a misfortune." He pulled on the lobe of his half ear. "One of their wagons overturned, and a young lady was . . . well, wounded mighty bad. They'll have services for her tomorrow."

"Services? You mean she's dead?"

George nodded. "That's right. She didn't make it through."

"Merciful heavens! Let's get down there and help them poor people. They'll need a warm meal and a pot of tea to steady their nerves." She arranged herself on the wagon seat, and said to Luke, "Let's go, boy. Time's a-wasting."

"Yes, ma'am." Luke got the team underway, and the rest of the party followed.

When the Binghams arrived, they found the Julander camp already set up, with fires going and bubbling pots hanging from tripods.

James sought out Brother Jeff and introduced Mrs. Bingham and the rest of the party to him.

"We're obliged for the help your men gave us this afternoon," Brother Jeff said to her. "We're beholden and would like you to partake of our meal with us." He beckoned to a tall, calico-clad woman with fine dark eyes. "This is my wife, Becky Julander. Mrs. Bingham, ladies, she can show you where we're going to serve the food."

Mrs. Bingham nodded to Mrs. Julander, looked around the tidy camp, and turned back to Brother Jeff. "Mr. Julander, you seem to have matters under control."

"Yes, ma'am. We've been practicing a good long time now. We've come from Mississippi."

"Why, we're from Virginia, ourselves."

"Is that a fact? Come with me, ladies," Mrs. Julander said, and Mrs. Bingham and the women moved off after her.

James said, "Your people aren't weepin' and wailin' like I expected they would."

Brother Jeff pursed his lips. "It's hard to lose a friend, that's for sure, but we have a bright outlook with our faith and our teachings. I'd like to tell you a bit about them after supper." He motioned to the other men. "You gentlemen are included in the invitation."

James stroked his moustache. "I reckon I'll listen," he said.

Robert nodded. "I don't mind talking a bit of religion."

George and Ned looked at each other. George made a sour face, but Ned quirked an eyebrow. "I reckon our souls are saved, but we'll hear what you have to say."

"It appears you'll have a crowd," James said, and went to look after his animals.

Chapter 29

Ned grabbed a tin plate from a stack and got in the line of men that approached a kettle at the first fire. Jessie wasn't in sight, or he would have cut the line to be with her. *She's likely serving food down the way*, he thought. When he got to the kettle, he sniffed the aroma of stew, and his mouth watered. He looked up to hold out his plate, and nearly dropped it.

A tall girl with long brown hair stared back at him, a smile playing on her lips. "How do," she said, and ladled the stew onto his plate.

Ned tried to return her greeting, but his heart seemed to have left his chest to clog up his throat. He swallowed, nodding to the girl. The firelight swirled in her dark eyes. "If you need more, come back, you hear?" she said, and gave him a slow wink.

Ned nodded again. Although he couldn't speak, his body seemed more alive than it had ever been, warmth spreading through his vitals and limbs. He moved past the girl, looking back to memorize her face and form. Who was she? What was such a beguiling creature doing in the wilderness? He kept his gaze on her as long as he could, and when the line came to the next fire, he accepted a biscuit from Jessie's hand and hardly knew it. Then he realized who she was: his betrothed, his beloved, his Jessie. He pushed down the warmth and tried to smile at her.

"Jessie," he said. The smile finally came, feeling forced and false. Before he could say more, the press of the man behind pushed him along the line.

Jessie. I'm going to marry Jessie. I love her. I've always loved her.

His head turned, as though he had no volition, to stare back at the dark-haired beauty at the first fire. *Who is that girl?*

Maggie felt a touch on her sleeve. For a moment longer she let her gaze follow the handsome, curly-haired man who had just stood before her, but was passing down the food line. She locked her knees to keep from falling, from melting away into a puddle. Her heart raced.

"Maggie!"

The voice in her ear made her snap upright, the ladle waving in the air. She let out her breath in a rush and looked up at her mother. Mama looked sad.

"Maggie, what are you thinking?" Her mother's voice was so low a whisper that Maggie leaned sideways toward her to hear it.

"Come again, ma'am?" Maggie replied in an equally low tone.

"You winked at that young man."

Maggie's eyes widened. She blinked. "I did?"

"You did, missy. He's going to think you're a bold flirt."

"A flirt? Oh no, Mama. I didn't mean anything of the sort." She dished a ladleful of stew onto the plate of the next person who came through the line. She could feel the heated flush of embarrassment on her face and neck. "I reckon I . . ." She stopped, then started over, still whispering. "He seemed so nice, but kinda shy-like. Tongue-tied. And so nice. And shy." Her words came out in fits and starts.

"Nice. And shy." Something caught in her mother's voice, and she coughed.

Maggie glanced at her again. Mama looked like she was trying to stifle a smile.

"So you winked at him."

"If I winked, I couldn't help it, Mama. He appeared to be so, so . . . nice."

"And shy?"

"Yes, shy. I reckon I was surprised into winking. I had no thought to be bold or brazen, Mama. He's just . . . so nice."

Her mother's light touch on her arm became a pat. She said in a strangled voice, "He does seem nice," and walked away as if she had an urgent errand to attend to. Maggie heard her coughing again. Mama surely was acting odd. Maggie sighed and looked down the line, but the fair-haired stranger was gone.

Chapter 30

Due to the combined efforts of both parties, the meal was tasty and filling. Soon the women began to clear away the food and the dishes.

Jessie found herself in the company of Mrs. Julander, who stood over the dishpan. The older woman handed Jessie a tin plate to wipe dry, and said, "I feel too young for you to be callin' me 'Mrs. Julander,'" she said. "I hope you'll call me 'Sister Becky,' or 'Miss Becky.'" When Jessie nodded her assent, she continued. "It's odd that both of our parties are travelin' in wintertime. What puts you folks so late on the trail?"

Jessie took the plate and swiped at it with a worn tea towel. "We've had hard luck with our wagons, Miss Becky, and sometimes we had to stop and work for supplies." She sighed. "It's been a long journey."

Miss Becky laughed. "It that a fact? It sounds like your luck was similar to ours."

"Yes. Now we're crossing paths. You're going up the trail and we're headed down." Jessie handed the plate to Hannah, who made a stack of the tin plates with one hand while she cradled her baby in the other.

"Maybe we're meeting because God has a purpose in mind."

"What do you mean, Miss Becky?"

"Maybe he wants us to talk together," Miss Becky said, and smiled. "You know, He loves us and wants the best for us."

"He does? I always thought God was a sort of gruff spirit who likes to torment us." Jessie wiped another plate and gave it to her sister.

"Oh my, no! God's not like that at all, my dear. He's your

Heavenly Father. He loves you like your earthly father does."

"My father's dead. That's one reason we left Virginia. His legs was shot off, and he couldn't defend us from the Yankee louts invading our town. Then he died, and my sis—" She broke off speaking, glanced at Hannah, and straightened her shoulders. "Here we are, a long time later, and we're nearly to Albuquerque. I'll be so glad when I can sleep in a real bed again."

Miss Becky shook water from her hands. "I'm sorry about your father, and the trouble you've had on your journey. God does love you, and he won't ever give you more trials in this life than you can handle with His help." She took up the water-filled dishpan, swirled it a bit, and tossed the water behind her toward the rear of her wagon. A goat's offended bleats cut through the air.

Miss Becky laughed, and called out, "Sorry, old Mike." She turned to Jessie and Hannah. "I forgot our billy goat was tied to the back of the wagon just there. He's a bit of a rascal, and we have to tie him up or he'll eat everything in sight." After a bit, the animal fell silent. She put away the pan, grabbed up a flour-sack towel and dried her hands, then said, "Let's go sit and talk a spell. Do you mind that?"

"Oh, no. You say things that make sense."

Hannah asked, "May I come too?"

Miss Becky smiled. "Certainly. I want to get a better look at that precious babe."

James sat down off to the side of a campfire, absently patting the dog on the head until it lay down with its nose between its paws. Robert came over and sat near James. George and Ned joined them.

Brother Jeff took a seat, placed a Bible in his lap, and said,

"We had a pair of preachers come to our county several years before the unpleasantness started. My wife and I were new married, but we let them stay with us for a while." He smiled. "They gave us a book to read, and they held meetings around the countryside for a few weeks. Becky and me felt convicted that we should become Saints."

"Saints?" Robert raised his eyebrows.

"We believe that the same gospel Jesus Christ preached has been restored to the earth again. The members of Christ's church called themselves Saints, and we do, as well." Brother Jeff rubbed the Bible. "A lot of folks 'round about took exception to that. We lost a few friends."

"That's a hard thing," James said.

"We found other friends in the members who joined the church. Most of them are in this party."

"Where is it y'all are going?" George asked. "Oregon? Wyoming?"

"We're bound for the Great Salt Lake Valley."

George sat back. "I thought only Mormons lived in that country." His voice had a hard edge.

Brother Jeff moved a bit in his seat, but didn't seem to take offense at George's manner. "That's a name we're given from time to time. We're members of the Church of Jesus Christ of Latter-day Saints. Like I said, we call ourselves Saints."

James stroked his beard. "So you're Mormons. I have a relative who followed that path, or so my ma told me. That was twenty-odd years ago, before I was born."

Brother Jeff laughed. "Our path, as you put it, has many doctrines to recommend it. We believe our first prophet, Joseph Smith, received a vision while he was just a lad. He saw God and his Holy Son. Brother Joseph was chosen to restore Christ's Church and the power of God to earth. That power is called the priesthood."

Robert said, "You say he's a prophet, like the ones in the Old Testament? I thought all the prophets were dead."

"The old ones are for sure, but many of them prophesied that after a falling away, the truth would come again to men. We believe that began to happen in 1820, when Brother Joseph had his vision."

"So he's a prophet, living and breathing and talking to God?" Robert moved his foot around in the dirt for a moment before he spoke again. "That's an amazing thing."

"It is amazing and wonderful, for a fact, but he was reviled and hated, and finally killed by a mob."

"I have some experience of mobs," James said, and looked away, a bitterness descending over him at the thought of the men rushing down the hall of the hotel in Trinidad.

Brother Jeff gazed beyond the fire. "We heard about Brother Joseph's death, his and his brother's, while we were trying to get up funds to move to Illinois to join the Saints. That news set us back some." He looked down at his clasped hands. "We didn't know what would happen to the Church with the prophet dead. We had contact for a while, and kept saving our traveling money. We found out Brother Joseph had given the power of God to lead the Church to others, so it kept on going. Later, we heard the Saints had been driven out of Illinois and went west."

"Why didn't you join them?" Ned spoke for the first time.

"We tried, but with crop failures, and one thing and another, we couldn't ever seem to scrape together enough money. We had our young ones and it took a lot of doing to raise them. Finally, we got the cash together, and were fixin' to leave, but the fighting started, and we were stuck in Mississippi."

The dog stood up and woofed, and James patted it on the head and said "Quiet, now," but it slipped from under his hand and left the fire. James looked at Brother Jeff. "It must be sweet to you folks to be so near your goal at last."

"We've had our hard times, but you're right. In a few more months, we'll be safe with the Saints."

The men spoke together for several minutes. James recalled something that had caught his attention when he heard it said at the accident scene.

"When your young sister died, a man comforted Miz Eliza by saying, 'We'll join her to us in Zion.' What did he mean by that?"

Brother Jeff tipped down his head and stared at his feet for a moment. After a while, he looked directly at James and said, "I'll tell you that, but first, let me give you a little background." He hesitated a moment as he looked around the circle. "You might find some of our teachings a mite odd. For example, we believe that husbands and wives can be bound together in marriage for eternity, by the priesthood power given to men. Love doesn't stop when someone dies, so why should a marriage end?"

Startled, James half rose to his feet. His heart pounded in his chest. This was exactly what he'd been telling God. He sank to his seat again, heaved a great sigh, and said, with a voice that sounded to him as though he were being strangled, "I don't find that odd at all."

Brother Jeff peered at him. "You've lost your wife," he said. It was a statement.

"Yes. About New Year's. She was a good girl, and didn't deserve to die so young."

Brother Jeff leaned forward and squeezed James on the shoulder. "I'm sorry to hear of your loss, very sorry."

"Much obliged," James said, looking up at last. "Please, won't you tell me more about marryin' forever?"

Chapter 31

The three women found seats beside one of the fires. Miss Becky asked, "May I hold your dear little one?"

Hannah nodded and gave her the baby.

As Miss Becky cradled the baby in her arms, James's dog came up to sniff at her, then lay down beside Jessie.

"Ooooo, you are so precious," Miss Becky cooed to the infant, counting its fingers. She kissed him on the forehead, then cuddled him against her bodice. "I'd forgotten how good it feels to hold a baby to my breast," she whispered. "Mrs. Fletcher, you are so blessed to have this sweet little bundle fresh from the arms of God." She admired the child for a few more moments, then passed him back to his mother.

"Do you really believe what you said before, Miss Becky?" Jessie stroked the dog's head. "That God loves me?"

"I do. You two are sisters, isn't that right?"

Jessie and Hannah nodded.

"Think about your feelings for each other, for your family members, for that baby. How do you suppose you got those feelings of love and kinship? God put them there. You are his children."

"Doesn't God punish us when we've done something wrong?" Hannah asked, looking down at her baby. "Something really bad?"

The expression on Miss Becky's face softened as she looked at Hannah. After a moment, she said, "I think sometimes we punish ourselves enough that God doesn't have to. I reckon you've had rough experiences in your life. Maybe some you're regretting. Our loving Father provides a way to wipe out all our sins and blunders."

Jessie fidgeted with the fringe of her shawl, thinking about the man she had killed way back in West Virginia. Hannah's mention of doing wrong things had suddenly brought an apparition to her mind of the man's grotesque form splayed out before her on the forest floor. Ned had said the man needed killing, but a foul taste filled her mouth. Would she go to hell for shooting him?

Miss Becky had continued talking, and Jessie shook her head to free her mind of the evil remembrance so she could catch up.

"And his true church is on the earth again. Baptism into his church brings forgiveness from God, a newness of soul, a cleansing as though you had just been born. You need faith in the Lord Jesus Christ and his restored church, and a repentant spirit, to receive baptism in it."

Hannah stirred in her seat, and Jessie glanced over at her. Hannah's face held hope for the first time in months, Jessie thought. *What did she do that was so awful she needs a baptism? The bad things happened to her.* A thought struck her, and she sat upright. *Did Hannah kill the man who attacked her? Robert always says the brute was dead when it all ended, but he never gives details.* She looked away. Were she and Hannah both murderers?

Hannah voice broke into Jessie's thoughts. "You're right about me having a rough life. I've done regretful things, and I want to know more about receiving forgiveness."

Miss Becky stared off into the distance for a moment. She looked at Hannah and said, "I have a little book I treasure a great deal. I would like to give it to you. It will show you how other families have gone through many hard trials, and how God has helped them to bear their burdens." She got up and left the fire for a few minutes. When she returned, she had a small book in her hand.

"This is called The Book of Mormon. It's scripture, just like the Bible. It will help you know that God and his son Jesus Christ are real, and that they love you. When I read it, I received much comfort in my heart. I hope it will do the same for you." She leaned over and held out the book.

Hannah took it and stroked its cover. She looked up at Miss Becky and smiled wistfully. "I don't know if I can take your precious scriptures, Miss Becky." She tried to give the little volume back.

"I'll get another book in Zion," Miss Becky said, her hands up to refuse the return of the book. She stood up. "Now then, my husband is talking to your men about our faith. I reckon we should go over and let him tell you more."

"We have another teaching that might give you comfort," Brother Jeff told James. "We believe that we can perform ceremonies like baptisms and marriages, and such, by proxy, for our dead loved ones. A living person stands in for the dead. That's what Brother Martin was talking about when he spoke to his wife."

James thought for a long time, digesting the man's words. "I recall Paul mentioned baptizing for the dead in the Bible. I don't understand about Brother Martin, though. What kind of proxy ceremony will they do for him in Zion?"

"That's the third teaching I want to tell you about. Do you recall in the Old Testament that Isaac had more than one wife?"

James nodded. "I recollect several of the ancient prophets who did that."

George hooted derisively. "Solomon had so many he needed to build himself a palace to keep them in."

Brother Jeff chuckled, but sobered as he spoke. "We believe God gave a commandment to the Saints to do likewise, for a few of the men to provide homes and look after more than one woman. Laurie Sue is Sister Eliza's blood sister. Brother Martin meant he's willing to have Laurie Sue sealed to him as a wife, if the new prophet, Brother Brigham, gives permission, of course. That is a comfort to Sister Eliza, to know that Laurie Sue will belong to someone forever as a wife, even though she's dead."

"That's an astonishing thing, Brother Jeff," James said.

George got to his feet. "Astonishing? Unbelievable. I think I've heard about all I care to. Heppie is wife enough for me."

Brother Jeff rose as well and thanked George for listening. George made a face, tugged on his brother's coat sleeve, and said, "Come along, Ned. I don't reckon we're cut out to be Mormon converts."

James saw confusion on Ned's face as he got up. He agreed with his brother, though, and the two strode off toward their camp.

When the three remaining men had taken their seats again, James said, "Let's back up a tad bit. What you're sayin' is that God wants our marriages to last forever?"

Brother Jeff nodded. "I do say that."

"And He gave your prophet the power to do that? 'Seal,' you said?" James noticed that Robert was leaning forward, intently taking in the conversation.

"Yes," Brother Jeff agreed.

"And if that wasn't done before a body dies, it can be done afterward?"

"Yes."

"I could be a married man forever?" James paused, tugging on his beard, then smoothing it. "Could I take another wife besides, a live one?"

"Since your first wife is dead, you wouldn't need the prophet's permission to marry again."

James rubbed his chest slowly, feeling the explosive pounding of his heart. "The things you tell me burn like a fire."

"That's the Holy Ghost witnessin' to you," Brother Jeff said.

"Do you reckon I can join your church?" James asked.

Brother Jeff opened his mouth, but a voice in the darkness interrupted. "I'd like to join, have the baptizing," Hannah took a step into the firelight. "Robert? Please?"

Robert jumped up and went to her side. "Yes." He looked at Brother Jeff. "I would like that, as well."

James and Brother Jeff were on their feet as Miss Becky and Jessie entered the circle of light.

"I can arrange that," Brother Jeff said. "I'll find a place in the river, and we can baptize you tomorrow, after the funeral service."

"How much water do you need for that?" Jessie asked.

Miss Becky put her hand on Jessie's arm and said, "John the Baptist used the Jordan River for Our Lord's baptism. He was immersed, totally covered. You might remember, the Holy Ghost came down like a dove, and then God Himself spoke."

"I've read that," James said. "I'll take the baptizin'." He looked over at Jessie, uneasy that she was present when he had another question burning in his soul.

The baby let out a cry, and Hannah began to rock him back and forth. "He's hungry." She gave a great sigh. "I look forward to tomorrow," she said, smiling at Robert. "Good night, Miss Becky. Good night, Brother Jeff. Jessie, we'll walk you back to camp."

Jessie looked from James to Hannah, uncertainty showing in her face.

James thought, *Does she want the baptizin' too? I reckon Ned will tell her no if she asks his permission. That's not my concern.*

She hesitated, finally walking away with Robert and Hannah. He turned back to Brother Jeff and his wife.

"How do I get Amparo—that's my wife, Amparo—sealed to me forever?"

Brother Jeff said, "That takes a bit more work. You'll have to go to Zion with us to see about that. I can scarcely wait to get there and have Becky and the kids sealed to me."

James's head fell forward and his words trickled slowly from his lips. "I gave my word to take these folks to Albuquerque. Maybe after that . . ." He felt a constriction of his heart as hope diminished.

"At least we can get you started with baptism, Brother James." Brother Jeff took Miss Becky's hand and nodded to James. "It's not full dark yet. I'll go find a fittin' place in the river and maybe dam it up a bit."

Jessie looked back as she walked away. James stood beside the waning fire, talking to the leader of the Mormon group. His head was down in a dejected pose, and she stopped for a moment to watch him. Brother Jeff took his wife's hand, gestured with his head, and left the fire. James ran his fingers through his hair, and Jessie ached to go to him, to comfort him, to hold him close to her heart. Remembering her promise to Ned, she balled her fists, turned away, and followed Hannah and Robert back to the wagons.

Chapter 32

After he left the fire with George, Ned checked the picket pin on his horse and spread his blankets near the Bingham's wagon. He chatted a bit with Luke, and looked around for Jessie, but she wasn't back from the Mormons' camp yet. He shrugged his shoulders and sat on his blankets, preparing to bed down.

Before he pulled off his boots, a thought struck him. James Owen hadn't returned either. Had he enticed Jessie to listen to Julander's outrageous claims? He had better go over and bring her to safety.

Ned pushed himself to his feet and shrugged into his coat. He wouldn't be surprised if it froze tonight. The Mormons would be hard-pressed tomorrow to dig a proper burial hole for that young girl who had died.

Once Ned was past the Bingham's fire, he walked in darkness. The stars glittered above, but the light they shed wasn't much to navigate by. A couple of people, Robert and Hannah, from the sound of the voices, passed him at a distance, going the other way.

Ned moved up to the fire where he'd sat with the men, talking to Julander. It smoldered by itself. Julander was gone. Owen was gone. Jessie wasn't there.

He stopped, unsure what to do next. Maybe Jessie had slipped past him in the darkness and was safely out of harm's way. He felt a bit foolish, chasing her all over the landscape like this, but he'd always been her protector, and he wasn't about to stop that now. Especially with Owen in the picture.

Maybe I'm making a mountain out of a molehill, he thought. *Owen's got that dead wife he's moping after. If he wants to join the Mormons and go with them, it's all the better for me.*

A figure came toward the fire, carrying a bucket that sloshed water over the sides. It was the girl he had met in the food line. Ned felt his body tightening, but tried to ignore it as he hurried to help her with the bucket.

"Here now, let me carry that for you," he said, stretching out his hand to take the handle.

The girl smiled in the waning light. "I ain't goin' no further," she said in a melodious voice that cut deep into Ned's soul. "I come to put the fire down."

"I can take care of that," he said, reaching out and taking the bucket from her slender hands. She stood still and surrendered it, and when their fingers touched, Ned felt as though he'd been lightning-struck. The girl was so close that when he inhaled, her scent filled his nostrils. He noted that she smelled of wood smoke and violets. *Violets? Here in the winter wilderness of New Mexico Territory?*

"I'm Ned Heizer," he said, listening to his voice rise up the scale into a boyish octave. What on earth was happening to him? Why didn't he step back out of her way and let her get about her business?

Ned figured the moon slipped up the horizon behind him, because the girl's face gradually glowed with a soft light.

"My name is Maggie," she said, taking air in a fetching manner that raised and lowered her shoulders and chest. "Maggie Julander."

Ned swallowed. This beautiful girl was Jeffrey Julander's daughter, and all that separated them was a bucket of water. He stepped sideways to get a bit of distance, put the pail down, took her hand, and said, "I'm very pleased to make your acquaintance, Miss Maggie." He was also very pleased that his voice stayed in a normal register this time.

"Mister Heizer," she acknowledged, giving his hand a tiny squeeze before she let it go.

Everything about Miss Maggie's comportment was pure innocence, but there was a heady undertone of bewitching backwoods humor, a quirk to her mouth that told him she liked to laugh, to take joy in life.

Joy in life. That's something I've been missing of late. The admission scared him, made him feel disloyal and a bit out of sorts. Digging into the mass of his fears, he discovered that the thing jolting him the most was that he truly *had* been missing joy in his life. He should be over the moon with happiness. Not so long ago, Jessie had finally said she would marry him. He'd agreed to her condition of waiting, but even the prospect of having to damp down his desire to be her husband hadn't dismayed him.

Or maybe it had.

Whatever was going on in his courtship, it didn't seem to matter right now. Miss Maggie's very presence expanded his senses and made him feel glad to be alive.

Ned shook himself mentally. Staring at Miss Maggie wouldn't finish her chore.

He bent and picked up the water bucket, smiling at the girl. He couldn't stop smiling at her. He circled the fire, pouring water onto the margins, then into the heart of the blackened coals. Wisps of steam arose, and his nose sampled the odor of ashes.

"Did I do that right?" he asked, handing the bucket back to Maggie.

"I reckon that took care of the job," she answered. "I'm obliged, Mr. Heizer."

Ned realized that he hadn't let go of the bucket when Maggie put out her hand to take it back. Their fingers both curled around the wire bail, side by side, their thumbs touching. Her skin was cool, but his hand felt like fire. He stopped breathing.

When he straightened his fingers at last to release the thick, curved wire, the empty bucket swung down to hang in Maggie's hand at her side, rocking back and forth so slowly that it seemed as though time had been altered by his suspended breath.

The moon bathed Maggie's face in white light. She was smiling. Ned knew he was smiling. Pixie lights danced before his eyes until he become conscious that he was in danger of passing out. He took a long, gasping breath, nearly strangling with the desire to touch her again. He must not do that. The moment had passed. All that was left was to wrench himself away, back to his camp, and let her go about her nightly routine.

"Miss Maggie," he said in a shaky voice. "Good night to you."

"And to you, Mr. Heizer," she replied, her voice barely above a whisper.

Maggie turned away, slipping off like a phantom and breaking the spell that had kept Ned rooted to one spot. His jaw felt slack, his legs rubbery. He'd never before experienced the lightness, the elation that permeated his very skin. He wondered how he was going to survive until he saw Miss Maggie again.

Hannah put the baby to bed, touching the tiny widow's peak with a kiss. She turned to Robert. "I'm going to have my sins washed away," she said, breathless at the wonder of it.

"Sins, my love? I find no sins in you." Robert stretched his length in the quilts, holding out his hand to help Hannah down beside him.

"I have a great many. That man, killing him. Not wanting the baby. Turning you away from my affections." She ticked them off on her fingers.

Robert took her hand and kissed each finger she had touched. She quaked with joy, but lest he misunderstand her quivers for fright, she turned her head and kissed him on the mouth.

"I shall be clean," she murmured against his lips. "Jesus will wash me in his blood."

"And I—"

"You have no faults, Robert."

"I warrant I can conjure a good many."

"No you can't," she said, kissing his neck, listening to his sudden intake of breath. "Isn't lust a sin?" She giggled.

"Not in the marriage bed," Robert whispered, and tickled her until she laughed out loud.

"You'll wake the baby," she gasped.

"That *would* be a sin. Good thing it will be washed away tomorrow."

Chapter 33

James awoke to a faint rhythmic thump that he later found out was several of the Mormon men swinging pickaxes to dig Miss Laurie Sue's grave. He sat, rubbed the sleep from his eyes, and got to his feet. Grabbing his boots, he tipped them upside down, shook them to remove any nighttime visitors, and put them on. He rolled his bed into a tight bundle and tied it onto the mule's pack that sat beside his saddle.

He gathered the rest of his gear and packed it up. Then he remembered. The Bingham company wasn't traveling anywhere today. After the Mormons held a funeral service for Miss Laurie Sue, he, James Owen, was fixing to walk down into a pool of cold river water and wash off his sins. It was a first step toward making Amparo his wife forever—no matter how long it might take to have it done.

He realized that for the first time in several weeks, he wasn't experiencing the never-ending grief he'd been carrying like a sack full of rocks tied around his heart, the grief about Amparo's not being with him. He figured it still would hurt later, but right now, thinking on his baptism, his heart jumped in his chest, free of restricting pain.

James took a deep breath and let it out slowly in a white plume. His lungs tightened around another breath of the crisp, cold air. Last night, he'd made this decision a matter of prayer. He had a comforting feeling in his chest about his choice to join the Mormon faith. If only Amparo were here—he knew she would receive the preaching about marrying forever with joy and acceptance. *Para siempre.* She was big on the notion of forever.

The Bingham women pooled their supplies with the Mormon ladies that morning, and breakfast consisted of boiled salt pork, beaten biscuits, and milk gravy. James got in line for the food behind Brother Jeff. He heard the man ask that four biscuits be tied up in a cloth, and when Jessie handed him the bundle, he put it in his coat pocket.

Jessie glanced up at James and put three biscuits on his plate, but she didn't say anything to him. He wondered again if she had the urge to become a Mormon. It'd seemed like she wanted to say something last night before Hannah whisked her away.

James looked at her a moment, wishing Ned Heizer had stayed in the north after the war. That might have uncomplicated things a tad bit. He asked, "Will you be at the baptizin' service?"

Jessie's eyes darted from side to side. She straightened her shoulders and put on a smile. "I wouldn't miss seeing you lose your sins for all the world," she said. Her light tone seemed forced. As he moved down the line to get his gravy, he wondered why it mattered to him if she would be there or not. How could he yearn for Amparo one moment and the very next be concerned about Jessie's whereabouts? *Life is complex*, he thought, and stuffed a biscuit into his mouth.

After breakfast, James joined the parade of people carrying seats to the spot where the Mormons had dug a grave off the side of the road. As he settled himself on his saddle, four men brought Laurie Sue's body, which had been sewn into a shroud made of canvas, to the front of the gathering. He got to his feet in respect for the dead as the men laid their burden beside the grave, and he sat down as they took places in the congregation beside their wives.

Jeffrey Julander went to the front, turned to face the crowd, and directed the Mormons to sing an old familiar hymn, "Rock of Ages." A woman in the audience gave a pitch, the Mormons began to sing, and the members of the Bingham party joined in. A hush fell on the group as Brother Jeff called on one of the men to offer a prayer.

The man arose and took off his hat. The other men followed suit, and as the Mormon got deep into his prayer, he spoke of being grateful for their trials along the trail and of their faith in a loving Savior. He asked for comfort for the family who had lost their kin, and peace for the hearts of all assembled there. He ended the prayer and sat down. The congregation followed suit.

Brother Jeff took charge again. He breathed slowly for a moment, and James wondered what he was waiting for. At last he said, "We're gathered to mourn the sudden passing of our sister in Christ, Laurie Sue Purdy. She may not have made it to Zion, but now she's in Paradise, greeted by Our Lord, Jesus Christ.

"We are left to wonder why she was taken and to do our duty as Saints to comfort each other, particularly Sister Eliza, who is mighty heartsick."

Brother Jeff took a slim book from his pocket and opened it to a part that he'd marked with a scrap of paper.

"Thus saith the Lord about the last days," he said, and began to read from the book. "'Mine indignation is soon to be poured out without measure upon all nations; and this will I do when the cup of their iniquity is full. And in that day all who are found upon the watch-tower, or in other words, all mine Israel, shall be saved. And they that have been scattered shall be gathered.'" Brother Jeff looked over at Laurie Sue's shroud for a minute, then resumed reading. "'And all they who have mourned shall be comforted. And all they who have given their lives for my name shall be crowned. Therefore, let your hearts be comforted concerning Zion; for all flesh is in mine hands; be still and know that I am God.'

"Brethren and Sisters, in this passage the Lord God of Israel declared that the day will come when all who mourn will be comforted, in that day when he gathers us in. We look forward to that blessed event." He closed the book over the scrap of paper, put it into his pocket, and spoke again. "The prophet Alma proclaimed that we as members of God's kingdom have a deep feeling and a sacred duty to comfort each other in our times of grief. He was speaking to the people at the waters of Mormon, urgin' them to take heed of their Christ like feelings of love and concern and to be baptized and become His Church."

Brother Jeff put his hand into another pocket and drew it out empty. He frowned, patting all his other pockets. Whatever he sought wasn't to be found, and Brother Jeff walked over to Miss Becky and asked, "Do you have your Book of Mormon?"

"Oh," she exclaimed. "I don't have it. I gave it to Mrs. Fletcher." She turned in her seat and asked Hannah, "Did you happen to bring that little book to the meeting?"

Hannah blushed, but nodded, took the Book of Mormon from her pocket, and handed it to Miss Becky.

"I'll give it back to you," Miss Becky whispered, and delivered the volume to her husband.

Brother Jeff opened the book, found the place he wanted, and read, "'Behold, here are the waters of Mormon and now, as ye are desirous to come into the fold of God, and to be called his people, and are willing to bear one another's burdens, that they may be light; Yea, and are willing to mourn with those that mourn; yea, and to comfort those that stand in need of comfort, and to stand as witnesses of God at all times and in all things, and in all places that ye may be in, even until death, that ye may be redeemed of God, and be numbered with those of the first resurrection, that ye may have eternal life— Now I say unto you, if this be the desire of your hearts, what have you against being baptized in the name of the Lord, as a witness before him that ye have entered into a covenant with him, that ye will serve him and keep his commandments, that he may pour out his Spirit more abundantly upon you?'"

James restrained himself from rising to his feet and calling out, "Yes, this is the desire of my heart!" He shifted in his seat and looked around, saw Jessie staring at him, and wondered if he had said it out loud. He broke into a sweat despite the coolness of the morning.

Brother Jeff shut the book with a thump and gave it back to Miss Becky.

"Are we not commanded to be faithful in carrying out our duty? Yes, and we do it out of love, one for another, even as Christ loved the Church for our sakes.

"Now we will lay the body of our sister in the grave, here beside our trail, but the memories we will take with us are of a sweet sister who was faithful in all her dealings, kindhearted, hardworking, and cheerful in adversity. We will commend her spirit to the keeping of Our Lord, and pledge to remember our time with her on earth with glad hearts."

Brother Jeff gestured to the four men who had earlier carried the body to the graveside. They came forward, took up the shrouded body, and gently laid it in the bottom of the grave. Then they picked up shovels and scooped the earth into place.

James looked away while they filled the grave, remembering all too clearly the similar labor he had performed just days before, in a place not so far away. His heart thumped hard in his chest, and he gripped his hands together until they ached.

When the men returned to their seats, Brother Jeff spoke again. "We have among us today several who wish to be baptized like those people of Alma's day and time. When we have concluded this service, those who wish to do so may gather on the side of the river to witness the baptisms," he said.

Brother Jeff ended his sermon with a few more thoughts and scriptures that James had never heard before. He led them in singing another song, one that the Bingham party didn't know. It included a verse about dying "before our journey's through," but all being well, as it was a happy day, free from toil and sorrow. James felt buoyed up, even though he had nothing to do with the family who mourned.

Another Mormon gave a prayer, and at the "Amen," the people rose to their feet and gathered around Sister Eliza, who dabbed ineffectually at her streaming eyes.

As the Mormons comforted the woman, James felt the grip of conflicting emotions. Grief, joy, and apprehension swirled together in his head, and he hoped he could maintain a steady countenance among these strangers.

Brother Jeff approached with the Fletchers close behind him and touched James on the elbow. "Are you ready?" he asked. "If so, follow me." He turned and strode toward the river's edge, taking off his coat as he walked. He stopped at the bank to remove his boots.

James hesitated a moment, his stomach churning. Then he went after Brother Jeff, stripping off his coat, as well.

The rocks put in the stream yesterday had done their work, and a fair-sized pool of water stood behind the temporary dam. Brother Jeff greeted those who had approached and called for another prayer.

This time, the Mormon who prayed asked for blessings upon the converts, that they would be able to have clear minds to learn more of the doctrines of the kingdom, and for a safe journey through life until they could join the Saints in Zion.

James stood stiffly alongside Robert and Hannah. He looked over at them. Their heads were bowed as they followed the prayer. Hannah, in particular, seemed relaxed and serene, patting her child on the back and swaying. James shut his eyes and bent his head.

The prayer ended, and Brother Jeff waded into the pool. He put out his hand and gestured for James to join him. James took off his boots and followed. The shock of the cold water when he entered the stream ran up his legs and spread into his chest, but James persevered until he stood beside the Mormon leader.

Brother Jeff smiled at him, and gave him quick instructions concerning stopping up his nostrils when the time came. He raised his arm and called James by name, said he was commissioned by Jesus Christ to do this baptism, told him to hold his nose, and laid him down in the water. James's weight pulled Brother Jeff off balance on the slick rocky bottom, and he went under too. They both came up sputtering and laughing.

"Whew! I do feel clean!" James said, shaking his head. Water drops spattered into the creek's flow. "So now I'm a Mormon?" he asked, and began to shiver in the chilly breeze. Oddly, his heart felt warm, though his skin bristled with gooseflesh.

Brother Jeff smiled. "Almost. We'll give you a confirmation by the laying on of hands. After that, you'll be a Saint." He turned James toward the water's edge, and James picked his way across the rocks. Brother Jeff beckoned to Robert to enter the water.

When James reached the creek bank, Jessie surprised him by holding out a blanket. He took it, thanked her, and wrapped it around himself. Ned came and took Jessie's arm, as though he wanted to remove her from the area.

James heard her whisper, "I want to watch, Ned." The man dropped his hand, but stayed at her side.

By then, Robert had made his way to Brother Jeff, who repeated the process of praying and baptizing. Robert came out of the water, shouting for joy. Brother Jeff patted his arm, beamed, and sent him back to the bank. As he approached, Hannah handed the baby to Mrs. Bingham and stooped to pick up a blanket. She gave it to Robert and stepped into the creek for her own turn.

"Watch your step, ma'am," Brother Jeff said, as he helped Hannah enter the pool of water. He repeated the same ceremony and, when he had finished, helped Hannah out of the water. Robert embraced her and wrapped her in the blanket, wiping a few tears from her smiling face.

James looked around. Where would the laying on of hands that Brother Jeff mentioned take place? Several Mormon men had moved away from the river and surrounded a chair someone had brought to the site. Brother Jeff joined them after toweling the water off his legs and torso and shrugging into his black coat. He waved a hand at James.

James gave the blanket back to Jessie and went to sit down on the chair. The men put their hands on his head. The hands warmed him. Brother Jeff spoke, his voice soft, but firm, as he pronounced the words that confirmed James a member of The Church of Jesus Christ of Latter-day Saints and gave him gifts and blessings from heaven.

At the end of the prayer, Brother Jeff patted James on the shoulder. He leaned over and whispered, "You are a member of God's Kingdom. Now we're going to give you the priesthood and ordain you an elder. Remember, we spoke of this power of God," he added.

James nodded, a lump in his throat.

Again, Brother Jeff's voice was soft and steady as he prayed and gave James the priesthood.

James was no longer cold. He sat beneath the warm hands of his brothers, soaking in the words and the feeling of overwhelming strength that caused him to shake a bit. The simple words seemed to come from God Himself, and sank forcefully into his soul.

Brother Jeff said, "Amen," which the other men echoed.

James said, "Amen," rose to his feet, and embraced Brother Jeff. "Thank you," he whispered in his ear. "I'm mighty obliged."

"You're welcome," said Brother Jeff. "I am most pleased to do it. Be faithful and true, and the desires of your heart will be met, if it is God's will."

James's heart soared, remembering his most precious desire: being one with Amparo forever. But that was a future promise, for a future time.

The other men embraced James in their turn, and he would have stepped away, but Brother Jeff said, "Join us in the circle to confirm the Fletchers. You have that right and duty now."

James expelled a lungful of air as the surprise hit him, but did as he was bidden, and placed himself between two brothers who had made room for him.

Robert sat in the chair. Brother Jeff confirmed him as a new member of the Church and gave him the Holy Ghost. Then he gave Robert the priesthood, as he had done with James, and invited him to join the circle for Hannah's confirmation. James and Robert looked at each other.

Robert grinned. "This is good," he murmured. "Very good."

James nodded. The strength he felt in the circle of men—brethren, he reminded himself—filled his chest with awe. He'd been a lone man for so long, all the way back to when he'd left his family. He'd missed his brothers, even after he married Amparo and gained her company. Falling in love with her had not driven out the yearning for family, for brotherhood. He sensed it here, the bonds of men united in purpose. His heart swelled throughout Hannah's confirmation until, when the brethren all said "Amen" together, he thought it would burst the walls of his chest. A few deep breaths helped calm him. This was very good.

A few moments later, Brother Jeff sat on a barrel in the Mormon camp and put a few blank pieces of paper on a makeshift desk in front of him. "Brother Harris," he asked, "you got that calendar you're keeping handy? What's the date today?"

Brother Harris went to fetch his calendar and proclaimed the day was Saturday, January 17, 1867.

Brother Jeff wrote out a certificate, stating that he, Jeffrey Julander, Elder, had baptized and confirmed James Owen on that date, and wrote another certificate as proof that he had ordained him an elder. He gave the two pieces of paper to James. "Keep them safe, now. When you make it to Zion, you'll need the proof of your membership and priesthood office in Christ's Kingdom."

"Thank you. I will do that." After reading the certificates over twice, James folded them carefully and thanked Brother Jeff again.

The man wrote other certificates for Robert and Hannah. "Please join us tomorrow at eight o'clock for Sabbath services," he said to the new Mormons as he passed one of the papers to Hannah. "We'll have the sacrament of the Lord's Supper."

Robert said, "I was hoping we could be on our way tomorrow."

"You'll be on the road before noon," Brother Jeff promised.

"Good. I reckon we'll be there," Robert promised.

Chapter 34

To James's surprise, Brother Jeff involved Robert and him in the Sabbath service the next morning. He asked Robert to offer the opening prayer. He knelt beside James and read a prayer over crumbled biscuit pieces that represented the body of Christ. After other men had given the bits of biscuit to the congregation, Brother Jeff pointed out the verse in a book of scripture called the Doctrine and Covenants that was the prayer James was to read. He did so, holding a large cup of water that stood in for the blood that Christ shed for mankind. This was passed to the Mormons as well.

James watched as Hannah sipped from the cup and passed it on. Her face glowed with joy. A feeling of comfort enveloped him, and he knew his decision to become a Saint was right.

After the Lord's Supper had been celebrated, Brother Jeff announced that their meeting would include testimonies from the assembled Saints. Then he sat down.

James looked around. What an odd statement. Wasn't Brother Jeff supposed to give a sermon?

A man got up and said how glad he was to take the sacrament of the Lord's Supper and renew his baptismal covenants with God. He had kind words for James and the Fletchers, accepting a new way of life and new beliefs. After a bit, he sat down.

Brother Martin arose and gave his testimony of love for the gospel of Jesus Christ and of all it meant to him. When he'd had his say, he wiped the moisture from his eyes, sat down, and took Miz Eliza's hand in his.

She stood up beside him and, weeping, spoke of her hope in

everlasting life and of the comfort she had in knowing her husband held the priesthood of God and that at the end of their journey, they could be sealed together for eternity. She wiped her nose on her apron, slipped a book from her pocket, and come toward James, who stood at her approach.

"This is Laurie Sue's Doctrine and Covenants," she said, holding the book out to James. "I reckon she don't need it now, and I think she would like to see it put to good use by a new brother in the gospel. Please take it in remembrance of her."

James received the book in both his hands and stood still, rubbing one thumb over the worn cover. "I thank you, Miz Eliza. I will keep it safe and study it carefully."

As she returned to her seat, James knew he couldn't sit down. He had to say something to these people. He made his way to the front and turned to the congregation.

"I want to give all of you thanks for the kind fashion you've received me as one of you. Brother Jeff thought I'd find odd the beliefs he told me about, but I have a burning conviction that they are God's truth. I'm mighty sure I don't know all your ways, or God's ways, but I mean to read and follow all the commandments in this book.

"I reckon I'm supposed to give a testimony here. I know my love for my wife didn't die when she passed on, and I'm mighty grateful to God to hear that He gave you a way to bind a man and wife together beyond the grave. I reckon that'll keep me sane for a good long time, until I can join you in Zion and make that happen for me and Amparo. In the name of Jesus, Amen."

His legs quivering like jelly, James headed back to his seat before they could collapse. As he walked, he glanced over the congregation. Jessie sat at the back, and he didn't know how long she'd been there. She didn't meet his eye. Her head was bowed a little forward, and her wheat-colored hair rippled beside her cheeks.

He bit his lip and took his seat. Hearing him profess his love for Amparo in a public meeting probably cut her to the quick, he thought, but reminded himself that Jessie was pledged to marry Ned Heizer. His feelings about another woman shouldn't be any bother to her. Still, he struggled to reconcile the facts with his emotions.

Unsettled, James turned his gaze to the front and gave attention to the other Saints who spoke. Hannah abruptly handed the baby to Mrs. Bingham and stood.

"I'm so grateful to have my sins washed clean," she said, and sat down as fast as she had popped up. She grabbed the child and kissed his tiny brow.

After a while, Brother Jeff called for a hymn, and the meeting ended with another prayer.

Before James could leave to tie the pack on his mule, Brother Jeff clapped him on the shoulder and shook his hand.

"Well done, Brother James. I thank you for your help during the meeting."

"I wondered why you asked me. You have so many brothers who know what they're doing."

"Y'all needed to learn how to administer the ordinances in the Church. I've called Brother Fletcher to be the presiding elder to the Saints in your party. You're going to be a mighty small congregation, but I hope you will be able to learn more about the gospel and convert a few others before you come to Zion."

James bit his lip. "That may be," he said, and straightened his shoulders. "Thank you for your instruction, Brother Jeff. It's been a great enlightenment to me to have come across you folks. I'll surely miss you." He half turned, but Brother Jeff stopped him with a hand on his arm.

"I've told you all I can think of that you need to know. Let the scriptures be your guide when you have a question, Brother James. Have a safe journey."

James clapped Brother Jeff on the shoulder and moved away. Across the road, the dog was running around the wagons, and George had the teams hitched up and waiting. James walked swiftly to his horses and mule. Although he cherished the knowledge he had gained during their several days' stop, it would be good to be on the trail again. The sooner he got the Bingham party to Albuquerque, the sooner he could be on his way to Zion.

Chapter 35

After the birth of Robert's son, James gave his tent to the Fletcher family. His new custom was to bunk down beside one of the fires. Several nights after they parted ways with the Mormon travelers, Robert had pitched the tent near their wagon.

The baby cried at midnight.

James awoke and lay listening to the intimate sounds: the wail of the hungry infant, Hannah waking and rustling around in the tent as she picked up the baby, the sudden cessation of noise, then hungry gulping sounds as the child nuzzled at her breast. His belly tightened.

Rolling over in his bedroll, he decided it wasn't lust that inspired his unease. He had no eye for a married woman, especially not one nourishing her young babe. It wasn't the thought of her breast that bothered him. He had seen women nurse their children before. He closed his eyes and tried to get back to sleep, but the feeling persisted. Suddenly he knew what rankled him.

I want children.

His longing deepened and turned into an ache. He had always wanted to be a father, to teach his children what he had been taught through his growing years. Ma had made him a God-fearing man. Pa had taught him practical skills. Dealing with his brothers, both the older and the younger, had helped him learn to get along with others, and that family was the best, the most important group of people he could associate with.

Family. Robert looked forward to the birth of his child. I want that same pleasure.

He had talked a bit with Robert, and admired the man's enthusiasm for providing a good life for Hannah and their baby. "A good life in a new land," he had said.

Robert will do that, he told himself. *He has the gumption for it.*

James turned the other way in bed.

I want a family forever, he thought. *Amparo's taught me that.* A cold wave raised bumps on his skin as it passed through him from head to toe. *I want a family, a wife to give me children, a woman I can love as I've loved before. Not someone to replace Amparo—no one can take her place. I need someone to stand by my side and share the rest of my life.*

Jessie's face loomed before his mind's eye. He sighed deeply, recalling the passion he'd once felt for her. *I surely was a lustful young stallion. Six little beans! I hurt Jessie so bad by leaving her behind in the Shenandoah.* Another sigh quivered through his frame. *If I'd stayed, I'd likely be a father now.* A knot of regret wrapped around his heart. He moistened his lips. *I want a livin', breathin' passel of kids I can hold in my arms, teaching 'em how to rope and gentle a horse, and comforting 'em when they fall down. I want Jessie there, birthin' 'em, motherin' 'em, kissing their skinned knees and . . .* He held his breath until he felt dizzy, then exhausted the air from his lungs and took in a great, shivering chest full of air. *Kissing me in the night. I want Jessie back, and Ned Heizer can go—*

Mules tales! He didn't want to swear, now that he'd got God's forgiveness for his sins, but the thought of Ned Heizer holding Jessie in his arms made his head feel near to exploding. *I may not be good enough to kiss Jessie's little finger, but I'm a danged sight better for her than Ned Yankee Heizer.*

A resolve started to grow in him, a commitment to make things right with Jessie, to somehow show her the depth of his affection. He had to turn her heart away from Ned. He had to make her love him again.

Chapter 36

James scouted the trail ahead of the wagons, keeping a sharp eye on the sky as it grew dark with heavy clouds. The wind began to rise, cold and fierce, gusting against him and the horse, and threatening to push them off the trail. He tied his neck scarf over his hat to keep it in place and pulled gloves from his pocket. Then he turned the sorrel's head out of the wind and started back toward the small train.

George rode out from the wagons, his eyes dark slits in his face. By the time the two met, the wind was howling, and flakes of snow were swirling around their heads, dusting the shoulders of their coats.

"What's up ahead? We need a campground."

"There ain't a good, sheltered spot, except . . ." James stopped shouting for a moment, adjusting his collar.

"Except what?" George held on to his hat with one hand and kept a firm grip with the other on the reins of his dancing horse.

"Down a piece there's a big Mexican outfit, a *hacienda*, my wife called it. They're good folks." James's muscles tensed as he awaited George's response.

George frowned. "Mexicans? Are they honest?"

"Don Pedro is a big landowner and a kind, decent man." James covered his lower face with his hand and breathed into it to warm his nose and mask his dismay at George's prejudicial attitude. "He helped me out once."

"I reckon we can't be choosy in a storm like this."

"No." His voice was flat as he continued. "We don't dare be choosy."

"Lead the way." Luke was driving the first wagon, and

George turned around to inform the boy about the change of plans.

James headed his horse straight into the wind, fighting it as it wheeled around to escape the icy blast. "Hi! Get up there, horse!" he muttered. "You'll be in a nice warm stable soon." He slapped the sorrel on the flank. The animal bucked a bit, but it was weary, and James was determined, so it soon followed his direction and continued along the road. A popping sound drew his attention, the impact of the horse's hooves striking the frozen snow.

A few minutes later, James turned the tiring horse into the lee of a small stand of trees where a trail left the road. The shelter wasn't enough for all the wagons, and James didn't dare stop. Luke drove his team in James's wake, and the other two wagons followed.

The temperature fell rapidly as the snow swirled around in the icy wind, leaving the ground white in some places and bare in others. George rode forward and told James he was going to spell his wife at driving the team.

"Mrs. Heizer can't feel her hands. How much further do we have to go?"

"I ain't been to the house, George, but I reckon it can't be too distant."

"Well, keep us on the trail. If this wind dies down, the snow will cover the path."

James barked a laugh. "It would be warmer, though." He could feel the hairs in his nostrils freezing stiff in the cold, and he covered his nose with his hand for a moment. His old wounds ached, and he rubbed his side. "Go take care of your wife," he said, and George rode back to the wagons.

James moved closer to the first wagon and used a rope end to chivvy the lead horses onward. "Luke!" he called out. "Use your whip, boy. We got to get out of this storm."

The boy nodded, handed the lines to his sister, and turned to get his whip from the wagon box. Jessie slapped the lines on the rumps of the horses, and James called out, "Hi! Giddap! Hey!" to the horses before he went ahead to pick out the trail.

Fifteen minutes later, the half-frozen travelers arrived at the arched gateway to the Chaves headquarters. James dismounted to open the wrought iron gate. It screeched as he pushed it aside. When all three wagons had passed through, he closed the gate, got back into the saddle, and rode up the white lane behind the wagons.

When the wagons stopped before the long, low adobe buildings, he approached the house. Don Pedro Chaves stood on his porch out of the storm, bundled in a bearskin coat.

James got off his horse.

"I know you, yes?" Don Pedro asked when James approached.

"Yes, sir. I'm James Owen. I was in Santa Fe some weeks back." He took off his right glove and held out his hand.

The older man's face lit up as he recognized the name as well as the face, and he extended his hand to James. "Oh yes, yes." He shook hands with warm regard. "At La Fonda." Don Pedro craned his neck to look at the people getting out of the wagons. "Tell me, where is your dear wife?"

James made a harsh sound. "She met with a . . . bad . . . accident," he said, pain pinching his voice. "She died in Trinidad."

"No!" Don Pedro crossed himself. "That cannot be!"

James plunged ahead, ignoring his rising grief. "This is the Bingham family and their kin. I'm taking them to Albuquerque." James gestured at the Binghams. "Can we shelter here?"

"*¡Cómo no!* Yes, of course! Please, bring your friends inside."

"Thank you." James turned to the family. "He says we're welcome. Go ahead in. I'll look after the stock."

"No, *joven*, my men will see to them. You are frozen. Please enter. Tell me of your misfortune. *¡Ay!* Such a young girl to die!" He crooked a finger and gave an order to the man who appeared, and the servant hurried off to do Don Pedro's bidding.

Jessie stumbled down the wagon wheel. Her fingers were numb. She couldn't feel her toes. Would she ever be warm again? She shuddered as she approached the covered porch, rubbing her fists along her arms, trying to regain feeling in them.

Her first sight of the man who stood greeting James made her open her eyes wide. Although he must be very old because his hair was silver, his brown face bore few deep wrinkles. He carried himself straight and tall, almost like a general, she imagined. She couldn't sense any malice in the man, for he smiled and made gestures of welcome to her mother, clearly inviting her inside the house. *Mighty gracious of him*, she thought.

When everyone was out of the storm, the man stood beside the roaring fire in a massive fireplace and spoke to the party in accented but formal English.

"I am Pedro Chaves, Peter Chaves in English. Everyone calls me Don Pedro. Welcome to my humble home. It is at your service for anything you will need. Come to the fire, ladies. Get warm." He turned to James and beckoned toward the women. "Now, who are these lovely ladies, Mr. Owen?"

James made introductions, including the men of the party, as well as Luke. Don Pedro turned to Mrs. Bingham. "*Señora*, my wife and the cooks will have a meal ready very soon. May they bring you hot chocolate?"

Jessie watched as Ma's look of apprehension fled, replaced

by astonishment. "Chocolate! My lands, Mr. Chaves, it has been years since I tasted chocolate! You are very kind, sir."

"It is nothing, *señora*, a small token to offer my guests." He motioned to a leather armchair in front of the hearth. "Please, sit and warm yourself."

"Thank you, sir. Girls, come around and thank Mr. Chaves for his generosity."

Heppie went and made a curtsey, and Hannah nodded to the man as she held her baby close. Jessie hesitated and glanced around. James had stepped back to allow the women to approach Mr. Chaves. Ned and the other men ranged themselves at the back of the group. How did James know this man?

Jessie put away the question to ponder later and stepped forward. She thrust out her hand to shake his like a man would do and said, "Thank you, sir. We appreciate your hospitality."

Don Pedro took her hand and shook it, grinning broadly. "You are most welcome."

Jessie smiled, ducked her head, and turned away. The man's openhandedness puzzled her. *Why's he bein' so kind to us? We showed up unannounced and unexpected. How did he come to know James?* As she wiggled the questions around in her brain, Jessie moved over to stand beside her mother, who had sat down in an armchair.

Jessie rubbed her hands together and looked around the room. Hannah and Heppie were seated on stools close to the fireplace. George knelt on one knee beside Heppie, spreading his hands to the fire's warmth. Across the room, Don Pedro gestured toward a leather couch, and Robert and James took seats on it.

Jessie felt a touch on her elbow. She turned her head to meet Ned's gaze.

"Are you getting warm?" he asked. "I worried that your

fingers would get frostbit, not having gloves."

Jessie looked at her hands and waggled her fingers. "I reckon they're doing fine," she said. "Still a mite cold, but I've got feeling in them now. I was worried when they were numb."

Ned took Jessie by the elbows and turned her around to face him. He cupped his hands around one of hers and chafed it. "This will take the chill off, honeybunch," he said.

Jessie allowed him to rub her hands, first one, then the other, and back to the first. He moved his hands up her arm, and she felt a twinge of uneasiness. Ned was being overly friendly, especially with her mother sitting right there beside them.

"Ned," she murmured. "Leave off. I'm all warm now."

One of the corners of his mouth moved slightly downward. He opened it as though he were going to reply, but closed it again and dropped his hands from her arm. He nodded, and said, "As you wish."

Jessie rolled her eyes toward her mother, hoping he would take a hint. She wasn't sure Ma could see what Ned had been doing, with Jessie between them, but the touch of his fingers on her upper arms had unsettled her. Yes, she had promised to marry Ned, but that didn't mean he was permitted to become so familiar. He probably wanted to kiss her, but she hadn't allowed that intimacy. Only one man had kissed her, and— She put her hand to her lips. *Only James Owen.* She looked behind her. James sat on the couch across the room, his fingers twisting against his thighs. She could tell he wasn't listening to Don Pedro or Robert. He looked up, meeting her eyes.

She turned her head, feeling guilty as she pushed away her tumbling thoughts. She shuddered, aware of Ned's concerned eyes on her. Glancing sideways, she caught sight of a stool like the ones her sisters sat upon. She took a breath and smiled brightly up at the man who would be her husband.

"Ned, will you draw up that stool for me? I'm a bit weary."

"Of course," he said, and went to do her bidding. She bit her lip. *How can I forget about James Owen? He's always nearby.* She rubbed a cold spot on her arm. *How am I ever going to make a life with Ned if James stays on in Albuquerque?*

Ned put the stool at her feet and Jessie sank onto it. The leather seat had absorbed warmth from the room, and the heat felt comforting through her skirt and undergarments. "Thank you."

He settled down cross-legged on the floor beside her and jerked his head in acknowledgement of her thanks.

Words jumped out of Jessie's mouth when she noticed that Don Pedro and the other men had stood up. "Why is that man being so good to us?" She took a sharp breath, annoyed at herself for letting her thought free.

Ned looked surprised, then scowled. "He seems friendly with Mr. Owen. Maybe he owes him a favor."

Jessie shrugged. "I reckon there's no way of knowing."

"Honeybunch." Ned reached up and put his hand on her arm. "You appear puzzled at Mr. Pedro's kindness, but I reckon he won't do us any harm."

"I wasn't worried about harm coming to us. He's mighty generous to a pack of strangers."

James left the room, following a servant man. She yanked her eyes away from him, focusing on her betrothed.

Ned patted Jessie's arm. "Don't go twisting your brains into a knot, honeybunch. Sit there all comfy cozy, soak up the warm air, and quit thinking so hard."

Honeybunch? Is Ned going to call me honeybunch all our lives? Jessie shuddered. *I don't like that pet name.*

"You're shivering. Shall I rub your arms again?" Ned asked.

"No, no, I'm fine." She folded her arms across her chest. *Honeybunch? James never called me that. He had more sense.*

Drat! Why am I thinkin' about James again? She put her hand to her forehead and rubbed a spot above her right eyebrow. *Jessie, you hate and despise James Owen. Because of that, you gave your word to Ned to marry him, and that's all you need to think about.* She stopped rubbing her face, looked down at Ned, and gave him half a smile. *I reckon we'll do as well as most folks, pulling in the same harness, as long as he doesn't call me honeybunch!*

James sat at Don Pedro's invitation and looked at the other side of the room. Ned stood close to Jessie, chafing first one hand, then the other between his own. His hands wandered up her forearms, rubbing circulation back into them. Each intimate gesture felt like it drove a thorn into James's flesh. He wanted to leap up, cross the room, knock Ned Heizer on his backside, and take Jessie away from him.

This is how Carl felt, watching Ellen and me. A jolt of fire flashed through James's veins at the thought of the woman who had been betrothed to him, and had married his brother. *I tried so hard to forget Jessie, to learn to love Ellen.* He looked at his hands, twisted together against his legs. *I should have seen the way of it and given her up to Carl with a bit of grace. Now I've lost Jessie to a Yankee. No, worse than a Yankee. A Virginia turncoat.*

Don Pedro said something to him, but James couldn't tear himself away from his thoughts to answer. He looked across at the folks arranged around the fireplace once more. He realized Jessie's eyes were fixed on him, and he felt a rush of blood into his head. *She don't love him. She gave him a promise, but she don't love him. Just like Ellen promised to wed me, not givin' me her love with her word.* The bitter irony hit him like a physical blow, and he rocked backward in his seat. Grim truth took possession of his soul. *Jessie don't love him, but she's wary of me. I hurt her when I left her behind. Pa set me up to marry Ellen and I lost her to Carl, but later I did marry someone. A gal I didn't yet love.* He swallowed down the gall that had risen in his throat as he listed his sins against Jessie.

Now Don Pedro and Robert had risen to their feet, and James scrambled to stand.

"Gentlemen, you are weary. I am selfish to keep you from your beds." He addressed himself to a servant who had come into the hall. "Ramón, are the fires lit?"

"*Sí, señor. Todo está listo,*" said the man, and James mentally translated his words as assent. But he remembered *listo* as signifying bright or quick. That couldn't be right.

He screwed up his courage and asked, "Don Pedro, what does *listo* mean?"

"Ah *joven*, it can mean clever, but Ramón intends to say that all things are in readiness. If you will go with him, my young friend, he will take you to a sleeping room." He turned to Robert. "Please, if you will wait a moment longer, Ramón will bring you, your *señora*, and your little one to another." He turned back to include James. "We have many rooms here in the *hacienda*. We don't often have the opportunity to fill them with guests. This occasion is a great joy to me." He put out his hand and shook with James. "Thank you for coming."

As James followed Ramón down the long corridor, his thoughts turned to the girl he'd married. *Amparo, I came to love you dearly. What Brother Jeff told us gave me a lot of comfort. There's a way I can be with you again when I'm dead. But girl, there's something you got to understand. I'm still alive, and I want Jessie!*

Ramón opened a door and ushered James into a small bedroom with a fire burning at one end. He bowed slightly to James and left the room.

James went right to the bedstead and put his war bag down beside it. He stood above the bed, remembering how he'd thought his life was at an end when Amparo died. His body stiffened at the remembrance of laying her to rest. That ordeal was over, he reminded himself. Now, because of the new ideas he'd accepted, he could go on living. He could have hope.

I'll need to win Jessie back, he decided, and thought of how he'd gotten her to love him before. His cramped shoulders gradually loosened as he recalled the sweet days of courting Jessie, singing to her on the swing in her folks' backyard, kissing each one of her fingers between verses of his love songs. How long had it been since he'd raised his voice in song?

"I sang to Pa's Texas cows," he said aloud. "I never sang to Ellen, nor to Amparo, but I sang to those dim-witted cows."

He sank to his knees to offer up his nightly prayer, asking for calm in his soul and for a way to gain back Jessie's trust so he could win her from Ned.

They stayed the night, and the next day too, as the blizzard roared on for nearly twenty-four hours. Don Pedro had made sure everyone was comfortable in snug rooms of both the house and a guesthouse. The animals were housed in tight adobe barns and suffered no ill effects of the cold. The dog, after making the acquaintance of Don Pedro's dog pack, spent most of its time lying in front of the warm hearth.

When the storm blew itself out, James ventured from the house to look around. Where was the road? All signs of the trail they had traveled yesterday lay under deep snow. He went back into the house, stamping his boots on the tile floor.

Don Pedro met him in the great room and took him into his office, where a desk with a pile of ledgers stacked on a leather blotter sat comfortably close to a potbelly stove. He ushered

James to an armchair in front of the desk and went to a sideboard where stood a decanter of brandy and several glasses, one with an inch of liquid already in the bottom. "Such a storm we had, no? You will stay again this night." He offered James a drink.

Declining the liquor, James said, "We don't want to put you out, sir."

Don Pedro picked up his glass and took it to the desk, where he sat in a swivel chair. "*¡Ay, señor!* We enjoy our guests. You are no trouble. None whatsoever." He smiled and twitched his moustache. "You can help me improve my English."

James laughed at that. "I'm no great shakes as a scholar, sir."

Don Pedro chuckled. "You learned English at the knee of your *mamá, joven*. It makes a difference."

James nodded at that thought. "I reckon it does, at that. My ma tried her best to raise us up as good, Christian citizens, with a lot of country wisdom mixed into the ABC's."

"I think, *mi jovencito*, that your *mamá* is a very great lady." He lifted his glass. "Cheers, my friend James. That is what they say, *no*?"

"No. I mean yes. In polite company, that is."

Don Pedro sipped his drink and smiled again. "My language is somewhat confusing, *no*? When I say no at the end of a sentence, I ask you to agree with me."

James smiled. "Confusing, yes, but awful purty. Sometimes, when Amparo got goin' speaking your tongue, the sound was musical, like bells tinkling." He rubbed his chin. "I miss her. I miss her a lot, sir."

"I can see that, *joven*. If it helps to know it, when you lose a loved one, as the years go by, the pain is less. You begin to remember only the good times, to cherish the sweet memories." He stopped and gazed into his tumbler. "My youngest son died many years ago."

"I didn't know that, sir. I'm sorry for your loss."

"He was a good son, very obedient, very kind. Since that time, I have tried to live a worthy life to enable him to enter heaven." Don Pedro moved his hand through the air. "That is what the priest counseled me to do, along with giving liberally to the church, of course. Surely my sacrifices have made that difference to my son."

James held silence, wondering if Don Pedro's religious penance bore any relationship to the circumstances leading to his own marriage.

Don Pedro smiled. "My memories of my son are now sweet, as I said, *joven*, but it has been many years. I wish that you may find peace sooner than that."

"Thank you, sir. I have a question for you. Is it a common practice in your religion to pledge to do something to get your loved ones to heaven?"

"It is. Why do you ask?"

"I reckon that's what my wife took on her. Her pa was recently dead, and when we met in Colorado, she was mighty insistent that she had to marry someone, anyone. The blacksmith said she'd made a vow. Do you reckon she was worried about gettin' her pa to heaven?"

Don Pedro pursed his lips. After a long moment he spoke. "You have made clear some of those words you had me translate at La Fonda, *joven*. You married the young lady to fulfill her vow?"

"That seems to be the case, sir."

"So, you made a convenient marriage."

James tucked his chin into his chest, then looked up at Don Pedro and squared his shoulders. "I reckon. At first."

"You grew to cherish your wife?"

"That's so."

"Were her last days happy ones?"

"I—I reckon so, sir. They were for me."

"*Bien. Muy bien.* That is good. I renew my wish that you may find peace and comfort as time passes." Don Pedro stirred in his seat. "Will you remain alone? It is not good for a man to be alone."

"I'm thinking on that problem, sir. Turning so soon to someone new seems like bein' unfaithful to all Amparo meant to me."

"You must take your time to grieve, *joven*, but not too long. Find a good woman to marry."

"I'm workin' along those lines."

"There is someone in your company? The bold *señorita*, perhaps?"

"She's spoken for."

"Ah! But is she married? May not a woman dance with anyone she chooses until she is at last wed?"

James felt his body tighten at the thought of Jessie's marrying Ned. "Perhaps, sir. I'd purely hate to see her end up with the man who claims her hand."

"You know her well?"

A memory of Jessie's sweet lips under his swept over James. "She's a friend from long ago," he said, knowing he was blushing. He hoped his beard hid his reddened face.

"Ah." Don Pedro let his breath out in a long sigh. "More than a friend, I believe. Or so your face tells me."

James leaned over to hide it, clasping his hands between his knees.

"You have good words, my young friend. Use them. Convince her you are the better man."

James looked up. "I reckon I need to try." He rolled a shoulder. "My feelings are tied in knots, sir."

Don Pedro nodded, and suddenly he chuckled. "They will be forever, *joven*. Remember, women are incomprehensible. We cannot know their minds. We can only strive to bring them happiness."

James quirked his eyebrow. "Is that meant to cheer me, sir?"

Don Pedro laughed, picked up his glass, and drained it. "At the root of all, your heart is happy, my friend. You should not stay in misery." He got to his feet and James joined him. "I have enjoyed our conversation, but I must get back to work. Please, tell the others of my invitation to stay another night. If you cannot tell which way to travel, you must remain here a little while longer, yes?" Don Pedro's eyes twinkled. "We also say yes at the end."

James chuckled. "I'll tell them of your offer. Thank you, sir. *Your* heart is very large."

Chapter 37

The weather warmed during the night, and the travelers left the following morning, after expressing their gratitude to Don Pedro for his kind hospitality. The wagons jolted along the snow-covered path that led to the main trail. With the snow melting, fence posts marked the way to the main gate. Don Pedro had sent a rider ahead to greet them when they reached the portal, and he guided them along the track toward the road and saw them on their way.

The party spent two days pushing through windswept plains and snow-clogged passes. On the third day, James rode ahead of the wagons, checking the trail for any remaining drifts. He turned in his saddle to look at the wagons trundling along a half-mile behind him. The snow had held off, and they were making good time along the road. Glorieta Pass was ahead of them. Soon enough, they would be in Santa Fe.

As he settled straight in the saddle once more, James clucked to the sorrel horse, and it sprang forward at his urging. He wanted to see what was along the road. If he found water, their night camp would be much more pleasant. His thoughts drifted over his many camps, both in the South and here in the West. The night camp before the fight at the courthouse, waiting for the Yankees to come up to battle. The camp on the prairie where he watched his fiancée Ellen leave the fire with his brother Carl. The camp at Fort Union with Amparo in his arms and joy in his heart. His cheeks reddened at the memory of their lovemaking, sweet and tender. *Oh God!* he groaned to the heavens. *How can she be gone? How can I bear being in Santa Fe without her?*

He closed his eyes, letting the feeling of desolation sweep

over him. When it had reached his toes, he lifted his head and squared his shoulders. God had a promise of joy for him. Someday . . . someday Amparo would be his again, for all time! As his heart lifted, he stood in his stirrups and gave a shout of exultation, punching the sky with his fist.

The sorrel shied, and James sat in the saddle again, chuckling at his exuberance. *Ain't I the silly one! Robert is goin' to come see what I'm yellin' about, for sure.* He patted the animal's neck. "Sorry, boy. I didn't aim to startle you."

Several miles on, James found an inviting location for their night camp. Water flowed from a crack in the side of a wall of rock, creating a pool that invited travelers to stop and refresh themselves. A stand of oak trees offered shelter and wood. If he remembered correctly, Santa Fe was but ten miles or so along the trail, and they would be able to reach it tomorrow.

When he rode back among the wagons to let Robert know he'd found a campsite, James noticed Jessie walking along the trail, heedless of the mud, braid-crowned head bent down, a serious expression on her face. She carried a book and glanced at it from time to time. Her arm dropped to her side, and she bit her lip in concentration. Ned Heizer was nowhere in sight.

He remembered Don Pedro's advice, and his stomach flipped over. A short time ago he'd been thinking of Amparo. In a few minutes he'd have to turn his whole attention to Jessie while Ned was elsewhere. He gulped and went to find Robert.

When James had finished giving his report, he rode up beside Jessie. Dismounting, he walked beside her for a few paces, holding the sorrel's headstall in his right hand so the fractious horse was a good distance from the girl.

"Something worryin' you?" he asked.

She jumped and said, "Ah!" and he realized that she had been so engrossed in her thoughts that she hadn't known he was present.

"I didn't mean to alarm you," he said, putting out his hand to steady her. His fingers shook as he touched her back.

"James," she said. They no longer walked. He no longer touched her.

"Were you woolgathering?"

She looked at her feet. "Hannah loaned me the book Miss Becky gave her. I been reading in it about a young man named Nephi." She stopped talking, lifted her head, and looked sideways toward James.

He said, "Robert told me about him. He was a prophet."

"Robert told Hannah about your prophet, Brother Joseph, and the new one, Brother Brigham." She looked at her feet again. "She told me about them. I reckon it's a good thing to have a prophet."

"Are you studying on the Mormon religion, Jessie?" James's chest felt tight with anticipation.

She looked him square in the face. "Maybe."

"Is Ned going to permit that?"

Jessie's eyes went wide. "Ned's not my keeper! I can decide for myself what religion I'll follow."

James felt like dancing a little jig at her gumption, but restrained himself. Instead, he dropped his chin and looked at his boots. He thought maybe a smile was in order, to go with the "good words" he'd selected to say, and when he lifted his head, his lips curved upward.

"I'd show respect for your choices, if I was your man."

Jessie inhaled sharply.

He knew he'd surprised her. He could only hope she wasn't put off by his daring words. She began to walk again, and he strolled along beside her, matching his stride to her shorter one.

She stopped abruptly, and he turned to face her.

"You know I told Ned—"

"I know," he said, cutting her off. "You haven't married him.

Not yet." He let the bald fact hang in the air, and watched as she digested it.

Jessie lifted her chin.

James suppressed a groan. She intended to be contrary.

"You have other concerns on your mind," she said. "You love your wife."

"I do," he agreed, and instantly knew he'd stepped in a deep hole. Hush! That was the wrong thing to say.

Jessie's face went pale. She turned away and raised the book in front of her eyes. After a moment, she said in a voice as cold as the wind, "Good day, James," and walked away.

James almost felt icicles forming on his eyebrows. He mounted his horse and took his post at the front of the wagons again.

Ned rode up from the rear as soon as he noticed James Owen talking to Jessie. Before he reached the two, Jessie walked away, her face in a book, and Owen got on the sorrel and left. Much as he'd like to pound Owen's face into the mud, Ned felt relief at not having to confront him. The day's weather was ideal for traveling, cold and crisp, the only detriment being the muddy condition of the road. The sooner they got to Albuquerque, the sooner he and Jessie would be wed, and Owen would be out of the picture.

The thought of marrying Jessie made Ned grin, and with that expression on his face, he caught up to her.

"Afternoon, Jessie," he said. "Was Mr. Owen bothering you?"

She lowered her book and shrugged. "No. Not so much a body should take notice."

Her words, though spoken in a mild tone of voice, seemed like a reproof, and Ned felt his grin stiffen.

"Just you call out for me if he vexes you again," Ned said. "I don't want him hassling you."

Jessie looked at him. "He wasn't hassling me, Ned. Only conversing a bit."

"Well, don't let him become a problem." He rode along beside her as she put the book in front of her face again. "What's that you're reading?"

"A book Hannah lent me."

A guarded note in her voice made him crane his neck in an attempt to see the title.

"When did Hannah come by a new book? It's not from those Mormons, is it?"

Jessie closed the book and put it in her pocket. "What if it is?" She walked forward, not looking at him.

"You want to be cautious of those Mormons, honeybunch. They've got some strange ways."

"What are you sayin', Ned? They seemed like normal folk."

"Well, for one thing, I count baptizing a body entirely down in the water on a mighty cold day powerful strange."

"Hannah wanted that, washing away her sins."

"I'm glad you have more sense."

"Don't make light of Hannah."

She spoke sharply, and Ned drew back, regretting his choice of words.

"I'm sorry. I didn't mean to slight your sister. I misspoke."

They moved on in silence for a time. Finally Ned said, "Jessie, honeybunch, we're drawing nigh to Santa Fe. Don't you think we could get married there?"

The furious face she turned on him took him by surprise. Her words shook him no less.

"I told you we'd wait until we got to the end of the trail, Ned. You agreed. Let's not be hasty in changing things around."

"Albuquerque's not that far distant, Jessie. You wouldn't run much risk of, well, gettin' in a family way and bein' all discommoded."

Jessie's face flushed. "Don't linger here, Ned. I don't want a disagreement between us."

He nodded, and turned his horse aside, flustered at her show of temper. Whatever was making her irritable? *I'll wager Maggie Julander is more tractable*, he thought. *She would heed my cautions about odd folk.* Ned let his thoughts dwell on Maggie for a moment, then clapped his hand against his cheek. Maggie was already one of those "odd" folks. Maggie was a Mormon.

He rubbed his jaw. The stubble of his beard felt like sandpaper on his flesh. Jessie had spoken the truth: the Mormons had seemed to be normal, not according to the tales he'd heard of them having horns and tails and the like. He'd seen no horns coming from Maggie's head, no tail proceeding from her shapely— He stopped himself from following that notion, but his wayward body was already warm from thinking about the dark-haired girl.

What ails you? he castigated himself. *Jessie's going to be your wife, not Maggie Julander. After all the work it took you to win her over, you'd best fix your fancies on the prize.*

He called me honeybunch again! Jessie thought as she walked away from Ned. She repressed her desire to scream into a slight "Ahhh!" *Won't he ever learn?*

At once she felt ashamed. She wasn't being fair. She hadn't mentioned to Ned how much she disliked the pet name. She would tell him tonight. She reflected a moment, whether she'd also treated James a bit too sharply, and decided she had, although with good reason. *I did trick him into saying so, but he still cares for that dead Mexican girl.* She took a deep breath. *His wife. What business does he have making up to me, anyway, telling me how he'd respect my selections in life? I'll stick with Ned, thank you very much, James Owen. Ned loves me!*

Jessie spent the rest of the afternoon walking along with her nose in Hannah's book, fascinated by the account of ancient people taking a journey of their own. Once, she stumbled and fell, scraping a knee, but the burn of the abrasion seemed small compared to the trials she read about.

That evening, Ned came around and joined her where she sat beside the fire, mending a tear in her skirt. She didn't look up as she said, "I'm sorry I snapped at you today."

Ned patted her hand. "That's fine, honeybunch. I reckon we can wait to get married."

Jessie sighed and bit her lip. "I simply cannot abide you calling me honeybunch, Ned." She gave a shiver. "Can you please refrain from sayin' it?"

Ned must have seen her slight convulsion, for he put his arm around her, saying, "Are you taking a chill? Can I bring you a blanket or the like?"

"Ned," she persisted. "Stick to the point. Will you stop using that pet name?"

"Of course, honey—" He stopped himself abruptly. "I reckon I can if I'll put my mind to it." He grimaced. "Anythin' else about me you've taken a dislike to?"

Finished with the mending task, Jessie bit through the thread, wove the needle into the cloth and flexed her fingers. "Well now, you do seem a mite prickly when James Owen is around. I'd favor seeing you two on a more affable footing. He is your old friend."

Ned compressed his lips, then licked them. After a moment, he spoke in a rough voice. "That's not something I can promise. We don't see eye to eye."

"You can be civil to him."

Ned cocked his head sideways. "I reckon I can do that, so

long as he understands that when this journey's done, you're marrying me."

"I said so, didn't I?" Jessie replied, shrugging. "What James understands or doesn't understand is not in my power to guarantee."

Ned seemed satisfied, and after spending another quarter hour in Jessie's company, he went off to check the stock.

When Ned had gone, Jessie took the needle from the cloth and flicked it with her thumbnail as a thought came to her. *What does James understand? It's certain that he made a point to seek me out this afternoon. And the thing he said! If he was my man.* She brought her hand toward her face, remembering the long-ago touch of James's lips on hers, but she pricked herself with the needle and dropped it.

"Oh drat!" she said, cross with herself. She pulled a piece of wood out of the fire to light her search for the needle, then got on her knees and carefully felt over the ground beside her seat.

"What's amiss?" James Owen stood beside her. He leaned over and took the wood from her hand. "Have you lost something?"

His voice brought her upright, and her face flushed as she recalled where her thoughts had recently strayed. When she tried to speak, nothing issued from her throat. She cleared it and tried again, dismayed at the squeaky sound. "I dropped my needle. It's the only one I have."

"I'll help you look." He knelt down alongside her, holding the firebrand first high, then low. Though they spent several minutes going over the ground thoroughly, the needle remained lost.

"That is so vexing," Jessie said as she climbed to her feet, ignoring James's proffered hand. "But I thank you for making the attempt." She turned her head away from James and wiped her eyes, not wanting to share with him that her frustration had brought out tears. She glanced back at him just as he spoke.

"It's the least bit a man can do," he said with a lingering look at her, and walked away into the darkness. He left Jessie feeling faint and breathless, wondering what he'd meant to imply. The warmth in her vitals confirmed her notion that he'd continued his tactic from the afternoon. James had set out to court her.

Chapter 38

The next day, James arose early and checked the same ground he and Jessie had covered the night before. He found the needle and was about to seek out Jessie and give it to her when he noticed that Ned had her attention.

James gritted his teeth and carefully wove the needle into the inside lapel of his coat. He had plenty of time later to give it back.

He went to saddle the black mare, but he found that another horse had bitten her on the hock during the night, and she was not fit to ride without treatment and rest. He shook his head over the matter, patched up her wounds, and saddled the sorrel.

Just as James put his foot in the stirrup, the dog chased a raccoon into camp, and they both ran under the sorrel's belly. The horse began to buck, and James, losing his grip on the saddle horn, flew into the air.

He woke up some little time later to the sound of Heppie Heizer's screams, seeing Jessie's anxious face leaning over him. Actually, Jessie had two faces, and they swirled in front of him, along with those of the rest of the party who crowded about him.

"She-ah," he said, trying to rise up.

Jessie pushed him back to the ground with gentle hands. "Lie still," she said. "You busted your head."

"I've got to hunt." His voice came out in a croak, startling him. His fingers explored his head, and came upon a knot wet with blood. He looked at his fingers. There were several too many of them.

"Not today," she insisted, although her voice shook. She

turned away for a moment, saying to the crowd, "I'll get his bed made up, if some of you will carry him over."

James closed his eyes, heard the voices of assent. His head did ache. So did his back. He flexed his extremities and they all worked. None of his bones seemed broken. He opened his eyes again and raised himself up on one elbow. "Jessie?"

Again, she pushed him down. "James, don't you rise up and hurt yourself more. Stay still. Soon's I lay out your bedroll, Robert and George will bring you to it."

"Stop dancing around, Jess."

Her forehead—foreheads—furrowed in concern. "I'm still as a statue, James. It's your eyes that are rollin' around. Stay still, now. You'll be right as rain after you take a rest." Her voice still shook a bit.

He shut his eyes, dizzy from the effort of trying to sort out which image of Jessie was the true one. He knew he would regain his strength by and by, but right now he felt that emptying his stomach might settle it down. He fought the impulse. He'd mess up Jessie's dress. That wouldn't do. That wouldn't do at all. Six little beans, but his head hurt!

James sensed movement as Jessie stood up, but he kept his eyes closed. He remembered how much she disliked blood and wondered if she, too, was battling with her stomach. Still and all, she seemed determined to take care of him.

After a while, somebody grasped him under the arms and someone else grabbed onto his legs, and they lifted him off the earth. Except for a moment when his trousers bumped against the dirt, the trip seemed uneventful. Be that as it may, James was grateful to be on solid ground again. The swaying motion had increased his nausea to the point that he didn't know if he could keep down his breakfast or not.

He couldn't.

Hush, he hadn't felt this weak since, well since he'd been laid up in the jail in Pueblo Town.

A cool, wet cloth touched the corner of his lips, wiping away the muck he'd vomited up. He opened one eye. Jessie was beside him again. One-and-a-half Jessies, now, not two. Seeing any number of Jessies was a long sight better than looking up from a jail cot and seeing Rand Hilbrands's face.

"There now," Jessie said. "Feel better?"

James closed his eye and nodded, then wished he'd kept his head still. He breathed out to keep the nausea at bay. After a few moments, he whispered, "Anytime you're around, I feel better."

He felt a fleeting pat on his shoulder, a little shove. "Go on with you, James Owen! Here you lay with a broken head, and you're trying to sweet-talk me." Even as she spoke, Jessie lifted his head slightly and dabbed at the wound.

"Nah," he said, teetering on the edge of a black void. "No sweet talk. I want you around for all my life and always."

Jessie inhaled sharply.

James felt light as air, his head suspended in Jessie's still hands.

He felt the wash of her breath on his face as she let it out. Her fingers began to work quickly to bind up his head as she said, "I'm betrothed to Ned."

He opened both eyes, lifted his hand, and touched her cheek. He let his hand fall to his side. "He don't give you enough respect."

"James!" The whispered word exploded in the still air. "Is the pot calling the kettle black?"

He understood her meaning, and struggled against the looming darkness to find words to lay her worries to rest. "I've always found you irresistible, Jessie."

"How can you? You love that . . . Amparo girl." She bit off the words.

"Don't you care for Hannah and Heppie both?" James closed his hands into fists, fighting to stay conscious. "Luke and Max? Your ma and pa, as well?"

"Oh," she said, her voice a quiet squeak. "I reckon I do."

"I have mighty tender feelings for the two of you," he whispered. "But you're here, warm and alive. You can't say—flat out—you're not fond of me." His voice trailed off, but he made a final effort and added, "I need you."

James felt his hands relax. He let the blackness enfold him.

Jessie tried to say, "I'm not fond of you at all," but her voice wouldn't come out of where it lodged in her dry throat. When James's muscles went slack, she gasped and put her hand over his heart to see if it was beating. The rhythm was strong and regular under her palm. He still lived.

She hastened to finish the bandage around James's head, his last words echoing in her heart. *I need you.* What was a body supposed to say to that? Ned had never said he needed her. She didn't think he needed anyone to get along in life. He always carried an air of self-assurance. Maybe he could manage without her. *I said I'd marry him, though.* She rocked herself up onto her feet and looked down at James. *Even if James needs me, I gave my word to Ned.* A frantic feeling came over her, and she felt her face creasing into furrows. *Who do I need?*

Ned hurried over to take Jessie's arm when she moved away from James Owen's bedside. "Can't you let your ma tend to Owen?" he asked.

Jessie looked up at him and shrugged off his hand. "I'm handy at taking care of wounds," she said.

"What was all that talking about?" Ned felt his face settling into a frown.

"Ain't you full of questions."

"Yep. I see what's going on. He's always hounding you."

"The man took a fall, Ned. He's half out of his head. Concussed, I reckon. A little talk might keep him lucid."

"Just take care he doesn't hog all your time."

Jessie made a motion of denial with her hand. "I reckon I'll spend most of it catching up on the laundry. There's a good washing pool here. A day or two off the trail won't harm us."

"Well, I don't agree. We could pack Owen into a wagon and keep traveling on." He smiled down at Jessie. "I'm anxious to get to the end of the trek."

Jessie put her hand over her mouth. He could see a frown behind her hand. "Don't be unseemly, Ned."

"What's unseemly about wanting to get married? I do look forward to that, missie." He had more to say, but Jessie had started off, walking away from him. "Hey!" he said. "I mean no disrespect."

"Disrespect. Humph!" Jessie said, putting her head down and striding quickly toward her wagon.

Ned threw his hands into the air. "Jessie?" She didn't answer.

Another traveler came down the road late that afternoon, a slovenly man riding an ungainly roan horse and leading a string of three sorry-looking pack horses and a haltered gelding. Ned, who was pouring water from a bucket into the water barrel on the Bingham's wagon, watched the fellow ride up to the Bingham party's encampment. Robert strode out to meet him, and the man asked for permission to stay nearby. Robert gave it.

The stranger settled his animals for the night before he wandered over to Mrs. Bingham's fire when suppertime drew near. Ned, still hauling water, saw him approach.

"Howdy, ma'am," the stranger said, stopping and tipping his beat-up felt hat to Mrs. Bingham. "My name's Lester. Alphonse Lester. I have a clutch o' hen fruit here I'd be willing to trade for a meal." He held up a once-blue bandana, lumpy with eggs, and looked around the camp, counting the people with little nods of his round head. "They won't stretch for omelets to feed your kin, ma'am, but you could make a nice cake with 'em."

"Mister Lester, set down and take a load off your feet," replied Mrs. Bingham. "I ain't seen eggs in a long while. Fresh, are they?"

"Two days old, ma'am. I traded for them back a ways."

She tapped her nose with one finger. "You've had them two days. How long did they sit before you acquired them?"

"Oh no, ma'am. They're next thing to fresh. I saw them laid, bunked down in the stable as I was." He scratched his nose with his free hand and added, "I'm a trader, traveling these parts, making one trade here, another trade there. Folks know I'll be around from time to time."

Mrs. Bingham nodded. "As the eggs are reasonably fresh, I reckon we can deal. That is, if you don't mind beans and venison for supper."

"I'd be mighty pleased with beans and venison, Mrs. . . ?" The word hung in the air.

"Bingham. Mrs. Joseph Bingham."

Mr. Lester nodded. "Pleased to acquaint myself with you," he said, handing over the bandana.

"Ned," she called over her shoulder. "Would you be so kind as to stow these in the grub box?"

Ned took two steps and relieved Mrs. Bingham of the parcel. "Surely, ma'am," he said, not taking his eyes off the trader as he did her bidding.

"Your son, ma'am?"

She hesitated, then said, "Near kin."

Ned approved of her not spelling out the relationship. It was none of the man's business.

Mr. Lester took a seat on the ground, again looking at the camp, his eyebrows raised in a speculative manner.

Ned thought the man was a bit too interested in his surroundings. A sense of unease raised prickles on the back of his neck. Instead of moving off toward the spring to get more water, he grabbed a stick, sank down on his haunches, and stirred the fire. When he got up, he noticed that Mr. Lester's eyes were fixed on one location. He looked in that direction. Jessie sat beside James Owen's bed, blowing on a spoonful of gruel. She'd unbraided her hair after wearing it up all day, and it rippled down her back like a waterfall made of sun-kissed wheat.

"Now that's a mighty comely sight!" Mr. Lester said, and Ned whipped his head back around toward the man.

The hungry look on the trader's face surprised Ned, and his distrust strengthened. He hovered around the fire, looking for tasks to keep him in camp so he could watch the trader.

After supper, instead of getting to his feet and going to his own campsite, Mr. Lester drew a pipe out of his pocket and lit it. Ned gritted his teeth. *Will the man never leave?*

"Are you folks traveling far?" Mr. Lester asked. "Winter ain't the best time for making good progress."

Robert answered him. "We're nearly to our destination."

"Oh, would that be Santa Fe?"

"No."

Ned felt his respect for Robert Fletcher growing. Being closemouthed was the proper way to treat this interloper.

"The hot springs down yonder?" Mr. Lester tilted his head and gestured with it in a westerly direction.

"We've got kin waiting for us where we're going." Robert had a slight frown on his face.

He's getting irritated with the man, Ned thought. *Good.*

"Hmmm," said the man. "I can see you folks been having a hard time of it. You know, I'm a trader. Maybe I can help you on your way."

"How's that?" Robert asked.

The man leaned back. "You're short a horse. I have a nice gelding I picked up along my way. A first-rate draft animal. Strong. Pulls good, and all day long, sweet as you please. You wouldn't go wrong trading for it."

George bent forward. "We don't have much in the way of goods. What kind of trade are you talking about?"

"You have something here in camp that brightens my eyes." The trader motioned with his head. "Sitting right over there. That young gal." He stared at Jessie.

Ned bounded to his feet and stood above the man. "You disgust me," he shouted. "Get out of our camp!"

Chapter 39

A few days later, James led the party into Santa Fe. They parked the wagons in the plaza, the historic end of the trail from Missouri.

Robert came up to James and said, "You've been here before. Where's the best place to buy foodstuffs? We're low on flour."

James moved his head carefully to look around and get his bearings, relieved that his head had stopped swimming during the day's travel. "I wasn't here long. Just a couple of days." He pointed. "If I remember right, there's a mercantile shop two or three blocks over."

"Do you need anything? I'd like the company," said Robert.

"I'll go with you. I have a few things to buy."

"Good. Ned and George want to stay with the wagons, in case that trader they ran off shows his face in town."

"What was that all about, anyway?" James asked. "I was fairly well out of touch when the yelling started."

As they walked along, Robert told James about the disgraceful proposal the trader had made. "Ned was all for dumping him in the pond, but George talked him out of it. He said it would ruin the water for all time."

"Six little beans!" James exclaimed. "Did Miss Jessie find out what was going on?"

"I believe young Luke teased her about it."

"I wish I'd been up to pounding the fellow. Sounds like my nemesis did a good job on his own."

Robert's face took on a quizzical look. "The man's manners were lacking, that's sure, but what's your interest in the subject?"

James didn't say anything for a couple of minutes. His teeth tugged at his bottom lip. He released it and said, "I want Jessie back."

"What?" Robert stopped in the street.

James turned around to face him. He nodded. "I want to marry her."

"But you've recently lost a wife. Isn't it early to want another?"

James took a step closer to Robert. He kept his voice low when he replied. "I reckon some would say that. It's a fact I'm not finished grieving for Amparo, but I'm running out of time, Rob. Heizer's anxious to marry once he gets to Albuquerque." He smacked his leg. "I care too much for Jessie to let her go into a marriage she's dreading."

"Dreading? Are you sure?"

"Watch her with Heizer. They quibble all the time. There's not the air of a loving couple hanging about them."

Robert began to walk again. "So you're rescuing her?"

"No." James strode along beside Robert for a few steps before he spoke again. "It's not that at all. I have a great . . . tenderness for Jessie. I regret leavin' her behind when I came west. I took the coward's way, lettin' Pa run roughshod over our wishes."

"Your pa's a mighty commanding figure of a man."

"He is that."

"Hard to stand up to a man so strong."

James snorted. "I'm shamed that I didn't. Now I have a chance I never thought would come my way. I need to win Jessie back."

"To ease your pride?"

"No. I love her so much I ache inside. I can't twiddle my thumbs and let Heizer have her."

Robert slapped James on the back. "Luck to you, my friend."

James responded in kind. "Thanks." He gestured toward a side street. "Down that way is the grocery shop."

James drifted around the store, his heart turning into a leaden lump in his chest. He'd been in this place only weeks before, stocking up on food to make the trip back to his pa's homestead— with Amparo. The small span of time since that occasion held such a range of shattered hopes, broken dreams. Now he was here again, harboring altered expectations, different desires. *Hush! Life ain't easy.*

He mentally shook himself, noting how he'd been blessed during the past weeks. *I never thought to see Jessie again. Nor to take upon me a new religion with power and promises.* The sweetness of the two events drove the hard lump from his chest. *I'm a lucky man. Besides Ma, there are no finer women on earth than Amparo and Jessie.*

James trailed his fingers over a bolt of cloth and smiled at his fanciful notion. *I don't have no guarantee yet that Jessie will have me*, he thought.

An idea hit him, and he felt inside his coat for the needle he'd pinned there a few days before. It was in place. The fall from the horse hadn't dislodged it. What was it Jessie had said? This was her only needle. He grinned and started toward the back of the store.

Ned watched Robert Fletcher and James Owen walk back into the camp with parcels. He limped toward where Jessie stood near the fire, helping her mother with supper. He wanted to be nearby in case Owen had any thoughts of approaching her. "Whew," he said to himself. All this watch-care over his intended bride took up a lot of time and energy. If only he could be certain Jessie wouldn't have her head turned by Owen's fancy words.

"Evening, Jessie," he said when he reached her side.

"Evening yourself, Ned." Jessie stirred the soup in a large cauldron hanging on a tripod

"Is there anything you need? Water?"

"No, Luke filled the barrels this afternoon."

"That's good. He's a hard worker."

"Aren't we all," Jessie answered.

Ned bit his lip as silence fell upon them. How come it was so hard to strike up a conversation with Jessie? After all these years, surely they had a lot to talk about. Mrs. Bingham was in earshot, though, as well as Heppie and Hannah, and strolling down memory lane didn't seem the thing to do with a passel of listeners. Neither he nor Jessie had been out of camp to explore the town, so that didn't offer a new topic of discussion.

He tried again. "Nice sky."

"It does appear to have a clear light," Jessie said.

Ned could only agree. He looked around. Owen stood over his pack, giving him a look of exasperation. *Good!* He would remain here whether he could find a task to do or not. Anything to thwart Owen's desires.

He took a step away from Jessie and squatted near the edge of the fire, spreading his hands to it as though they were cold. They weren't, but no one needed to know that. He rubbed them together, acting out his role for the women.

"You should wrap up in a quilt if you're cold, Ned," Jessie said.

"No need," he said. "I'll be comfy in a minute or two."

Just then, James Owen approached the fire and began to whistle an old tune. Ned looked up in time to see shock registering on Jessie's face, driving out the color. *What's going on?* Ned wondered. *What does "Annie Laurie" mean to her?*

"Ned," she said, her voice urgent. "I believe I need more firewood. Please, would you fetch me a big ol' log?"

He looked at the woodpile a few yards away. "You have wood."

"I need more. Please?"

He nodded and stood up, knowing he was being sent away. *Damn James Owen!* he thought. *What's he got up his sleeve?* He glowered at his rival as he passed him. Owen smiled back and took a step closer to Jessie.

As soon as Ned walked off, Jessie turned to James and hissed, "Don't be foolish, James Owen."

In reply, he softly sang, "'Maxwelton's braes are bonnie where early falls the dew. And 'twas there that my fair Jessie gave me her promise true.'"

Jessie felt a touch faint. "That's all past and gone."

He shook his head and continued in a voice so hushed he almost whispered the words: "'Gave me her promise true that ne'er forgot shall be. And for love of my fair Jessie I'd lay me doon and dee.'"

"Stop it. Ma will hear you."

"Does that matter?"

"You left me behind." Jessie tried to turn away, to give him her back, but she made the mistake of looking at his eyes, and a quiver ran through her body, rooting her in place.

"I own to being foolish several times in my life, but never so much as then. When I heard you tell me to go, I lost heart."

James stood so near that Jessie could have reached out and touched his cheek. She struggled with that impulse as he continued. "I was a fool to listen to you and to Pa. I should have stayed with you or fought Pa to bring you along."

"James." She shook her head in confusion as her insides churned. *Ned loves me, Ned loves me*, she repeated several times in her mind. *James is simply jealous.*

"I have something for you," he said.

She shivered at the intensity of his voice.

He pointed to the center of the plaza. "Meet me at the town

well after supper, and I'll give it to you."

Before she could refuse, James was gone, striding away with a confident air as he whistled the refrain to "Annie Laurie" again.

"Six little beans!" she muttered, using one of James's favorite exclamations. Curiosity zipped around the corridors of her mind as she tried to imagine what James would bring her. It suggested first one thing, then another. *If James is really jealous* . . . She gave the soup a vigorous stir and knew that, despite her misgivings, she would be at the well.

After supper, Jessie's reservations nearly got the better of her curiosity.

James only wants to turn your head, she told herself as she dried her hands on her apron. *If he cared a fig, he would—* Her thoughts in disarray, she wondered what he *would* do if he truly loved her. Well, one thing was clear. If she didn't go meet him, she never would know what he had in mind. For sure, she wouldn't receive whatever he had bought for her in town.

At last, curiosity won out. Jessie took off her apron, unbraided and brushed out her hair, and slipped away from the camp.

Although the plaza was large, it took her only a few moments to find the town well, with its washing troughs for accommodating laundry day. She spotted James sitting on the edge of one of the troughs, a lighted lamp at his side. She stopped for a minute, a flood of memories making her heart leap into her throat and constrict her breathing. She almost smelled lilacs. *No!* she thought. *I don't want to remember that!* She nearly turned to run, but she must have made a sound. James looked up and saw her, and he smiled, lamplight caressing the creases on the lit side of his face. *If he says my name, I'll be lost*, she thought.

"Jessie," he called. His voice matched his smile.

"Hello," she managed to say, wanting to run and hide at the same time that she desired above all things to be swept away by her memories to a past that should have been her present.

James got up and approached, took her hand, and brought her to the circle of light. "I wasn't sure you'd come," he said. "I'm mighty pleased you did."

His smile had not faded. In fact, it seemed to Jessie to be wider than before, brightening his eyes. Even so, he seemed oddly vulnerable.

She hesitated before answering. She didn't want to seem petty, but finally the only thing she thought of to say was, "You said you had something for me."

James laughed. "I did say that." He let go of her hand, indicated that she should sit down and, when she had done so, sat beside her.

He reached inside his coat and wiggled something loose from the facing of the lapel. "I found your needle," he said, and held it out so she could see it. A short tail of thread trailed from the eye.

"You did?" Jessie smiled. "You found it! Thank you, James."

Instead of giving it to her, he leaned back and thrust his free hand into his pocket, bringing out two small objects. One was a packet of pins that he transferred to his other hand. "I didn't want you to lose the needle again, so I bought you this." He unfolded a scrap of cloth to reveal that it was pierced with three bright new needles. "It's sort of a sewing kit, without the scissors and thread." He paused. "Maybe I should have gotten you those too?" His voice trailed off, uncertain. He asked, "Did I do wrong?"

Jessie held herself very still, afraid to answer, but her immobility was in vain. His thoughtfulness made tears spring to her eyes. She wiped at them, but they trailed down her cheeks. She looked up. The anxious, little-boy expression on his face was too much to bear. She began to sniffle, caught in a whirlpool of gratitude, tenderness and affection.

"Hush! Now I made you cry," James blurted out, his face crumpling.

"No! You done . . . That was so sweet. You didn't have to. But you did."

"Don't cry, Jessie. This is all backward. I wanted you to be happy."

"I am," she bawled, unable to stop the tears and the emotions that fed them.

"But you're cryin'."

"Yes," she agreed. She wished James would put his arms around her, but sensed that his confusion had him spellbound. She had no claim on asking him to comfort her, so she kept on crying, and he kept making soothing sounds. He didn't touch her, which she realized was because he had his hands full of prickly objects. That thought struck Jessie as funny, and she began to laugh.

A moment later, James joined her in merriment. He stuck the found needle into the cloth with the others, and put the cloth and the pins into her hand. "Ah, Jessie," he said, after one long spell of hoots and chortles, "It's mighty nice to laugh with you. I wish you'd marry me."

Jessie shot to her feet. That would not happen, much as she wished it could. She'd promised— *Oh Lordy, why did I promise Ned I'd marry him? Did he hear us laughing? He'll come over and find us making merry together!*

"I must go," she said, and gathering up her skirt in one hand, ran back toward the camp.

Chapter 40

The party left Santa Fe the next morning amid flurries of snow that continued intermittently throughout the day. They made ten miles before coming to a water hole edged with white. Ned went to fill his canteen, but James warned him off and led the wagons past the water. When James had left, Ned turned his horse and approached the hole. He was kneeling to get water when James rode up.

"Don't drink that!" he called.

Ned got to his feet, feeling the rise of irritation in his stomach. What gave James Owen the right to tell him where to whet his thirst? "What's your problem, Owen?" He balled his hands into fists.

"That's bad water. You don't want to drink it."

"Who says I don't?" Ned blustered.

"See that white rime?" James was off his horse, kicking the coating that rimmed the water tank.

"A little ice. Maybe snow."

"No. It's alkali. I saw the like in Texas."

"I've never heard of it." Ned bent over, scooped up a handful of water, and drank it. The taste was noxious, but he couldn't spit it out in front of his rival. He did allow some to dribble out the side of his mouth.

"No!" James exclaimed, and pulled Ned away from the water tank. "It poisons the water."

Ned swallowed, then shook himself away from James's hold. "It's not so bad."

"Don't be a fool, Heizer." James got the canteen from his saddle and held it out to Ned. "You'd best get some good water into you and dilute that mouthful you took. You're going to be sick, but you probably won't die if you'll do that."

"I'm never sick," Ned shouted, angered at being called a fool. Then he fell to his knees and retched, his mouth burning. He heard James's sharp inhalation of air. Ned cursed himself for letting his ill humor lead him to reckless behavior. When he'd finished throwing up, he wiped his mouth with a shaking hand and whispered, "You have the right of it. Will you help me get on my horse?"

"Gladly," James replied, offering the canteen again. "First, drink deep."

Ned took the canteen, washed out his mouth, and spit. He took another mouthful and swallowed it, regretting his hardheadedness as he realized the alkali water had burned his throat as well as his mouth. He chugged down the liquid in the canteen, mentally blessing James Owen. The man could have shrugged his shoulders and left him to do what he wanted, but he stepped in and tried to prevent the injury.

Ned handed back the canteen and said, "I am a fool. I'm beholden to you."

James nodded once, but didn't say anything as he helped Ned get on his horse.

By the time Ned dismounted in camp that evening, he knew he was in trouble. He'd been dealing with retching and the trots ever since the incident at the water hole. James Owen had always seemed to be nearby to help him get on and off his horse, never saying much, but assisting when he was needed.

Ned slid to the ground, unsteady on his feet, wanting to collapse into a heap, but knowing he couldn't do that before he found privacy for another bout of affliction. He limped toward a stand of trees at the edge of the clearing, one hand clutching his cramping belly. Beads of sweat trickled down his cheeks. *Where's George when I need him?* he thought.

"Heizer?" came James Owen's voice from behind. "Do you need aid?"

"No," Ned groaned. "Send my brother."

"I'll do that," James said. Ned heard the crunch of his boots on dry twigs as he retreated toward the camp.

Ned went about his business as best he could while clinging to a tree to keep from falling. When he'd finished an attack of dry heaves, he fell on his hands and knees and gave himself up to the weakness that caused his entire body to quiver. A moment later, George came running through the grove.

"Ned? Where are you?"

"Here," he said, his voice rasping in his ears. "I'm here."

George hauled him up and got himself under Ned's arm. "Holy Nellie, what ails you?"

"Bad water," Ned managed to whisper.

"Water? You didn't drink that alkali poison Owen pointed out, did you?" George half walked and half carried Ned toward the camp.

"Uh-huh."

"No wonder you look like a calf with the scours. Let's get you bedded down. I'll ask Mother Bingham if she has a remedy."

"It burned my throat," Ned muttered.

"Don't talk. Heppie! Miss Jessie!" George called. "Make up a bed for Ned. He's bad off."

Ned winched as George pulled him over rough ground at the edge of the clearing. "Hold up. Belly hurts," he said, panting.

George held him while he fought against the gripping pain in his gut. Thankfully, his body had run out of perfidious fluids, and after great effort, he found enough strength to assist in getting himself into camp.

After a time, he found himself lying in his blankets with

Jessie pressing a cool, wet cloth to his cracked lips. "Oh, Ned," she exclaimed. "Didn't you know that water was bad?"

He shook his head a fraction of an inch, without strength to speak.

Jessie said, "Thank you, Ma," and twisted to accept something from Mrs. Bingham. She put a spoonful of liquid against his mouth. "Sip this. Ma said slippery elm and chamomile will ease your burns. She knows her remedies."

Ned accepted the liquid and felt it slide down his throat as he swallowed. Jessie spooned it into his mouth until the cup was empty, murmuring all the while, "Is that better? Does it soothe?" without waiting for an answer. She set the cup aside and began to wipe the sweat from his forehead with her cloth.

After a while, she patted him on the shoulder and said, "You need to sleep. Rest will restore you." Then she began to croon a lullaby in a soft voice.

A lullaby? Something about having Jessie sing him to sleep disturbed Ned, but he drifted off before he could work it through.

Robert decided they would remain camped until Ned had recovered. They spent the next two days tightening harnesses and mending clothes.

Ned drifted in and out of sleep, hearing scraps of conversation, feeling the soothing slippery elm tea roll down his throat, knowing Jessie came to tend him when she noticed he was awake. Where was she when he was asleep? Letting James Owen court her?

Jessie hadn't accompanied him to the trees. George, or occasionally, James, had done that duty. She'd know what he had to do and when he had to do it, though, and that unsettled Ned. A body should have some privacy, even from the girl who loved him.

When he awoke from a nap on the afternoon of the second day, Ned's mood matched the dark gray clouds overhead. The only light in the sky diffused through the clouds on the western horizon. *Late afternoon*, he thought. He assessed his health. His mouth and throat no longer burned. His bodily functions had regularized. *Tomorrow we can push on*. He looked around. No one had noticed he was awake. *Good. Time I proved I'm up to traveling.*

Ned threw the quilt aside, got to his feet and, wavering just a tad, limped away from the camp. Nature was calling, and he sure wasn't going to let Jessie know how unsteady he felt. He couldn't put himself through any further discomfiture.

How much frustration can a man stand? he asked himself. *Does Jessie care for me or not? You'd think James Owen hung the moon, the way she talked to him when he was laid up. "James, don't you rise up and hurt yourself," and "I blew the heat out of this gruel for you." Sounded like a cat purring, her voice all soft and sweet as cream, like that Maggie talked to me.*

He stopped short. Maggie. What made him think of Maggie Julander? Memories popped into his mind. Maggie. Tall—almost as tall as Ned himself. Slim, with dark hair falling over her shoulders like a waterfall in deep shadows. Sun-browned arms. That Mississippi lilt to her voice. The yearning way she had looked back toward him when the Mormons left. *No, Ned*, he told himself. *You're going to marry Jessie.*

"Jessie," he moaned as his mind reviewed the past days when he'd lain abed, mouth and throat burning until she'd brought him the tea. *She sang me lullabies. Lullabies! Same as she did Luke! I'm not her man. I'm her big brother!*

He chewed on that thought for a moment as he took care of his business. *Does she love me? Maybe. Maybe like I'm her protector, yes, her big brother. I've looked out for her for years, made sure she didn't come to any harm ever since we were youngsters. Don't we suit each other?*

A biting question entered his thoughts. *Do I love Jessie?* "Of course I do!" he exclaimed to the wooded landscape. "There's no doubt of that."

"Ned?"

He stiffened at Jessie's voice behind him.

"What's there no doubt of?"

"Jessie," he said, his brain whirling with the enormity of the idea that came upon him, the vastness of the consequences of what he knew he was going to do. He turned slowly to face her, the girl he thought he'd adored forever. The bottom seemed to drop out of his stomach. "Jessie," he said again. "We've been friends for a long time."

He watched the expressions changing on her face. Wariness. Doubt. Fear. Knowing he brought her to fear was like a punch to the head. He swallowed hard.

"Jessie. You don't have to marry me."

"What?" Her face reflected horror. "Ned, what are you sayin'?"

What would be better? Blaming himself or her? He watched Jessie shaking her head back and forth. Himself. That was the right notion. He squared his shoulders. "I'm releasing you from your promise."

"No. No no no! You can't do that! We're getting wed soon. When we get to Albuquerque." Her hands balled into fists, almost as if she would strike out at him in another minute.

He gulped. "I don't love you, Jessie. Not that way."

"You're daft! You do love me. You always have."

"Like a friend, Jessie. Like a good habit."

"A habit! I'm not a habit. I'm your—I'm almost your wife. You can't simply shuck me off like a dirty shirt."

"I'm not shucking you off, Jessie. I'm letting you go. You fancy James Owen over me."

"James Owen? What's he got to do with anything? He—I don't—he don't care a fig for me!"

Ned shook his head. "You're hiding behind me, Jessie. Using me to keep Owen at a distance so you won't get hurt again." He felt a slow burn of anger rising in his gut. "All a body has to do is look at his eyes to know he worships you."

"No." Her voice took on a mournful tone. "He loves that dead wife."

"He loved you first, dammit!" He stood as tall as he could, considering that his soul was bent over, crouching and curling into a ball at having to admit the truth. "Get it into your head, Jessie. We're done. James Owen has a better claim on you. He knows it and now I know it."

"I don't know any such thing! I won't let you throw me over."

He didn't see the slap coming, and it snapped his head to one side, stinging his face and his dignity.

Anger flared in him. "I should have traded you for the gelding," he said. At the look on her face, he compressed his lips and regretted his words, but they were in the air. He couldn't take them back.

"I hate you," she said, flinging the phrase like another slap.

"Good. You won't want to marry me." Ned turned and started toward the camp, his harsh thoughts blinding him to his surroundings. The last thing he knew was a tremendous pain at the back of his head, accompanied by a flash of red behind his eyes.

James heard the scream, recognized the fear in it, knew it was Jessie's voice. She'd slipped into the woods, following Ned Heizer. As James jumped up and headed toward the trees he wondered what was happening between them to make her shriek like that. Even Heizer wouldn't—

He almost stumbled over Ned's body. That raised the short hairs. *Hush, where's Jessie?* Her cries had been cut short as though someone's hand had clamped over her mouth. He peered into the trees ahead, and started as the old dog rushed past him, growling deep in its throat. He ran forward, keeping it in sight. George and Robert raised a cry behind him as they discovered Ned.

James heard a muffled wail ahead and to his left, and he turned in the direction of the sound. "Jessie," he hollered. "I'm coming!"

Whoever had taken Jessie moved through the woods at a quick pace, and James wondered if he was in a race with a horseman. Fear gripped his heart with a tight fist, but he dug deep into his strength and ran faster, dodging around trees, hurdling fallen logs, slapping brittle hanging branches away from his face.

Jessie screamed again. A man's harsh voice told her to shut up, but she disobeyed him, giving James a beacon to run toward.

Time had no meaning as he fought his way through the vegetation, his chest heaving, the puckered scar on his side burning in agony. *Jessie!*

He caught sight of her white apron through the screen of tree trunks. She was just ahead, beyond that copse of oaks. She struggled with a stout man on horseback. *Is that the trader?* James gulped air, found his second wind, and sped toward them.

The dog was barking, growling. A horse screamed, reared as the dog nipped at its legs. Jessie was falling, crying out as the man landed on top of her.

~*~*~

Oh God, oh God, oh God, Jessie prayed. *Not like Hannah!* She flailed with her elbows, scrambling from under the man's heavy body. *I won't let him!*

The man grabbed her ankle, dragging her toward him. She bent her other knee and kicked at him. He let go for just a moment, then clutched at her again before she could get free. He stood up and pulled her to his feet, swearing at the fleeing horse. She shrieked, and he put his hand over her mouth once more.

"None of that!"

Jessie shuddered as her captor yanked her along, kicking at the dog that nipped him. She'd been angry before this brute hauled her onto his saddle, angry at Ned for his imprudent, thoughtless words, for jilting her after all this time. Now she felt the anger rise in her again, beating back the fear that had partially paralyzed her brain.

She bit the man's hand, grinding her teeth into the flesh, tasting the brine of his blood. She gagged, and her teeth lost their grip as the man thrashed his arm in pain.

Despite having to take a second to spit out the trader's blood, Jessie grabbed at the man, wrapped her arms around his waist, and hung off him, a dead weight, trying to hinder his progress until James could catch up. The man tripped, flailed around, and halted, trying to beat at the dog with a club.

She'd stopped him, she realized, triumph surging through her body. She had the upper hand. She and the dog, she recognized, as it tore at the man's leg. Because of her efforts at hampering the trader, his stupid club wasn't having much effect on the dog.

James burst between two saplings and skidded to a halt. Jessie laughed at the astonished look on his face.

He launched himself into the fray, hitting the man over and over with his fists, and getting a glancing blow on his head from the club for his troubles.

The sight of blood streaming down from James's scalp almost choked her, but it didn't seem to deter him from playing the hero. He soon overpowered the man, bringing them all down to the ground in a heap.

"Jessie, turn him loose," James said.

She unwrapped her arms from the man and spit again, shuddering, but she wanted to laugh at James's commanding tone. She and the dog had got the best of the trader.

"*¡Quita!*" he told the dog. "Get off there."

Jessie scrambled away, and the dog sat on its haunches, still growling.

As James lugged the man to his feet, he said, "See if you can find his horse. Bring a rope."

"You ain't gonna hang me?" yelped the man.

"What outlandish notion took hold of your senses?" James shouted at the trader. "You can't kidnap a woman!"

"Your head!" Jessie said, reaching up with a corner of her apron to dab at the blood pouring down James's cheek. "You're bleedin' all over."

"Never mind my head. Get me a rope."

"I wasn't going to hurt her. I only wanted a bit of female companionship," the man whined.

"You picked the wrong female," James said, twisting the trader's hands behind his back. "She's mine."

Jessie sucked in her breath, not sure if she was annoyed at James's statement, or overjoyed.

After they got the trader to camp, Jessie stood on one side of the fire, patching up James's scalp wound. Hannah and Heppie huddled together on the other, working over Ned. Jessie noticed that as Heppie twisted to pick up Ma's remedy basket, a small round lump stuck out from her belly. *Heppie? With child?* She sighed. How long would it be before her turn came? Ned didn't want to be her husband. Was James in earnest, or had he merely been flirting with her?

Robert and George stood sentinel over the trader, who slumped on the ground nearby, his hands tied behind his back.

"What do we do with him?" George asked.

"We can't let him go." Robert scowled at the ground. "He's apt to go looking for another young lady to prey on."

James said, "Let's take him in to Albuquerque and let the law deal with him. We're only three days out."

Ned roused himself, shaking his head a bit. "Santa Fe's closer."

"We've passed Santa Fe," James said.

"I'm going that way," Ned replied in a quiet voice. "I'll take him with me."

George walked over. "What do you mean? We're bound for Albuquerque."

Ned got to his feet. "Y'all are bound for Albuquerque. I'm headed the other way."

Jessie felt James go still under her hands. As she listened to the hubbub of voices raised in denial, a sick feeling formed a knot in her stomach. *He knows Ned's leaving me.*

She turned her head, willing Ned not to continue, not to shame her, but he looked her way and pressed on. She held her breath.

"Miss Jessie and me ain't right for each other. I was wrong to hound her into giving me her pledge." He spoke to her. "I beg you to forgive me." He paused for a moment, waiting.

Ned's gracious words brought her no dishonor, no embarrassment or disgrace. She recognized his gift of freedom, and managed a nod and a thankful smile as the knot in her stomach untied.

Ned returned the smile, one side of his mouth tilting higher than the other. He faced the others again. "There *is* a little gal in the Mormon bunch I reckon is right for me. I aim to catch up to them and see if she feels the same."

George spoke up. "Are you sure, Ned?"

"Sure as I'll ever be."

"Well, brother," George said softly, "let's get you some provisions together so you can leave in the morning."

Jessie looked down at James and noticed that her fingers were covered in his blood.

He caught the direction of her gaze and picked up one of her hands. "I thought blood made you sick," he said.

Jessie ducked her head. "Not yours, it appears."

James got to his feet and pulled her away from the camp into the trees.

As Jessie went with him, she realized that his manner was much different from that of the young man who had paid her court in that faraway town in the Shenandoah Valley. His soul had grown. When the horse bucked James off, he had struggled to stay conscious long enough to convince her of how vast love could be. "I have mighty tender feelings for the two of you," he had said of her and Amparo, and she knew it was true.

There would always be Amparo, but she had left Jessie a gift. Because of her, James's heart was larger, deeper, big enough to hold Amparo and Jessie too.

James stopped and turned to face Jessie, his eyes glowing with intense feeling.

"Marry me," he whispered. "Soon as we get to town."

Joy flooded over her, wrapping her in warm swirls of emotion. She was free to say yes. She nodded, slowly at first, then quickly, bobbing her head until she felt giddy. "I reckon you're the only one who wants me."

James reached over, stilled her face, and wiped a smudge off her cheek. "More than life, Jessie Bingham." He began to sing, so softly that no ears but hers could hear, "'And for love of Jessie Bingham, I'd lay me doon and dee.'"

"That would be a great trial to me," she whispered, wiping James's blood off her hands with her apron. "But you came after me. You proved you're willin'."

Jessie looked around. Lightning crackled in the clouds to the west. Everyone in camp was gathered around Ned, arguing, discussing . . . ignoring the two of them.

She looked at James. He smiled at her, taking her breath away, filling her soul with wonder and elation.

He took her face in his hands and said, "I'm willin' to live for you, and with you, forever and always."

"Oh, James," she said, clinging to him. She closed her eyes. Sometime soon she would tell him that she knew how much Amparo had blessed her life. *She sent you back to me a much better man. My James*, she thought, feeling the warmth of his affection surrounding her heart.

He gathered her into the circle of his arms. Then he kissed her: long, and hard, and joyfully, and drove away the troubles of their trail of storms.

The End

Take a Sneak Peek at

That Tender Light

Light

The Origin Story of The Owen Family Saga
An Owen Family Novella

Excerpt from *That Tender Light*

As she lay dying, Rod Owen's mother made him promise to find a good, Christian woman to marry.

"Mind that she be a church-goer, Roderick, or me and your pa and all the ghostly shades of the Yancey and Owen families, God bless 'em, will haunt you till kingdom come."

Rod had sworn an oath to his mother and held her hand as the life went dark in her feisty eyes. Then, putting aside his deep grief, he bought her the finest funeral he could afford in 1838, and laid her to rest in the Mount Jackson, Virginia, cemetery beside his father, whose stone read, "Rulon Peter Owen, beloved husband and father," along with his birth and death dates.

A year later, he could finally afford a matching stone for "Nellie Marie Yancey Owen, beloved wife and mother," but had not yet found a church-going woman to marry.

Not that he hadn't tried.

He made his first attempt at courting with a fetching girl in Mount Jackson named Muriel Cathy, but he was too late. She only had eyes for the companion of his youth, Chester Bates, and soon married him. Rod could hardly refuse his friend's request that he attend him as his best man. He handed a circle of gold to Chester, and was obliged to observe as the man slipped the ring onto the girl's finger.

Once he had swallowed his pride and disappointment, Rod paid court for some weeks to Rebecca Penewit of Woodstock. The ride on horseback was long, and he wasn't sure how deep the girl's piety sunk into her heart, but she was comely, with yellow hair and blue eyes, much like his own. However, when he tasted the doughy, soggy apple pie she made especially for him, he ceased calling on her as soon as good manners would permit.

There had been other attempts, but he felt no lasting connection with any of the women.

Now, two years after his mother's passing, he rode along the Shenandoah Valley pike toward Front Royal, wondering how much leeway she would allow before she gathered the ghosts to disturb his sleep. He'd done his best to keep his promise, but with no kith or kin to help him on the increasingly prosperous farm outside Mount Jackson, he had little time to go a-courting.

Two days ago, Rod had received a letter from a wealthy young man named Madox who resided in Front Royal, asking him to come discuss a matter of business. A stranger looking at Rod's homestead would say his business was farming, but he would not be completely correct. Above all else, his business was horses. He bred them, trained them, and sold them, and his reputation in the field was spotless. He had learned all he knew from his late father. Someday, he hoped to have sons to teach in the same way he had been taught. But before he could have sons, he must have a wife, and his lack of success in that search pressed dismally upon his soul.

There was no denying he was lonely. He certainly could use a wife around the farmstead, but he resisted the thought of installing just any woman into his home . . . or his bed. He had certain standards besides the one his mother had set, that she be a godly woman.

He knew now that he wanted a slim, raven-haired girl whose apple pie would please his palate, whose wit would spark his intellect, and whose form would weaken his knees and quicken his pulse all the days of his life. She also had to be God-fearing. He didn't know of such a female within a hundred miles of home.

Rod shook his head as he jogged along on the horse. For the present, he should concentrate on whatever business young

Madox had for him. Perhaps when he had accomplished that task, he could widen his search for a fitting wife. ❧

ABOUT THE AUTHOR

Author Marsha Ward writes authentic historical fiction set in 19th Century America, and contemporary romance. She was born in the sleepy little town of Phoenix, Arizona, in a simpler time. With plenty of room to roam among the chickens and citrus trees, Marsha enjoyed playing with neighborhood chums, but always had her imaginary friend, cowboy Johnny Rigger Prescott, at her side. Now she makes her home in a forest in the mountains of Arizona. She loves to hear from her readers.

Connect with her at www.marshaward.com

www.ingramcontent.com/pod-product-compliance
Lightning Source LLC
Chambersburg PA
CBHW020907200626
46814CB00001BA/210